A MURDER IN PEMBROKESHIRE

The Vicky Blunt Welsh detective mysteries
Book #1

NICOLA CLIFFORD

THE
BOOK
FOLKS

Published by The Book Folks

London, 2025

© Nicola Clifford

This book is a work of fiction. Names, characters, businesses, organizations, places and events are either the product of the author's imagination or are used fictitiously. Any resemblance to actual persons, living or dead, events or locales is entirely coincidental. The spelling is British English.

All rights reserved. No part of this publication may be reproduced, stored in retrieval system, copied in any form or by any means, electronic, mechanical, photocopying, recording or otherwise transmitted without written permission from the publisher.

The right of Nicola Clifford to be identified as the author of this work has been asserted in accordance with the Copyright, Designs and Patents Act, 1988.

ISBN 978-1-80462-327-5

www.thebookfolks.com

A MURDER IN PEMBROKESHIRE is the first title in a series of detective mysteries by Nicola Clifford set in West Wales. Details about the other books, as well as the author's previous Mid Wales crime series, can be found at the back of this book.

Chapter one

A Dyfed-Powys Police squad car pulled up in the yard of Ynys-hir farm and Sergeant Vicki Blunt stepped out. The farm was situated on the outskirts of a village called Fron-Wen, a few miles from Haverfordwest in the west of Wales. Vicki reached back inside the car for her regulation bowler hat, zipped up her bright-yellow jacket, then set off across the frosty ground and walked towards the front door of the farmhouse. She was about to knock when it was flung open by a small, scruffy-looking man, bent by age. He peered up at her from beneath a greasy-looking flat cap.

'Got here at last then,' he said, his voice high and creaky.

'Thought you'd be quicker than this, truly I did. I rang 999 and was assured someone would come out. That was an hour ago.'

Vicki allowed him to have his say, knowing there was little point in interrupting the flow. In her experience, farmers always relished the opportunity to rant.

'I don't know what I pay you buggers for,' the man continued. 'Every year on our council tax bills there's a payment for your lot, and do we ever see a copper around here these days? We do not! We're sitting ducks on our farms, valuable kit lying around ready to be stolen.'

Vicki removed her pocketbook and pen. 'Mr Harding, isn't it? I'm Sergeant Blunt from the station in town and I attended as soon as possible.'

'What if I'd been attacked? Left flat on my back and bleeding?'

'The call handler reported there was no threat to life and that the situation was not ongoing. As I am sure you'll understand, sir, we have to prioritise calls. Now, if you could tell me exactly what the problem is, we can begin to deal with it.'

'I'll show you what the problem is. Follow me.'

The short man left the farmhouse and clumped across the yard in mismatched wellies which appeared to be too big for his feet. He dragged open a wooden door on a single-storey, stone building. The door had obviously dropped on its hinges and grated loudly against the concrete. Vicki shuddered. As a lifelong sufferer of misophonia, aggressive, irritating sounds were physically painful to her.

'In there,' Harding said.

'What is?'

'The pair of dogs that were causing the problem. They were rioting in my ewes first thing this morning so I shot them both. No owners in sight, of course. What I want you to do is check the microchips, required by law in Wales–' he paused to allow his point to sink in '–and provide me with the name and address of those owners.' He took off his cap and scrubbed the top of his balding head. 'Such a mess they've caused; animals savaged, others dead, and some pregnant ewes have lost their lambs.' He sighed heavily. '*Duw duw*, you should see it up there. Looks like a battlefield, there's blood everywhere.'

'I know how distressing something like this is and I will follow up on it, but even if the animals were microchipped, I wouldn't be able to pass on the details.'

'It was my bloody sheep that were killed. I'm not the one in the wrong here. I've got signs all over the farm about keeping dogs on the lead but does anyone take any notice? Of course not. This is down to bloody English townies.'

'You saw the owners then, sir?'

'What? No, just their dogs.'

'So I'm wondering how you can tell me the owners came from England.'

Harding didn't answer and Vicki sighed, trying not to add an eye-roll to the mix.

'As I've said, sir, I will take this matter seriously and I'll be in touch with a progress report as soon as I have something to tell you.'

'You'll be wanting the dogs then?' Harding bent, grabbed hold of the back legs of a scruffy mongrel and began dragging it towards the door.

Vicki averted her gaze. 'I don't need the bodies,' she said.

'Then how the hell will you check them for chips? Get the boot open, love, and I'll drop them in for you.'

Vicki was about to protest when her radio crackled and she heard her call sign. She caught the farmer's eye.

'Excuse me a minute, sir.' She turned away and answered the call. '8142.'

'Vicki, are you still at Ynys-hir?'

'I am, just about leave and head for the station.'

'Before you do, there's another call just come in, not far from your location. A dog walker has come across a car parked off the road one of the forestry access tracks. He says there's a young woman sitting inside.'

'Why do I need to attend?'

'The caller – one Evan Jones – said he couldn't make up his mind whether the woman is sleeping or dead, but either way, he hasn't been able to get a response from her. The car is locked.'

'Anything else I need to know?'

'Nothing. I'll send through the exact location.'

'OK, I'm on it.' Vicki looked back at the farmer. 'I'm sorry, Mr Harding. I've got another call and need to get off.'

'No problem,' the man said. 'The other dog isn't such a weight. I'll just load it in the boot with the first, then you can get off.'

* * *

Vicki drove through the lanes in search of a rough track leading into a patch of forestry not far from the farm. The morning was still cold and frosty, glassy shimmers of ice shone on the tarmac. Before long, she spotted a young man standing in the lane and he waved a hand. He was bundled in a thick coat, woolly hat, gloves, and a bright scarf. A cream-coloured, slightly overweight Labrador on a lead sat next to his feet. Behind the cattle grid at the start of the access road, a group of inquisitive sheep had gathered. Their misty breath hung in the cold air above their woolly backs and was lit by the low, pinky-yellow sun, like the smoke of a bonfire. As Vicki parked and left the car, their heads turned as one to study the newcomer, their nostrils twitching. A couple of ewes sneezed loudly and shook their heads, ears flapping from side to side.

'Morning, Mr Jones,' Vicki called. 'I've been told you have a car to show me?'

'Yes, a couple of hundred yards further up. Follow me and I'll show you.'

He turned away and Vicki fell in next to him, her boots crunching loudly on the frozen earth.

'Like to talk to me about what you've found, sir?' Vicki asked.

He nodded. 'I came across the vehicle about an hour ago. Like I said to the 999 switchboard, there's a young woman sitting in a car. I've tapped on the glass but she didn't move and I can't open any of the doors. She doesn't look well, to be honest, and that's why I rang in.'

The pair walked on around a slight bend and a small blue car parked on the edge of the track came into sight. Vicki walked closer. The engine wasn't running. She rested a hand on the bonnet but there was no detectable warmth, then she peered through the driver's window. The young woman's face was resting against the glass. Her eyes were closed, mouth slack, and a silver thread of spittle dangled from her bottom lip. Vicki tapped on the window.

'Hello, love,' she said loudly. 'Police. Are you OK?'

The woman didn't react.

'I tried all that,' Jones said, 'but she hasn't even twitched. I didn't feel right about breaking in.'

Vicki just nodded. She noticed how pale the woman was and knew something was very wrong. She removed the baton from her belt and, without extending it, struck one of the back windows. It took several blows before the glass cracked, then broke, and when it did, the scent of exhaust fumes billowed out. Vicki reached into the front seat, gave the woman a gentle shake, then placed fingers against her throat. Discovering the skin was cold, and unable to detect a pulse, Vicki straightened up and called in the incident. The call handler promised to send a CID officer.

'Any need for an ambulance?' she asked.

'No,' Vicki said, 'too late for that.'

'Suicide, do you think?'

'Not my call to make. I'll wait for CID and take a statement from the finder. Tell them upstairs to get a move on. I don't want to leave her out here any longer than we have to.'

By the time the statement had been taken, an unmarked Land Rover arrived containing DI Glyn Hughes and PC Kurt Helman, a relative newbie in uniform. Vicki groaned inwardly at the sight of Hughes; he was not her favourite person.

The heavy man left the truck and stomped closer.

'Sergeant Blunt,' he said, a nasty smirk on his lips. 'What can you tell me?'

'Not much, sir. This young woman here was found about an hour ago by this gentleman, Mr Jones. I broke a window to check on her condition and the car was full of exhaust fumes. The woman is dead, sir.'

'So, a suicide then? You've got me out for a suicide?'

'No, sir, a suspicious death. In my opinion, it is too early to make assumptions. That's why I requested backup.'

The inspector huffed and walked towards the car. 'Let's take a look then,' he said. Finding the doors locked, he reached in through the broken window, forced the catch with difficulty, and opened the driver's door. After a couple of minutes, he stood up. 'Well, you were right, she is dead. Did you find a hosepipe attached to the exhaust?'

'No, sir. Another reason I called it in.'

'Any note?'

'I haven't looked. I was anxious to preserve the scene.'

Hughes nodded. 'OK. You arrange for the body to be collected and I'll get someone out to take a look over the car before it's moved. Was the engine running when you arrived?'

Vicki shook her head. 'No, and the engine was cold.'

'Right then. I'll leave Constable Helman with you to wait for the meat wagon and mechanic. I have better things to do than this.'

'Do you want the vehicle recovered?'

'Depends on what the mechanic says. Keep me informed.'

Hughes walked back to the truck, got inside and drove away.

'What about me?' Jones asked. 'The wife will be concerned if I don't get home soon.' He held up a mobile phone. 'There's no signal out here to ring her. Emergency calls only.'

'You can get off, sir,' Vicki said. 'I have your details and will be in touch if we need to ask you anything further.'

Jones stared at the woman in the car. 'Do you think she killed herself?' he asked.

'Bit too soon to tell, but thanks again for ringing this in.'

'Only what anyone would do.'

He turned away, twitched the lead, and the dog trotted next to his side as he walked back towards the lane.

'How long do you think we'll have to wait here?' Kurt Helman asked. 'It's bloody cold.' He leaned on the bonnet of the car and shoved his hands in his pockets.

'Oi!' Vicki snapped. 'What do you think you're doing? This is a potential crime scene.'

'I reckon she topped herself. Women often do that.'

'Just get off the car. As to your earlier question, I have no idea how long we'll be here, but get used to it. Much of coppering involves a lot of hanging around in the cold.'

Chapter two

After a hard day at the station, Vicki was finally able to clock off, and drove home to Fron-Wen. She parked outside a large, detached house, walked up the front path and slipped her key in the lock. She removed her coat and dumped it on a hat stand.

'Susan, it's me,' she called. 'Fancy a cuppa?'

'Please,' a woman answered. 'I'm in the library.'

Vicki went to the kitchen, made the tea and carried two mugs to the book-lined room at the rear of the house.

An older woman sat behind a leather-topped desk. She looked up as Vicki entered, removed her half-moon glasses and smiled. She was dressed in a thick cardigan which sported a large brooch in the shape of a bumblebee. Her grey hair was frizzy, an actual style difficult to determine.

She was in her mid-sixties and laughter lines creased the skin of her face.

Vicki placed the mugs on the desk and leaned forward to brush a kiss on the older woman's cheek.

'You look done in,' Susan said. 'Difficult day, *cariad*?'

'I'm knackered. First, I was sent out to a farmer who had shot dead a couple of dogs that were worrying his sheep. That was followed by the discovery of a dead woman in a car, parked on a forestry track away from the road. A dog walker found her.'

Susan nodded. 'Yes, it's always a dog walker who finds the bodies. Although' – she chuckled – 'it's the dogs that do the finding, but not having thumbs they can't phone the police.' She sipped from her mug. 'So, what is it? Suicide, misadventure, suspicious circumstances?'

'Not my decision to make.' Vicki perched on the edge of the desk. 'That bloody man, DI Hughes, attended. Out of everyone available at the station, they send me Hughes. He couldn't organise a conga in a holiday camp, that one. Useless article.'

'You've made your feelings perfectly plain on that score; many times, if I remember rightly.'

'We should never forget that an innocent woman is languishing in prison because of that disgusting man,' Vicki said.

Susan chuckled. 'Like we are ever allowed to forget. What *you* conveniently forget is that she was found guilty by the court.'

'Because the investigation was flawed, badly run by that man, and evidence was lost and tampered with.'

'Not that you've been able to prove any of that.'

'I know I'm right, but I agree that proving it has been a problem. I was outranked, and a junior officer backed him up – too afraid not to.'

'And that's why you're back in uniform. You were lucky not to be demoted, dismissed even. You can't, *really* can't cast serious aspersions on a senior officer without cast-iron proof.'

'I had a witness until Hughes worked on her and she changed her story.'

'Another theory you haven't been able to prove. I still think you should resign,' Susan said. 'With your experience and your transferrable skills, you'd be an asset anywhere. Trust me, you'll never move up the ranks with this on your record.'

'I'm not going to throw in the towel, no matter how often you tell me to. I'll never be able to uncover the truth if I'm outside the organisation, and besides, I don't want to do anything else. I enjoy being a copper.'

'Then you're the rod for your own back. I understand why you want to put things right, but that isn't always possible, no matter how hard you try, or how much evidence you uncover. Whistle-blowers have never been well-regarded in the force and you know this too.'

Vicki nodded. She drained her mug then stood. 'I need a bath and food, in that order,' she said. 'Shall I cook supper this evening?'

Susan shook her head. 'No need, *cariad*. One of my friends dropped in earlier with a lasagne, just needs heating up. Why not share it with me?'

'Sounds good, thanks. I'll stick it in your oven on a low heat and be back down in an hour.'

Vicki went to the kitchen, found the pasta dish in the larder and slipped it into the warming oven of an old Aga. Back in the hall, she opened a small door at the bottom of the stairs and went up to her apartment. She had lived there for a couple of years and had no plans to move.

Susan had been a chief inspector before she was injured in action and invalided out of the force on a full pension. Vicki moved in shortly afterwards and the arrangement worked well. The self-contained apartment on the first floor made use of rooms her ex-boss rarely entered, and the rent was cheap. Susan sometimes needed assistance when her reduced mobility was difficult to manage. Vicki had been more than willing to help, and not just because of the rent reduction. Susan Thomas had spent her whole working life in the force, starting as a cadet. Having put in forty years, her knowledge of all things copper was immense, and she was more than happy to act as mentor to an officer thirty years her junior. And of course, they were good friends.

Vicki stepped into the hall, which had been the landing, switched on the radio, then headed for the bathroom. She put the plug in the bath, turned on the taps, added a handful of Radox crystals to banish the cold from her bones, and looked forward to supper.

Chapter three

Vicki hauled herself out of bed the next morning and groaned. Susan had opened wine to go with supper and Vicki knew she should have stuck to a single glass, not helped to empty the bottle. She took a quick shower, gulped down a strong coffee to wake her up, then got dressed and left her apartment. There was no sign of Susan downstairs so Vicki left through the front door and went out to the car parked on the drive. The windscreen was coated by thick frost, so she unlocked the door and cranked the engine. With the blower on full, she scraped at the ice until the glass was clear enough to see through, then strapped herself in and set off for the station in Haverfordwest. She wrinkled her nose; the dogs she had transported the day before had left a nasty smell, which seemed to have grown stronger overnight.

She took the drive slowly, not only because of the ice on the road, but the early spring sun was low in the sky and made her squint. Due to the early hour, she didn't meet any traffic, apart from a truck and trailer loaded with feed for sheep. The driver squeezed into a pull in and let Vicki pass. She raised a hand and soon found her way to the main road. When she arrived at the station, she glanced at her watch, saw she had time to check on the case she had picked up yesterday, and ran upstairs to the CID department. DI Hughes was already in so Vicki wound her way through the desks to his office and tapped on the door.

He glanced up from his computer screen. 'Oh, it's you,' he said.

'Just wondering what progress you made yesterday. Do we have a name for the woman found in the car?'

'Yes, we do, she had ID on her.' He rummaged on his desk, finally locating a tatty notepad. 'Christina Page, thirty-four, a teacher at the local primary school. Her family has been informed. She's currently with the pathologist for a quick look-over, but he said it does appear she was overcome by exhaust fumes. We'll know more later today.'

'What would you like my lot to do?'

'Gather some background. Talk with the school, Christina's neighbours, friends, and another chat with her mother would be a good idea. You know the drill. I still think she topped herself, but we didn't find a note. Gathering info regarding her recent movements would also be useful.'

Vicki nodded. 'I'll get them on it. I'm just about to give the morning briefing. Anything else on the list?'

Hughes sifted through a pile of folders and removed a sheet of paper from the middle. 'Pretty quiet overnight but there are a few calls needed. All on there, knock yourself out.'

Vicki took the paper and gratefully left the office. She hated having to breathe the same air as Hughes and was sure he felt the same way.

She walked back downstairs and into the squad room. About a dozen officers lounged on plastic chairs and looked up as she entered.

'Morning, all,' Vicki said and took her place at the head of the room. 'As you know, we found a deceased woman in a car yesterday not far from Fron-Wen. No definite cause of death available yet, but I'm informed the path lab is working on it. We do have the woman's identity though. Christina Page, she was a teacher at the local primary school. CID want us to make inquiries into her background. That will involve house-to-house, a chat with her mother, and a visit to the school to talk to those who knew her.'

She looked around the room and saw nodding heads.

'Anyone know if a vet came out yesterday to run a scanner over the dead dogs I brought in?'

A young female officer spoke up. 'Yes, Sarge. No chips found in either animal.'

'Mr Harding won't be happy. Can you get out there this morning, Ruth, and give him the good news? Take someone with you.'

'Yes, Sarge.'

'The only other thing on the list is trouble on the Barton Estate. We have multiple reports of anti-social behaviour so a few of you need to get out there. Make yourselves visible and talk to the locals. See if you can discover the names of any culprits and reassure the residents. Information gathering only at this point. Right, then, let's get on, and stay safe, everyone. Constable Helman, I want you with me this morning. We'll visit the school, then call in on Christina's mother.'

The room emptied quickly. Vicki went to the locker room and dressed in her bright-yellow hi-vis jacket. She checked her kit, then removed her hat from the locker and went out to the car park. Kurt Helman was waiting for her by the car.

'Want me to drive, Sarge?' he asked.

'No, you're all right.'

They got in the car and Vicki pulled out of the car park. The roads were busier now with commuters on their way to work, parents dropping children at school, and numerous work vans and delivery trucks. Vicki navigated her way through the snarl-ups, finally arrived at St David's school twenty minutes later, and the officers were soon seated in the headmaster's office.

The man had introduced himself as Martin Llewellyn and was wearing a smart suit and a colourful, silk tie. Vicki thought he looked more like a banker than a teacher.

'Mr Llewellyn…' Vicki began.

The man held up a hand and smiled. 'Martin, please.'

Vicki tried again. 'Martin, we are here to speak to you about Christina Page.'

'Yes, I thought you might be. Such a tragedy. How can I help?'

'We'd like some insight into how Christina was during the last couple of months, whether you knew if anything was bothering her.'

'If there was anything, she didn't make it obvious. She was just as she always was, happy – bubbly even. She was an exceptional teacher, good at her job and wonderful with the children, mainly because she was so committed and dedicated.'

'Had she taken any sick time lately?'

'Not for as long as I can remember.' He smiled. 'Christina was a fit and healthy girl.'

Vicki felt the hairs on the back of her neck twitch at the inappropriate remark and took an instant dislike to the man.

'How long has Mo Page worked here?' she asked.

'Getting on for eight years.' He snorted. 'She was here when I joined the team three years ago and very willing to share her experience of the place, show me the ropes.' He leaned forward and lowered his voice. 'I know you're not supposed to have favourites, but she was by far the best teacher in the school. I'm devastated to lose her. Can you tell me how she died? I've had many calls from parents who are anxious to know what has happened.'

'I'm afraid not, sir. We can't release details until the investigation has been completed.'

'I understand.' Martin steepled his fingers in front of his chin.

'Can you tell me about your relationship with Ms Page?'

'We didn't have one. We were colleagues, nothing more.'

'Did you ever meet up after work, go for a drink perhaps?'

Martin shook his head. 'No, only at Christmas when such behaviour is obligatory.'

'So you'd never been to her home?'

'No, I haven't. Why are you asking?'

'Standard procedure in cases of suspicious death.'

'So you think someone murdered her?' Martin's eyebrows raised in shock.

'I said the circumstances were suspicious – different thing altogether.'

Vicki shut her notebook and got to her feet. 'One last question, did she have a favourite among the staff? A confidante maybe?'

'That would be Gareth Sinclair, he teaches the infants.' Again he lowered his voice. 'I should warn you he's... uh... a little effeminate.'

'Do you mean he's gay?' Vicki asked.

'Yes, he is.'

'And you felt the need to warn me?' Vicki stuffed her notebook into a pocket. 'Where do I find Mr Sinclair?'

'Why do you want to talk to him?'

'Because we're talking to everyone who knew Christina, so I'd be grateful if you could point us in the right direction.'

Martin huffed, left his desk and led the officers through the school to the staff room. He introduced Gareth Sinclair before heading back to his office.

Gareth was an incredibly tall, thin man, with a mass of piercings in one ear and a couple more in one of his bushy eyebrows. He shook hands with Vicki then moved towards a small grouping of upholstered chairs.

'Take a seat,' he said, 'and tell me what I can do for you.' He smiled weakly. 'I'll try to hold it together, but Christina and I were close, besties. I can't believe she's dead.' He pinched the bridge of his nose and sat opposite the officers.

'I'm sorry for your loss, sir,' Vicki said. 'Have you known each other long?'

Gareth nodded. 'We completed our teacher training together and were delighted when we were both offered posts here, which meant we could work together too.'

'Was she unhappy recently? Did she have something on her mind?'

'If she did, she didn't confide in me about it – which would have been unusual. We shared everything, always did.' He smiled sadly. 'I'm a dreadful oversharer, but Christina always had time to listen, quite wonderful she was.' He sighed. 'I helped her through the break-up with her husband a few years ago.'

'Was it an acrimonious split?'

'It wasn't good. She came home and caught him in bed with one of their neighbours, but Christina is… was… a strong woman. One of the many things I admired about her.' He took a deep, shuddering breath. 'The grapevine says she killed herself, committed suicide, but there's no way. She wasn't the sort to give up on life and had always lived it to the full.'

'Listening to gossip is never a good idea. We are investigating her death, but at this point we haven't reached any conclusion. How would you describe her husband? Did they divorce?'

'He's a horrible man, one of those macho types. He hated me for obvious reasons but Christina wouldn't allow him to affect our friendship. I really admired her for that, and yes, they were divorced. The decree absolute came through last year and we went out dancing to celebrate.'

He shuddered miserably at the memory and tears began to fall. Vicki placed a gentle hand on his arm.

'So you're telling me that there was nothing worrying her, and if there had been, you're sure she would have spoken to you?'

'She grumbled now and again about trolls online, nothing specific, and we all suffer stuff like that now and again.'

'Did she say who might have been posting?'

'No, she didn't, but this sort of people always use a moniker, never their real names.' He looked up, his eyes red and puffy. 'When you find out what did happen to Christina, would you let me know, please?'

'Of course, and we may have to speak to you again, depending on how the investigation progresses. Can you give me your contact details?'

'Sure. Happy to.' Gareth pulled a wallet from his back pocket and handed over a business card. 'Everything is on there. Who else will you be speaking with?'

'Everyone who knew her. We have a visit planned to talk to her mother.'

'When you see Jill, would you let her know how sorry I am and pass on my condolences? I'll let the dust settle before I call on her.'

'No problem. One more question. Did she have any issues with anyone on the staff here? Had she fallen out with someone perhaps?'

'Not that I'm aware of.' He leaned closer and lowered his voice. 'The only person she didn't like was the head, Martin Llewellyn.'

'Do you know why?'

'Said he was a creep, too touchy-feely for her liking. He had a bit of a thing for her and could be a pest.'

'Can you elaborate on "a bit of a thing"?' Vicki asked.

'We all knew he fancied her rotten, and fancied his chances.' He laughed, a bleak sound. 'He was the only one who didn't accept his chances with her were zero. She had mentioned making a complaint.'

'Do you think he was trolling her?'

'I doubt it. It's not his style at all; well, not that I know of.'

Vicki made a note, then got to her feet and held out her hand.

'Thank you, Mr Sinclair,' she said. 'You've been helpful. Once again, I am very sorry for your loss.'

The man nodded, wiped his face with a tissue and got to his feet.

'I'll see you out, unless there's anything else.'

'No, that's it, for now.'

Chapter four

Christina's mother hadn't been at home, so Vicki arrived back at the station earlier than she had anticipated. Kurt Helman slipped out of the car as soon as she had pulled on the handbrake and vanished inside the station. Vicki was walking through the back door when she heard her name called. She turned and saw a pleasant-looking man in his late thirties, dressed in navy-blue overalls and a police-issue waterproof jacket. She recognised Billy Marsden – a civilian who worked in the police garage – and smiled.

'Hey, Billy,' she said. 'Don't often see you here. Everything OK?'

'On my way to an audience with Horrible Hughes to give him an update regarding the car we picked up yesterday.'

'The blue Fiat found near Fron-Wen?'

'That's the one.'

'Find anything interesting?'

'Not so much interesting as odd.'

'Oh? Fancy telling me about it? I was the first on the scene.'

Billy looked over his shoulder then made himself comfortable against the wall. Vicki suspected he was fond of her but had kept their relationship friendly so far.

'Well,' he said, 'there were significant anomalies recorded on the OBC.'

'English please, Welsh if you have to.'

Billy grinned. 'Faults with the on-board computer. I plugged in the diagnostic kit to see if I could determine when the engine stopped, and when I did, a whole bunch of faults were displayed.'

'What sort of faults?'

'Random stuff. Some to do with the over-heating engine, others linked with doors and windows, problems with airbags, tyre pressure warnings. I won't bore you with the entire list, but it seems as though the OBC experienced a catastrophic event.'

'Is that why the engine stopped?'

'No, the vehicle ran out of fuel a few minutes after two o'clock, the morning you found it.'

'You know there was a woman in the car, found deceased?'

'Yes, I did. Suicide, I heard.'

'No decision yet as far as I know, and no obvious signs I saw. No length of hose for example, no note either.'

'She wouldn't have needed a hosepipe.'

'Why do you say that?'

'When I got the car on the lift at the garage, I noticed that the manifold – the big lump of metal that attaches the exhaust system to the engine under the bonnet – was missing bolts. It was so loose, it was almost wobbling.' He moved over as a couple of young coppers walked past. They nodded at Vicki.

Billy continued, 'The fumes from the manifold would easily be able to find their way inside the car, and if the driver couldn't get out…' He shrugged. 'The loose manifold should have been picked up on the MOT – two weeks ago.'

'Do you know where that was carried out?'

'High Road Garage on the estate on the other side of town.'

'Great, thanks. Enjoy your meeting with the horrible one, and if he asks, you haven't seen me.'

'Fair enough. How about a drink at the weekend? It's been a while.'

'I'll let you know.'

Vicki walked to the car and tutted when she saw Kurt Helman hadn't reappeared. She got in and set off towards the industrial estate alone.

* * *

High Road Garage was larger than Vicki had expected, it was also busy. Mechanics peered inside engine compartments, shone bright lights on the underside of vehicles on the lifts, and hit metal with metal somewhere in the back. Vicki parked close to the office and walked inside.

The office looked tired, reflected by a half-dead ivy desperately clinging to a set of dusty shelves. A few framed prints of old buses hung from scruffy wallpaper, and the carpet was smeared in places with oil. The space was divided by a long desk, behind which a couple of women shuffled paper. One looked up and her eyebrows rose when she spotted the uniform. She walked to the desk and smiled; her teeth too white to be genuine.

'Good afternoon,' she said. 'Can I help you?'

'I hope so,' Vicki said. 'I'd like a quick word with the owner, if that's possible.'

'May I ask what you would like to see him about?'

'I'm sure he'll tell you later if you ask him.'

The woman frowned, crossed to a phone on a nearby desk and punched in a number. Her long fingernails scrapped and tapped on the plastic buttons, making Vicki shiver.

'Mr Simpson, there's a police officer here asking to see you. Will you come out or shall I bring her through?' A pause, then, 'Yes, sir. I'll show her to your office.' She put the phone down and opened a small door in the desk. 'This way.'

The owner's office was at the rear of the building and in significantly better condition than the reception area; cleaner too, although the smell of oil was still present. A man in his sixties was sitting at the desk and got to his feet as Vicki entered, a welcoming smile on his face.

'Thanks, Brenda,' he said. 'Please, Sergeant, take a seat. Can I get you something to drink?'

'No, thank you, sir.'

'Is something wrong? Has one of my lads been up to something they shouldn't?'

'Not as far as I know, sir. This is more of a general visit in the course of an ongoing investigation.'

'Well, I'll certainly help if I can. What would you like to know?'

'Can you confirm your garage recently MOT'd a blue Fiat owned by a Ms Page?' Vicki handed over a scrap of paper with the registration number written on it.

Simpson took the scrap and woke up his computer.

'Ah, yes we did. Last cat in, a couple of Fridays ago. Is there a problem?'

Vicki ignored his question. 'Presumably it passed, but can you tell me if there were any advisories?'

'Give me a mo, should be on here.' He tapped at the keyboard some more, then leaned back in his chair. 'Not really, a couple of bulbs. The car isn't old and gets well looked after. We noted that it could do with a couple of new front tyres before the next test, but nothing else. Christina is a regular, so I know the car. We gave it a service at the same time as the MOT and didn't find any problems.'

'Did you do the work, sir?'

'Me? No.' He laughed. 'I'm a jockey turned trainer. The grease monkeys do the hands-on stuff.'

'Could I have a word with whoever carried out the service?'

'Yes, if you'd like to, let me just… ah yes… Ieuan Noonan. I'll give him a shout.' He stood then hesitated, looked down at Vicki and asked, 'Are you sure there's nothing wrong? I run a tight ship here, always have. Are you sure someone hasn't got themselves into bother?'

Vicki smiled to try to put the man at ease. 'Not to my knowledge, sir. I don't know whether you've heard, but Christina Page was found in her car yesterday morning. Unfortunately, she had died, and we need to investigate her death. We're just covering all the bases.'

Simpson dropped back on his chair. 'Christina is dead? How awful. How did she die?'

'That's what we're looking into.'

'Do you suspect foul play?'

'No, nothing like that, but I won't deny the circumstances aren't straightforward, hence my visit to you.'

Simpson got back to his feet. 'I shall miss that young woman, proper ray of sunshine, she was. How is her mother?'

'Do you know the family?'

'Yes, good customers and friends. We often invite each other to parties and get-togethers. I'll have to give Jill a ring. Right, let me go and find Ieuan.'

He left the room. Vicki stood and wandered around checking out business certificates, awards and a few framed photographs hanging on the walls, including one of

Simpson and a young boy, supporting a large, rod-caught salmon between them. More family photos were propped on the desk. The door suddenly opened. Simpson walked in accompanied by a young man in oily overalls who was wiping his hands on a scrap of rag. He was in his early twenties and looked nervous, not keen to catch Vicki's eye.

'Have a chat with the sergeant,' Simpson said. 'I'll go and fetch some tea, give you some privacy.' He patted his young employee on the shoulder. 'Don't fret, lad. You're not in any trouble.'

Ieuan took a seat and concentrated on trying to clean his hands.

'Hi, Ieuan,' Vicki said. 'My name is Sergeant Blunt and I work at the station in town. I'd like to talk about a service and MOT you carried out a couple of weeks ago on a blue Fiat.'

'Yeah, Christina's car. The boss told me what's happened and I'm gutted. She's been coming in since I started working for Mr Simpson – really nice lady.'

'Was any work needed, other than the service?'

'Nothing, it was all in good order.'

'Our police mechanic has discovered that bolts on the manifold were loose, and a couple missing, causing the manifold to "wobble about" was how he put it.'

'I didn't see anything like that, and I'd have noticed when I changed the oil and the filters. I always take a shufty around the engine compartment when I have the bonnet up.'

'Our guy also found multiple faults with the OBC. Did you notice anything amiss with that?'

Ieuan shrugged. 'Why would I? I steer clear of the computer. I'm a mechanic, not an IT specialist. All I did was turn off the service light and nothing flashed up.'

'No concerns at all then?'

'Straightforward job – as it should be. The car is only just three years old. The MOT was the first it had.'

* * *

Vicki drove back to the station and was about to check in with the troops, anxious to learn if any had made progress, when DI Hughes collared her.

'I need a word upstairs,' he said and turned away without waiting to see if she would follow.

She fell in behind him as he climbed the stairs to the second floor, and tried to keep her gaze away from the sight of his ample buttocks rolling from side to side as he hauled his bulk up the risers.

He went to his office, dropped on the chair behind the desk out of breath, and looked up at her.

'Billy Marsden was in earlier,' he said. 'Seems he has some concerns regarding the car recovered yesterday.'

'Yes, I am aware. We spoke on his way in.'

'Well, he thinks the car could have been sabotaged, mechanically and digitally, whatever the fuck that means.' He sighed heavily and leaned back in his chair, which squeaked in protest. 'Personally, I thought he was barking up the wrong tree, but then the initial autopsy report came in.'

Vicki raised her eyebrows. 'Oh? What were the findings?'

'The woman did die from carbon monoxide poisoning, but…'

'But what?'

'Bruises on her upper arms were noted. The pathologist said it looked as though she had been grabbed roughly, dragged maybe. He also found evidence of an injury to her head which may or may not have rendered her unconscious.'

'What are we saying? That a third party cracked her on the head, stuffed her in the car, drove it out to the wilds, then left her inside with the engine running to make it look like a suicide?'

Hughes snorted. 'I don't know what I think,' he snapped. 'All I know is that we will all have to devote precious hours – and some of the budget – to the case until we can properly explain the circumstances. As if we didn't have enough to do.' He rubbed his face. 'Any of your lot turn up anything useful?'

'I was about to debrief when you dragged me up here. I have visited High Road Garage though. Billy told me the car had been MOT'd a couple of weeks ago, so I went to have a chat with the owner and the mechanic who worked on the car. I'm satisfied that the faults Billy mentioned were not evident at the time.'

'So, if Billy is right, any tampering must have occurred recently.'

Vicki nodded.

'How did it go at St David's primary school?'

'Pretty much as you'd expect. I spent some time talking with her best friend on the staff and the headmaster. Neither had noticed a change in Christina's demeanour, and Gareth Sinclair – the friend – vehemently denied she would have killed herself.'

'Doesn't mean she didn't,' Hughes muttered.

'No it doesn't, but Christina was reported as being a happy person, someone who really enjoyed life. So far I haven't discovered anything that might have convinced her to take her own life.'

'What did her mother say?'

'She wasn't in when we called so it's first on the list for tomorrow.'

'OK, then. Go and find out what your gang have uncovered and I'll see you in the morning.'

'Yes, sir.' Vicki got to her feet. 'Should a SOCO go out to the track where the car was discovered? Have a sniff around in case there's any evidence of the suspected third party?'

'That would make sense, and I'll have someone re-examine the vehicle. Arrange that before you leave and we'll catch up tomorrow.'

Vicki nodded, opened the door and strode from the office.

Chapter five

Vicki pulled up outside the house in Fron-Wen, turned off the engine and gathered her shopping bags from the boot. She let herself in through the front door.

'Hey, Susan, where are you?' she called.

'I'm in bed,' Susan answered.

Vicki dumped the bags in the hall, tapped on the bedroom door and pushed it open. Her friend was propped up with a mass of feather pillows and bolsters, and had a book in her hand, which she rested face down on the bedspread before removing her glasses. 'You're late today,' she said. 'Everything OK?'

'Busy, that's all. Hughes nabbed me, which put me behind. More to the point, how are you?'

'Having a bit of an off day.'

Vicki perched on the side of the bed. 'Is the pain bad?'

Susan nodded. 'My back bones don't react well to the cold weather.'

'Have you eaten today?'

'Not really. Gwen popped in with scones and made a cuppa. The words "pain" and "appetite" don't go together.'

Vicki smiled. 'I went shopping on the way home, got some of that chocolate cake from the deli you like so much. Not that you can get anywhere near it until you've eaten some soup.'

'Stop talking to me as though I'm a child.' Susan smiled to soften her words. 'I'll see you in the kitchen, it's warmer in there.'

'I'll go and put the soup on.'

In the kitchen, Susan lowered herself into an easy chair with a straight back and cushions next to the Aga.

'I'd like to choose some new wallpaper for my room,' she said. 'I'm fed up looking at bloody bamboo. Stare at it for too long and it seems the stuff is moving. Makes me cross-eyed.'

'I've offered to put the spare telly in your room several times.'

'And I've told you – several times – that a bedroom is no place for a television. Besides, daytime TV would send me doolally quicker than anything. Now, get the soup on before I change my mind, put the cake somewhere I can feast my eyes on it, then tell me about your day.'

Vicki put a pan on the Aga and told her about the case she was involved in, and about the ongoing unrest on the Barton Estate. The anti-social behaviour seemed to centre around a group of young men in cars, and their hangers-on. Constable Ruth England – an unfortunate name for a Welsh copper with Irish heritage – had received many reports from residents about cars racing in the streets at night blasting loud music. Large amounts of alcohol and possible drug-taking had also been mentioned.

'There's always been trouble there,' Susan said. 'It was built in the sixties then quickly forgotten about.'

'It's been worse lately. I'll pop out there tomorrow, try to reassure the residents and collect some names. As always, names are in short supply.'

'Difficult to grass anyone up in a small place like Haverfordwest – everyone knows everyone else. Have a word with any old ladies, they're not usually backwards at coming forward.'

Vicki chuckled. 'Good idea.'

'So, Glyn Hughes is definitely investigating the woman in the car case?'

'He hasn't got much of a choice, with Billy Marsden raising issues and the autopsy showing Christina's death was likely to involve some form of foul play.' Vicki frowned. 'I just hope the bloody man handles this case properly.'

Susan finished her soup and eyed the cake on the dresser. Vicki noticed, got up and cut a slice, then poured tea from a hideously decorated pot that had been left in the house by the previous owners.

'Are you around at the weekend?' Susan asked around a mouthful of cake.

'I will be on Sunday, but I'm off to visit Emma on Saturday.'

Emma Hardwick, a twenty-five-year-old local woman, was in prison for the murder of her husband, a crime she insisted she didn't commit. DI Glyn Hughes had been the officer in charge of the case and, in Vicki's opinion, had made a mess of the investigation. He compounded the mess with inappropriate behaviour, for which he hadn't been reprimanded – yet. Vicki had been in court for the verdict, heard Emma's gut-wrenching howl of despair and saw her tears and made a silent vow to find some way to overturn the unjust decision. To have Emma exonerated and released.

'You never miss visiting her, do you?' Susan asked.

'I try not to. She doesn't get many visitors and prison isn't doing her any good. I'm afraid I'll go in one day to find she has melted away.'

'What do your bosses have to say about these visits?'

'Nothing. I'm pretty sure they don't know; after all, no one has ever asked me, and I haven't offered the information.'

'They could find out, obtain a list of Emma's visitors.'

'They could, but why would anyone bother? Hughes certainly wouldn't. He doesn't want the case mentioned in the station, he's worried his failings might come to light.'

'How long has Emma been inside now?'

'Coming up to eighteen months. I'm surprised she's made it this far, tiny little thing like her. She doesn't even come up to my shoulder.'

'You are rather tall.'

'Six foot isn't remarkable these days.'

Susan grinned. 'Yeah, whatever.'

'Will you get one of your mates over on Saturday? As always I'll have to leave at sparrow's fart, and won't be home much before dark.'

'Yeah, probably. While you're out the way I enjoy talking about you.'

'Charming. How's the cake?'

'Blissful. Thank you.' Susan put another small piece into her mouth. 'So, what's your next step regarding Christina Page's death?'

'Hughes is arranging a SOCO to re-examine her car, and I'm meeting another one at the scene in the morning. I'm hoping to find and recover evidence to prove someone else was involved.'

'It's a long shot, bearing in mind time has passed, but there hasn't been any rain so you might get lucky.'

* * *

At eight the next morning, Vicki turned onto the forestry access road and pulled up behind a white van with "SOCO" emblazoned on the sides. A little further on, she spotted an officer crouched on her heels, peering closely at the ground where the Fiat had been parked.

'Morning,' Vicki called. 'Have you been here long?'

'Morning. No, not long.'

'It's Sian Jenkins, isn't it?'

The woman smiled. 'Yes, that's me.'

'Found anything?'

'There's some tyre marks in the frozen mud that weren't left by the Fiat. It seems another vehicle pulled up next to the car.'

'That's interesting. Any clue what sort of vehicle?'

'We ought to be able to get some idea. The conditions are perfect for taking casts. When they're set, I'll take them back and check the database.'

'Do you think the marks were left the same day the car was found?'

'I'm guessing they could have been, but it's difficult to be completely sure. It doesn't seem as though this track has any regular traffic so, as I say, maybe. I'm just about to widen the search to the surrounding area.'

'Can I do anything?'

'Give me a hand if you like, but don't walk anywhere near the position the car was found in, and shout if you spot anything.'

An hour later, the tyre casts had set, and a couple of drinks cans, a crumpled tissue and a disposable vape were sealed in plastic evidence bags.

Vicki peered at their discoveries. 'All this looks as though it was discarded recently,' she said.

'Yes, I thought so too. We might get lucky with fingerprints and DNA. I'll make sure to let you know if the lab finds anything.'

'Thanks, but don't forget to liaise with DI Hughes. This is his case.'

Sian nodded. 'I still think of you as a DS, not a plain PS.' She smiled. 'Just to let you know, the rank and file are on your side. Very few were happy about the sentence that girl received.' She chuckled. 'The same few who weren't *un*happy when you were put back in uniform. How are you coping with that?'

'I'm still a copper, that's the main thing, and still on the same salary. It's only the work that's different, and I guess a change is as good as a rest.' Vicki snorted. 'Not like I'm getting one, CID is short-staffed.'

'I guess.' Sian sighed. 'If I can ever help with the Emma Hardwick thing, give me a shout and I'll do what I can. That was a dreadful verdict.'

'I'm visiting her on Saturday,' Vicki blurted out, then wanted to smack herself in the face for her lack of discretion.

'Oh? Have you been before?'

'Yeah, now and again. I want to try and get her released. She's innocent, I'm sure of it.'

'Maybe I can come with you one day, look at the problem from a SOCO's point of view.'

'You know, I might take you up on that. Thanks.'

'No sweat.' Sian slammed the back doors of the van shut. 'I'll be in touch.'

Vicki watched her drive away, then got into her car and followed the van back to the lane.

* * *

Vicki walked inside the police station and managed to make it to the squad room without bumping into DI Hughes. She was pleased to see most of her shift officers had their heads down, wading through information collected the previous day. PC Kurt Helman was an exception. He leaned back in his chair, feet on the desk, and rolled up small pieces of paper to flick at Ruth England. Vicki walked closer, knocked his feet to the floor and glared at him.

'What?' he protested.

'If you want to behave like a schoolboy, don't do it here! We're short-staffed and no one is going to carry you.'

'I was thinking, that's all.'

'Well, be more productive… and keep your feet on the floor.'

Vicki turned away and Ruth moved to her side.

'Can I show you something, Sarge?' Ruth said.

'Of course. What have you got?'

'I've been reading through the statements we took from residents on the Barton Estate. As I told you, no one gave us any names – although I'm sure they know who they are complaining about. Anyway, there are a couple of elderly sisters who live there; they moved in soon after the place was built. I reckon if you and I pop along for a chat they could be very useful, with the right encouragement.'

Vicki smiled. 'What sort of encouragement are we talking about?'

'Bag of pastries from the local baker's maybe? When I spoke with them, I knew they had more to say, and got the impression that no one can fart on the estate without Ena and Awel Williams knowing about it.'

'OK, I'm in. We'll go together.' She looked up and addressed the room. 'Right then, you lot, work through the paperwork from the Barton Estate case, and the door-to-door statements you collected regarding the suspicious death. A couple of you should go back to the estate, catch up with those who were out when you called the first time.' Kurt Helman got to his feet and Vicki frowned at him. 'Not you, Constable. Desk work for you for the rest of the week.'

'Hey. That's not fair…'

Vicki held up a hand. 'What did I say about schoolboys? Just get on with it and quit bellyaching. I'll be back before the end of shift and it would be good if you had something to show for your efforts. Come on, Ruth.'

Chapter six

Vicki asked Ruth to park on the edge of the estate, then left the car, put on her hat, and together they walked towards 28, Ash Grove, home of the Williams sisters. There weren't many residents out and about. Even though the sun was shining, a strong easterly wind cut the legs from beneath you. A group of teenagers at the end of the street huddled in hoodies, vaping and staring at their phones. The gang noticed the officers and quickly melted away without looking back. A couple of young mums, bundled together against the frigid air, pushed strollers, their babies hidden by protective canopies and sealed away from the wind. They didn't look at the officers either, but Ruth and Vicki were used to such responses.

'Do you have any trouble from Kurt Helman?' Vicki asked.

'Strange question, Sarge. What sort of trouble are we talking about?'

'Any sort. He's beginning to irritate me beyond what's reasonable. He looks about sixteen, even though he's in his early twenties, and behaves like a sulky kid.'

'I think he only joined the force cos his granddad was a copper. You can see his heart isn't in it.'

'So why does he stay, then?'

'You'll have to ask him, boss. I'm not keen, but he hasn't done more than try to wind me up. I can cope with that. Some senior officers are much more trouble than he is. Handsy, some of them.'

'Don't get me started,' Vicki grumbled.

She turned off the pavement, walked up a concrete path laid across a strip of what used to be lawn, and rang the bell of number twenty-eight. A few minutes passed before a croaky voice called, 'Who is it?'

'The police, Miss Williams. From the station in town.'

The door opened and a white-haired, short woman wearing a thick jumper and a woolly skirt peered out.

'Hello,' she said. 'Can I help you?'

'I hope so. Would it be OK to step inside for a minute? Better than talking on the doorstep.'

'Of course.' The door swung open. 'There's nothing wrong, is there? You haven't caught Ena shoplifting again, have you?'

Vicki was about to answer when the woman laughed.

'I'm kidding you. I'm Awel and we're in the living room. Would you like a cuppa?'

Ruth held up a carrier bag from the local bakers in town. 'Fancy a Danish pastry to go with it?'

'That's sounds lovely. *Diolch*, my dear. Do go through. I won't be long.'

'I'll give you a hand.'

Vicki tapped on the door of the living room then stepped inside and blinked. Ena was a mirror image of her sister; they were quite obviously twins. She looked up and smiled.

'I thought I heard someone mention the police. I guess you're here to pinch Awel for shoplifting?'

Vicki laughed. 'She already told me that you're the one who's been at it and, I have to say, you'll never get bail. Tea and cakes are on their way.'

'Such a treat. Now, tell me why you're here.'

'Constable England and I wanted a chat about the anti-social behaviour on the estate over recent weeks. We've had many reports but have failed to catch anyone actually causing the disturbance. As I say, many reports but no names. My constable tells me you and your sister have lived here since the houses were built, so I'm guessing you must know everyone.'

'That we do,' she said, 'but there are a few I wish we didn't know. The estate was always a little rowdy now and then, following a good win at the rugby, usually, but these days it's every night.'

'What is?'

'Cars racing up and down, kids out in the street spitting, swearing, and playing music at all hours. The girls are no better, hanging on the car owners' arms, starting cat fights… you name it.'

The living-room door opened and Ruth and Awel entered with a tray of mugs and a plate of sticky pastries. Vicki moved some magazines from a small table.

'We were talking about the yobs with the cars,' Ena said. 'The sergeant wants us to give her the lowdown. I was just telling her how things have deteriorated over the last couple of years.'

Awel sat next to the fireplace and nodded. 'Yes, they have that. Can't speak to the kids these days, I'm worried they might have a knife. Even if they haven't, you get a mouthful of abuse. Never like it in our day, when any adult could drag you home to your mother for a clip around the ear. Do that these days and the mother is likely to punch you in the face.'

'Yes,' Vicki said, 'I agree. Things have changed since I've been on the job, and certainly since when I was young. The changes must be huge for you.'

Awel nodded. 'Yes, indeed.' She smiled suddenly. 'We'll be a hundred at the end of August so we've seen massive change.'

'Wow!' Vicki said. 'That's an achievement.'

'It's easy,' Ena said. 'Just make sure to keep breathing.'

Vicki chuckled. 'I'll keep that in mind. Now, what more can you tell me about the troublemakers?'

'They like their cars, spend all night tearing around the estate, music blaring, and any day it isn't raining, they're out polishing and working on them. "Pimping them up" I believe it's called.'

Ruth stifled a giggle and focused her attention on her note-taking.

'They don't bother us, apart from the noise. We don't go out after dark, always worried we might turn into pumpkins, but the disturbed nights are wearing.'

'Is there somewhere they meet up during the day?'

'The car park behind the Hunter's Moon Inn at the end of the main street,' Ena said. 'There's a yard at the back and they gather there after closing time before they start roaring around the streets. At the other end of the estate, there are some lock-up garages behind the houses. That's usually where they are during the day.'

'That's useful, thanks,' Ruth said and made a note. 'Do you have any names for us?'

'Not really, they all use nicknames, but one of them lives opposite us, just across the road. He interests me.'

'Oh, why's that?' Vicki asked.

'Well, he never goes out during the day, but has very many friends who visit regularly. Shifty-looking lot, but maybe that's my age talking. Anyway, come night-time, he struts out of the front door like a popinjay and gets into one of the cars. I don't think he owns one himself, but he joins in with the mayhem every evening.'

'How many friends are we talking about?'

Awel pointed at a chair in the front window behind a net curtain. 'Take a seat and count some.'

Vicki picked up her half-empty mug and sat in the chair. Within minutes, a young woman walked up to number twenty-seven and tapped on the door. It was opened and she went inside. Five minutes later she was back on the pavement and a middle-aged man passed her and entered the house.

'Is it like this every day?' Vicki asked, scanning the street for any likely callers.

'Pretty much,' Ena said, 'until he goes out.'

'He's dealing drugs, isn't he?' Awel asked. 'No one has that many visitors, and we see the same people over and over again.'

'That might be what's going on. Drugs were mentioned in some of the reports we've received at the station.' Vicki saw the man exit and walk away. 'Does anyone else live in the house?' she asked. 'Does he have a family?'

'There was a young woman living there earlier in the year, but I can't remember the last time we saw her. Pretty little thing, long hair and chocolate skin. I always thought she lived on her nerves, looked wary, frightened even, but that's just my opinion. I could be wrong. There's an older woman living there too, blonde and fat. Might be the popinjay's mother.'

'This is useful information,' Vicki said. 'I'd like to take a statement from each of you – if you can spare the time.'

The sisters laughed and Ena said, 'We have lots of that. I'll go and get the kettle on again and we can make a start.'

* * *

Back at the station, Ruth headed towards the squad room while Vicki walked upstairs to brief DI Hughes. She found him in his office staring at his computer screen, and he looked up as she entered.

'Any luck with SOCO this morning?' he asked.

'It wasn't a waste of time. It looks as though a second vehicle had been pulled up next to the Fiat at some point. Casts have been taken of the tyre tracks for analysis. We also found some recently discarded rubbish – drinks cans and such. Sian Jenkins is going to have it all tested for prints and DNA. Nothing else. Has Billy Marsden at the garage been in touch?'

Hughes nodded. 'Yeah, the OBC is with Digital Forensics, Billy thinks it may have been tampered with. No prints found inside the car or on the manifold bolts.'

'When can we expect some results?'

'After the weekend, he said. Have you picked up anything from the estate residents?'

'Yeah, looks like there could be a dealer on Ash Grove, who also seems to be involved with the anti-social behaviour.'

Hughes snorted. 'That's always the way. Are you suggesting a raid?'

'Eventually we'll probably have to go that way, but the informants are two elderly women who live opposite the suspect's property. While Constable England and I were there, three individuals visited number twenty-seven and no one stayed long. I think we should gather information before we go in. Who knows, we may be able to get a lead on the supplier – if drugs are involved, of course.'

'Yeah, maybe. I'll run it past the guv and get back to you. You're off this weekend, aren't you?'

'Yes, sir.'

'OK then, we'll regroup on Monday morning, first thing. Anything else to tell me?'

Vicki was tempted to ask, "Isn't that enough?", but merely shook her head and left the office.

Chapter seven

Vicki snapped awake as her alarm clock sounded, and swore beneath the duvet. She wasn't at her best so early in the morning, but the long drive to HMP Eastwood Park near Wotton-under-Edge in Gloucester would take at least three hours, and she didn't want to be late. She got dressed, gulped down a coffee and poured the remainder into a flask to drink during the journey. She let herself out of the house and was pleased to see there had been no frost during the night, so she got into the car, cranked the engine and pulled away. The weather was overcast but dry, and early in the morning the roads were quiet. Vicki took the A40 and A48 before joining the M4 close to Llanelli. The radio was on but all the while Emma Hardwick was in her mind.

Emma had married a man fourteen years older while she was still a teenager. There were rumours that maybe she had been pregnant, but nothing had been proved and there was no child. Four years into their marriage, something happened. Emma had opened the door to the emergency services covered in blood, and incoherent. Her husband, Oliver, was found stabbed to death in the kitchen. During the interview, she insisted she had found Oliver on the floor when she returned home, but she had no alibi. She told officers she had been out for a walk, but no one was able to corroborate her story, as no one had seen her. The weapon – thought to be a chef's knife missing from the block in the kitchen – had never been recovered. A neighbour originally stated that she had seen a figure leave the house around the time of the killing, but on the witness stand, she said she must have been mistaken and had remembered a different day. The case for the defence collapsed. Emma was found guilty by the jury and the judge handed her a life sentence, ordering that she wouldn't be considered for parole until twenty-five years had elapsed – when she was nearly fifty. Vicki sighed and mentally reaffirmed she would correct the miscarriage of justice, no matter how long it took her.

The clouds parted as she crossed the River Severn into England and joined the M5. HMP Eastwood Park was in a village called Falfield, not far from Wotton-under-Edge, and Vicki took a comfort break while she was still a few miles away. The coffee in the flask beckoned and a leg stretch wouldn't go amiss either. She pulled in at the next lay-by, drank the coffee and wandered around a little to encourage the circulation in her legs. After a visit to the small toilet block, she tucked the flask back in the car and began the final stretch of her journey.

The prison had a long private drive that looked as though it might lead to a country estate. The name, Eastwood Park, made it sound like that too. A fairly understated sign on a metal railing next to one of the entrances announced the place was in fact a prison and young offenders unit. Some of the residential blocks on site resembled modern, housing estate properties separated by areas of grass, but the tall, green gates, with two coils of razor wire on the top, said different. Vicki parked the car, pulled on a warm, hooded top and made her way to the visitors' entrance. Over an hour later, after the endless searches, identity checks and a once-over from the resident sniffer dog, she was inside the visits hall waiting for Emma to appear.

A little while later, Vicki spotted Emma shuffle into the room and raised a hand. The young woman caught her eye and walked closer. She sat on the orange chair and faced her. She looked tired, worn down. Shockingly, she had cut her long red hair disturbingly short, and was wearing a badly fitting sweatshirt and a pair of baggy, too-long jogging bottoms. She smiled weakly.

'Hi, Vicki,' she said. 'How was your journey?'

'Uneventful. Made good time today, not so much traffic on the roads. How are things with you?'

'Same as always. Surviving.' She chuckled, a hollow, mirthless sound. 'I'm not getting much trouble these days. Most of the girls are on my side. Many of them wish they'd stuck a knife in their partners, so I get more sympathy than kickings.'

'Well, that's good.'

Emma nodded. 'My literary skills are still in demand, reading and writing letters, stupid poems sometimes. I'm even teaching some of the younger ones how to read, and I'm working on the prison magazine.' She shrugged. 'It keeps me busy.'

Her eyes reddened. Vicki could see the distress tucked behind the lids and her heart twitched. Emma shouldn't be in this place. Vicki knew with certainty that she wouldn't be able to cope if she was ever locked up, so it was difficult to understand how the young woman kept going with a minimum of another twenty-three years of jail time ahead of her.

'It's good that you have something to do, something positive,' Vicki said. 'I transferred some money to your prison account.'

'Thanks, but you don't need to do that, after all it must cost a fortune in fuel to get here. You don't have to keep giving up your time to visit me.'

'I'm happy to and I still feel guilty about you being in jail. The investigation was handled badly and I didn't do enough to help you at the time.'

'You did as much as you could and even then your bosses came down on you, put you back in uniform.'

Vicki waved the comment away. 'That doesn't matter. What does matter is getting you out of here.'

Emma sighed and scrubbed at her painfully short hair. 'I don't think that's going to happen. Why don't you just give up?'

'Because I don't want *you* to give up. You didn't kill Oliver! The person who did is still wandering around out there while you languish in this dreadful place.'

'Just don't let it take over your life – like it has mine.'

Vicki shook her head. 'I'm not going to stop until you're back out in the land of the living.' She changed the subject. 'I like your new hairstyle. You look like Sinead O'Connor, but it was a shock seeing it so short.'

'One of the girls had some clippers, and the prison has an explosion of nits, so it made sense. Not only that, I don't have to waste any of my spends buying hair products at the canteen.'

'Yeah, it does make sense. Right, I'll go and get some coffee and chocolate, then we can have a proper chat.'

Vicki went to the hatch and stood in the queue. From a distance she gazed at Emma, who was staring at her hands. The tiny woman looked like a doll, lost amongst the ranks of tables and chairs and other inmates. Vicki knew that no matter what Emma said, she would never leave her to rot. She would keep visiting until the verdict had been overturned and the young woman had been released.

* * *

The journey home seemed to last forever and the roads were much busier. As Vicki approached Cardiff, the motorway traffic increased and at times ground to a complete standstill. She swore and thumped the steering wheel. It was obvious a rugby match was being played in the Principality Stadium and she wished she had thought to check before booking the visit. Frustrated and weary after wasting well over an hour in the mayhem, she finally pulled into Sarn Park, a service area at the end of the motorway. She parked close to the entrance, locked the car and went in search of coffee, hoping a caffeine kick would wake up her. While she waited to be served, she sent Susan a text offering to pick up a fish and chip supper on her way home through town. Susan sent an enthusiastic reply and Vicki smiled. She walked back to the car, pulled onto the A48 and a while later, parked outside the chippy. She ordered two cod lots, well-wrapped to keep them warm, then hightailed it to Fron-Wen.

She announced her presence in the hall and heard Susan answer from the kitchen. When Vicki entered the warm room, she was surprised to see the table had been laid and Susan was pouring white wine into a pair of glasses.

'Hey, Suzy, looks like you've had a better day.'

Susan grinned sheepishly. 'I gave in and hit the morphine.'

'Should you be drinking then?'

'It would be difficult to feel much more wasted than I am already. I'm up to date with work so I don't need to use my brain for anything in the near future, which is just as well. The medication turns me into a dullard.'

'Nothing new come in?'

When Susan left hospital after her injury, she had set up a consultancy for all things security. She worked for any company or individual, if she could satisfy herself they weren't "scumbags" as she put it. She had even advised the police on a couple of occasions when her extreme curiousness proved useful on complicated investigations. With a full police pension coming in and a mortgage she paid off when the compensation cheque arrived, she could afford to be picky. She lowered herself gently onto a wooden chair next to the table.

'No, nothing new and no backlog.' She chuckled. 'I'm half expecting Glyn Hughes to ask for help with the Christina Page case. From what you've said, I'm not sure he'll be able to get to the bottom of it without assistance. It sounds too complex for a bear with so very little brain.'

'He won't ask you. He's too proud to admit he needs help.'

'Yeah, maybe.' Susan sprinkled salt on her food and added a hefty dollop of tartare sauce to the fish. 'How did the visit go today?' she asked.

'Just the same as all the others – depressing as hell.'

'How is Emma?'

'She's shaved her hair off, lost weight, and looks like the inmate of a concentration camp. She told me she got rid of her hair because there were lots of nits around, but I'm not so sure. I'm worried her mental health is slipping. If it is, she won't get any help inside. The prison doesn't have a great record in keeping their inmates safe.' Vicki rubbed her eyes. 'I can't begin to comprehend how anyone survives in a place like that, especially knowing you are innocent and facing over twenty years before there's the chance of release.'

'Are you sure you aren't harming her by instilling false hope? When the police arrived at her house that day, Emma opened the door and she was plastered in blood. Her hands, knees and shoes were covered in it.'

Vicki sighed. 'She stated at trial that she had dropped to her knees in the kitchen to try and stop the bleeding. The amount of blood on Emma was consistent with her doing just that. And of course the murder weapon has never been found, which makes the case shaky at best.'

'The chef's knife was missing. The wounds on the body were consistent – to use your word – with an identical blade.'

'But why would she stick a knife in her husband and then try to save him? That doesn't make any sense to me.'

'Horrified by what she had done, perhaps? There is no normal reaction in a situation like that. Emma gave moving testimony at her trial about the abuse she had suffered during her marriage, from a man who took coercive control to the next level. Terrible, what he did to her. She'd probably just had enough that day and lashed out with the knife in her hand. It could even have been an act of self-defence.'

'I thought you doubted her conviction,' Vicki grouched.

'I still do. The charge of murder was wrong, she should have faced a charge of manslaughter. Given the circumstances, I'm sure the judge would have been kind – even if the jury found her guilty.'

'She wouldn't change her plea and has always insisted she wasn't in the house when Oliver was killed.'

Susan dipped a flake of fish in the sauce. 'She may have been badly advised by her legal team. If you could make a case – adding what you know about the faulty investigation – she might be granted an appeal.'

'She shouldn't need an appeal. She's innocent!' Vicki said angrily and rubbed her tired eyes.

'I understand why you feel so strongly but remember, if you do manage to drag the case back to court, no one but Emma will thank you for it. The CPS – and Horrible Hughes – will make sure they give you the worst possible time.' Susan put a chip in her mouth then pushed the half-full plate away. 'Best way to tackle this, in my humble opinion, is to uncover a new and credible suspect.'

Vicki shook her head. 'I don't have to find the real killer, just cast enough doubt on Emma's conviction for it to be overturned. Anyway, considering the trail went cold two years ago, that's a big ask.'

'I know, but you have to agree it would be much easier if you could uncover a new narrative, and that would go better with a replacement suspect.'

Vicki nodded. 'Yeah, I guess. Tell me, do you know Sian Jenkins? She's a SOCO based at Carmarthen.'

'I met her a couple of times before I left; nice girl, I thought.'

'While we were at the scene where the Fiat was found, she mentioned she was aware I was looking into Emma's case and offered to help. She went on to say the rank and file were behind me; they weren't happy about what went on back then.'

'What sort of help is Sian offering?'

'Forensic-type stuff would be my guess, or just reading through the case to help me find the gaps. We didn't really discuss it, but she said she would visit Emma with me one day if I liked.'

'So, someone at work *does* know what you're up to.'

'Yes, Sian does!' Vicki snapped.

Susan sighed. 'I know you're tired but I must say this. Whatever you do, or whoever you upset in the process is your business, but you must not drag a junior officer with you. That's just not fair.'

* * *

The next morning was sunny with a stiff, salty breeze blown in from the west coast a few miles way. Vicki carried a laundry basket down to the orchard at the bottom of the garden, and hung wet clothes on a long line strung between the plum trees. She'd just finished pegging out the sheets from Susan's bed when she heard her name called. She looked back towards the house, squinted in the bright light and spotted a man in overalls walking across the damp grass.

'Hey, Billy,' she called. 'What are you doing out this way?'

'Just passing. Thought I'd see if you were in and beg a cup of that great coffee you make.'

Vicki chuckled. 'What if I said I was out of coffee?'

Billy put on a mock frown. 'Are you?'

'Course not, come on up the back stairs to the flat. I'll get the kettle on and you can tell me what you really want.'

She picked up the empty clothes basket to carry indoors. Billy wrestled it from her grasp, even though it wasn't heavy, and Vicki rolled her eyes. They walked up the narrow staircase and Billy sat next to the counter on one of the stools.

'Fancy a jammy crumpet for breakfast?' Vicki asked.

'Sounds great, thanks.'

Vicki rummaged in the bread bin and dragged the toaster out from a bottom cupboard.

'So, why are you here, apart from coffee and crumpets?'

'I wanted to speak to you about the death of Christina Page.'

'I'm listening.'

'Well, last night I went for a drink with the digital forensic guy, Eli Barnes, who is examining the OBC. He said the faults displayed weren't faults but instructions.'

'I'm not sure what that means.'

'The best way to describe it is the faults were programmed to occur.'

'So a design error or software error was made at the manufacturers?'

Billy shook his head. 'No, the OBC was tampered with recently.'

'Can he tell exactly when that happened?'

'No, the date/time stamp was one of the faults, but I reckon you're looking for an individual.'

'How would anyone do something like that?'

'They'd need access to the OBC, and enough knowledge, of course. The main faults were as follows: unable to turn off engine, windows and doors locked, and phone connection to the car disabled. Christina couldn't get out or phone for help.'

Vicki swallowed hard. 'You said something the other day about Christina not needing a hose because the manifold was leaking exhaust gases.' She took a deep breath. 'Now we know for certain she couldn't leave the vehicle, even if she was conscious.' She looked up at him. 'The autopsy showed signs of bruises on the victim's upper arms, and a blow to the head.'

'So this is definitely a murder case then?'

'It's certainly not suicide. Are you coming in tomorrow or shall I pass this on to Horrible Hughes?'

'Best not, Vicks. Don't want him to think we've been talking behind his back. I'll deliver the report first thing. How did you get on with SOCO at the scene?'

Vicki told him what had been found, but didn't mention Sian's offer to help with Emma's case, or about the visit she had made herself the day before. She experienced a shiver, maybe Billy already knew about it, maybe others did. The force's grapevine was vigorous and had a long reach. She gulped a mouthful of coffee and glanced up at the clock on the wall.

'Gosh, I'd better get on,' she said. 'There's another couple of washing loads to do before I'm finished.'

'Want a hand?'

'Don't be daft. I don't want you coming in contact with my smalls.'

'Uh, no, of course not.' Billy looked at his shoes, ears pink with embarrassment. 'I'll get off then. Might see you in the morning.'

'Yeah, you might, and thanks for dropping in. I appreciate the tip-off.'

Chapter eight

Vicki arrived early at the station the next morning. She had a busy day ahead of her and wanted to get the daily audience with DI Hughes out of the way as soon as possible. He had obviously just been to the canteen as she met him in the corridor outside his office. He had a mug in one hand and a silver foil package in the other that looked greasy. She prayed he wouldn't begin to eat before she had left. He shoved open the door with an ample hip and dropped onto his chair.

'Morning,' he growled.

Vicki nodded. 'What's on for today, sir?'

'I've authorised a couple of DCs to keep the Williams sisters company for a while to gather info on number twenty-seven, and Billy Marsden, the guy who works in the police garage, has just been in. In a nutshell, he said the computer in the victim's car had been hacked, so, bearing in mind the autopsy results, we are now treating the case as murder.'

'It always looked suspicious finding her like that. So you're ramping up the investigation then?'

'Yeah. I'd like you to take another trip out to High Road Garage and speak again with the mechanic. We know he had recent access to the vehicle, so maybe he also had a motive for murder. Make sure you interview the entire staff.'

'Will do. How is Digital Forensics getting on with Christina's mobile devices and laptop?'

Hughes stared at her and blinked. 'What?'

'According to the statement given by her friend, Gareth Sinclair, she'd been having trouble online and picked up some trolls.' Vicki returned his stare. 'Don't tell me no one is looking at them. Are her devices even in the station?'

'Her phone is,' he said. 'I found that myself on the seat of the car.'

'So, have you had it examined? Christ, the look on your face tells me you haven't. What the hell is wrong with you?'

Hughes sat up straighter and glared across the desk. 'You forget yourself, Sergeant. Speak to a senior officer like that again and you'll find yourself on a charge.'

Vicki surged to her feet. 'OK, so on the way to the garage, I'll call into Christina's place and collect her laptop.'

She ripped open the door and ran downstairs, swinging around the corners by hanging onto the metal banister. She couldn't believe what she had just heard. Horrible Hughes was at it again. Messing up another investigation with shoddy work. She burst into the squad room and the door bounced off the wall. Police Community Support Officer Dai Phillips left his seat by at least six inches and PC Kurt Helman grabbed his chest dramatically.

'Morning,' she said. 'First off, the death of Christina Page has been classified as murder. Consequently the investigation will be scaled up. While you're out today, keep your ears open and chat to the locals, you know the drill. Try to speak with anyone who knew her and ask around. We need to discover who might have wanted to kill her.'

'Maybe it was a stranger killing?' an officer at the back of the room said.

'No, I don't think so. This was planned, the tampering with the vehicle proves that. Someone had enough time – and access – to hack the computer and loosen the manifold. I think Christina knew her killer.'

Several officers nodded their agreement.

'Something you need to be aware of,' Vicki continued. 'CID are running a stake-out of 27, Ash Grove on the estate. Please, ensure that none of you does anything to compromise the operation when you're out there today. Now, I need a couple of you to man the phones and read through the statements we've already collected on both cases. Anyone seen Ruth England?'

'She rang in sick, Sarge,' Helman said and smirked. 'Woman's trouble, I expect.'

Vicki glared at him. 'Then you'll come out with me today… but you better not say any more shit like that.' She walked to the door and held it open. 'Off you go then, boys and girls, and take care.'

The room emptied and Vicki followed her officers, Helman on her heels.

'So where are we going?' he asked.

'Christina's place to pick up her laptop, then we'll pay a visit to Ieuan Noonan, the mechanic working at High Road Garage.'

'Want me to drive?'

'No, I don't.'

Helman shrugged and got into the passenger seat as Vicki started the engine and headed into town. She parked outside a small, terraced house with a tiny front garden and left the car. Blue-and-white police tape fluttered across the garden gate, more criss-crossed the front door. She tore the tape away, inserted the key she'd brought from the station into the lock, and walked into a short, narrow hall with a low ceiling. A few items of post were scattered on the coir mat. Vicki picked them up and placed them on a side table next to a phone. She noticed the message light was blinking so she pulled on gloves and pushed "play". A tinny voice announced,

> You have three new messages.

Vicki pressed "play" again.

> Hi, doll. Just wondering where you are. Give me a call when you get this.

A male voice. Vicki pulled out her notebook and scribbled down the date and time the message had been left – half past seven, on the evening before Christina's body had been discovered.

The second message had been left by the primary school's headmaster, and he sounded angry.

> Chris, it's Martin. I hope you're on your way. It's nearly nine and I have a class full of toddlers without a teacher. If you weren't coming in today, you should have called, this is not good enough.

Vicki made another note and listened to the last message, left at half past ten in the morning, a couple of hours after Christina's body had been found.

> Hi, *cariad*, it's Mam. I know you'll be at school now, but didn't want to bother you there. Thought you'd like to come over to Llangwm for supper this evening. It's been too long since we've had a proper chat, so I'll hope to see you later. Love you. Bye.

Vicki slipped the tape from the machine and sealed it inside an evidence bag. She was due to see Christina's mother later in the morning.

'What are we supposed to be looking for, Sarge?' Helman asked.

'Computers and other mobile devices. The place had already been searched before the case was deemed to be murder.'

'So, how come none of the stuff we're picking up now was taken then?'

'I have no idea. If you're that interested, why not ask DI Hughes? I'm sure he'll be happy to tell you.'

Kurt Helman frowned and headed upstairs. Vicki opened a door off the hall and found herself in a small living room-cum-office. A desk was positioned beneath the front window and a laptop sat on the surface, together with a mobile. She made sure the devices weren't plugged in then slipped them inside a large paper sack. A quick look around the room showed the owner had been neat and tidy. A collection of delicate glass animals marched along the mantelpiece, weaving between four brass candlesticks which looked as though they had been recently polished. In the alcoves were bookshelves, packed with novels old and new, reference books about nature, and large, heavy volumes containing photographs released by the National Geographic Society. Framed photographs that appeared to have been taken locally hung on cream walls. Vicki wondered if they had been taken by the victim and began a quick search in the cupboards. In a tall, corner affair she discovered a top-of-the-range digital camera and tucked it in a second evidence bag.

Finding nothing else to interest her, she went to the hall. She could hear Helman moving about above her head, so she walked up the stairs to the small landing. She pushed open the bedroom door and saw the officer with his hand deep inside a drawer, which looked as though it contained lacy underwear.

'What are you doing?' she asked.

Helman's head shot round, his eyes wide. 'Nothing. Looking for any mobile devices like you told me to.'

'Unlikely to be a laptop in her knicker drawer.'

'How would I know? I'm a guy. Who knows where girls put anything? My mam keeps a secret stash of cash in hers.'

'Not very secret if you know about it.'

Helman's face flushed pink and Vicki continued, 'I've found the laptop and a second mobile so we can leave. As I told you when we arrived, the place has already been searched so let's get on.'

Helman shoved the drawer closed, pushed past his boss and went out to the car.

Vicki took a last look around then followed him out. She placed the recovered items in the boot and set off for the garage where she found a spot on the forecourt reserved for cars awaiting an MOT.

She turned to look at Helman. 'I'm going to have a chat with Mr Simpson, the owner,' she said, 'before speaking to Ieuan Noonan. While I do that, have a wander around, chat to the workers and see if you can find out if any of them knew the victim. Don't make it obvious, and keep your ears open. Pay attention to anything they say.'

Helman nodded then left the car and Vicki went to reception.

'Morning,' she said as she entered. 'I'd like another quick word with Mr Simpson. Is he in?'

Brenda nodded, picked up the phone and spoke to her boss. She hung up.

'Mr Simpson said to go on through,' she said and returned to a mountain of what looked like invoices covering the top of her desk.

'Thanks,' Vicki said, slipping through the small door in the reception desk and making her way to the owner's office. She tapped on the door and pushed it open.

Simpson got to his feet and smiled. 'Sergeant Blunt. I didn't think I'd see you again so soon. Please, take a seat. Can I get you something to drink?'

'I'm fine thanks, sir.' Vicki sat. 'How are you?'

He grinned. 'Not bad. Busy – as always. Now tell me, does your visit have anything to do with Christina's death? Have you got any further with your investigation?'

'There have been developments.' Vicki took a breath. 'I'm very sorry to have to tell you that we are now treating her death as murder.'

'Murder? Oh God, no. Her poor mother. Do you know who was responsible?'

'No, sir, still working on it.'

'Dear, oh dear.' He rubbed his eyes. 'I can't believe it. Who on earth would want to kill her?'

'That's one of the reasons I'm here – to ask if you knew of anyone who wished her ill.'

'No, I don't know anyone who didn't like her. How awful.' He reached into one of his desk drawers, removed a small, silver hip flask and took a swig. Without thinking, he offered the flask to Vicki, who smiled and shook her head. 'No, of course not,' he said, 'you're on duty and it's too early. Sorry.'

'No need, I can see the news has shocked you. Is Ieuan Noonan in today? I'd like another word with him.'

'Yes, I'm sure he is. I'll go and give him a shout. Sit tight.'

A few minutes later, Ieuan entered the office. He nodded at Vicki and took a seat.

'The boss has just told me that Christina was murdered,' he said. 'I'm guessing you think I had something to do with it, well I didn't. All I did was service her car and I told you that when you were here before.'

'I know you did,' Vicki said, 'but I just need to make absolutely sure you didn't spot any faults with the vehicle. We believe it was tampered with in such a way that Ms Page was poisoned by the exhaust gases.'

'Well, it wasn't me, and I didn't notice anything when I did the service. It all looked fine to me.'

'Did you and Ms Page have any sort of relationship? For example, did you ever go out together for a drink, something like that?'

Ieuan frowned. 'God, I wish, she was gorgeous but way out of my league – I'm too young for her.' He got to his feet. 'I've got masses of work waiting, so if that's all…'

'Just one more question. Do you know any of the petrolheads on the estate? The guys with the flash cars?'

'Yeah, a few. Some come in here for MOTs and mechanical jobs they can't handle themselves.'

'Do you know if any of them were friends with Ms Page?'

Ieuan snorted. 'Hardly. Not her type at all. She was a classy woman and wouldn't hang around with any of that lot.'

'How about the lads here? Any of them have a relationship with her?'

'No chance. If anyone had they'd have bragged about it, and no one said a word.'

'OK, then.' Vicki got to her feet. 'If you do remember something, or hear anything, make sure to ring me. I assure you that whatever you tell me will be in confidence.'

'I'll bear that in mind, but I really don't have anything to tell you.'

Chapter nine

Vicki left the garage and dropped Kurt Helman at the back door of the station to deliver the items removed from Christina's home to Digital Forensics. After he'd emptied the boot, she pulled away and headed towards the village of Llangwm, where the victim's mother lived. The small village was close to the Cleddau Estuary, built on the side of the Llangwm Pill, a wide and slow-moving tributary a few miles from Haverfordwest. The weather had changed and thick clumps of drizzle drifted from dark skies and made driving unpleasant. Vicki parked outside a detached house not far from the church and left the car. She turned up her collar against the rain, put on her hat and walked through a pretty garden to the front door. She knocked loudly and it was soon opened by a short, dumpy woman, with puffy red eyes and a pale round face.

'Hello,' she said. 'I really hope you're here to tell me who killed my daughter.'

'I'm sorry, no. We're still investigating. I'd just like a chat about Christina if you're up for that.'

'I'm up for anything if it helps to bring my poor girl's killer to justice. Come in out of the wet and I'll put the kettle on. Difficult conversations are always easier over a cuppa, don't you think?'

'Yes, I do, thanks.'

Vicki stepped inside, shook the rain from her coat and removed her hat.

'Go through to the living room, I'll bring the tea in. Do you take sugar?'

Vicki nodded. 'Just one, please, Mrs Page.'

'Please, call me Jill.'

Vicki pushed open the door Jill indicated and stepped into a light, airy room with a large window. She gazed through the glass at a bucolic scene, watched the Pill sliding slowly past green fields, and spotted a couple of boats moored next to the bank. She turned away. A baby grand piano stood at the opposite end of the room, with many framed photographs placed on the shiny lid. Vicki examined them closely and discovered they were mainly of Christina from toddler to adult. She couldn't see any pictures of a father, or any siblings. It appeared Jill was alone with the tragedy of her daughter's death. The door opened and the short woman entered carrying a pair of mugs, which she placed on a low coffee table next to the sofa.

'Please,' she said, 'take a seat and tell me what you'd like to know.'

'I'd like to ask about Christina's friends. Did she have a boyfriend?'

'She stayed away from blokes after her marriage ended.' Jill dabbed at her eyes with a crumpled tissue. 'I can't say I blame her; the divorce was acrimonious and the process wore her out. She tried very hard to hide her distress, but a mother always knows. She was always a popular girl though, more so after she got rid of her useless husband, but she was damaged goods.'

'Yes, I can see why she'd think twice. I'm sorry to mention this, but one of her friends said she caught her husband in bed with a neighbour.'

'Yes, that's right, the bastard! He broke her heart and ever since then she's had an issue with trusting anyone else. Just as well really.'

'Why do you say that?'

'There were a few men, knights-in-shining-armour types who sniffed around. Blokes like that seem to find vulnerability a turn-on. Martin Llewellyn was one of them, made a right pest of himself from what she told me, never mind he's married with two little kiddies.'

'You're talking about the headmaster at her school?'

'Yes, he's a nasty, sleazy guy who wouldn't take no for an answer. Chris told me she was going to report him to the authorities but she was killed before she could do that.'

'Did he ever go to her house?'

'I have a feeling he might have, but she never said. My girl was very good at putting on a front; she presented a smiling face to the world, even when she was unhappy. It was difficult to work out what was really going on with her, she didn't like to worry me.'

Vicki made a note, then asked, 'Is there a Mr Page around?'

'No, he died when she was little. Brain tumour. It's just been the two of us ever since.' She sighed heavily. 'I didn't remarry, in case that was going to be your next question. Brian was the love of my life. I'm glad he's not here to see this, it would have been the end of him.'

More tears fell and Vicki gave the distressed woman a moment or two to gather herself.

'I'm sorry to stir all this up,' she said, 'but we really want to catch whoever did this to Christina and to do that, we need to ask these questions.'

'Yes, I understand. I'm sorry I'm such a mess.'

'No need to apologise, I appreciate how hard this is on you. Tell me, do you know Gareth Sinclair, her best friend at the school?'

For the first time, Jill smiled. 'Yes, I know Gareth, they were friends for years. If he hadn't been gay they might have married, a much better choice, but that's silly. If he hadn't been gay he wouldn't have been Gareth, if that makes sense.'

Vicki smiled. 'Yes, I understand. He seems like a good guy. I spoke to him at the school a couple of days ago and he mentioned the trouble your daughter had experienced with her boss. I didn't know it was bad enough for her to consider reporting him though.'

'Like I said, she was a private person, kept a lot of stuff close to her chest.'

'Gareth mentioned she had been bothered by online trolls. Did she talk to you about that?'

'Not really. She might have mentioned it a couple of times and said they didn't bother her, just annoyed her.'

'Did she say anything about the messages the trolls left?'

'She didn't go into details. I guess it was the usual abuse many women receive online these days, from people who can hide behind anonymity. If I had my way, I'd blow up the internet. I hear very little good about it. Bring back libraries and proper social interaction, I say. Ban all this chatting with online "friends" you don't know, and live in the real world.'

'I'm with you on that,' Vicki said. 'Social media causes such trouble and most of the cases we deal with these days have some online element.'

Jill sniffed and fought more tears. 'Do you think you'll be able to catch whoever did this awful thing to Christina?'

'I certainly hope so. As I said, we are working hard on the investigation and as soon as I have something to tell you, I'll return.'

The sobbing woman suddenly reached out a hand and grabbed Vicki's wrist. 'Thank you,' she said, 'for the investigation, and your visit. It's good to have someone to talk to.'

'Have you been offered a family liaison officer?'

'No, but I don't want a stranger here. I have some friends in the village whom I can call on, but they all have such busy lives. I don't want to be a burden.'

'I'm sure you wouldn't be, but let me give you my card. All my numbers are on there and if you think of something I need to know, or just want some company, don't hesitate to call. I'll pop in for a cuppa next time I'm out this way, if that's OK.'

'That's kind, thank you. You'll be welcome and I'll keep your card by the phone. Would you like another cuppa now?'

'No, thanks, I need to get back to the station, but I'll be in touch.' Vicki got to her feet. 'I can see myself out. Look after yourself and ring any time.'

Vicki left the house and, as she did so, a call came through on her radio.

'8142, where are you?'

'8142, Llangwm, been chatting to Mrs Page.'

'Well, you better get back here on the double, Vicki. Horrible Hughes is looking for you and he's not happy.'

'When is he ever? Any idea what he wants?'

'None at all, but make it quick. Something has really rattled him.'

'OK, I'm on my way.'

Vicki put the car in gear, wound through the lanes to the A4076 and put her foot down. Arriving at the station, she walked through the back door and stuck her nose into the squad room. It was empty apart from the officers battling the paperwork mountain. They looked up as she entered.

'DI Hughes is looking for you, Sarge,' one of them said. 'He's in a bit of a state.'

'Do you know why?'

'Not a clue.'

'OK, I'll be back. Keep at it.'

Vicki ran upstairs and found the inspector in his office, phone clamped to his ear, red-faced and sweating.

'Yes, sir,' he said and slammed down the receiver. He looked up. 'Where the fuck have you been?'

'Where you told me to be; High Road Garage, Christina Page's house, her mother's place in–'

'We've got trouble,' Hughes snapped. 'I've tried to keep a lid on it but the news will spread fast once it gets out.'

'What sort of trouble?' Vicki asked, wondering if Horrible Hughes had been caught acting improperly.

'One of your plods patrolling the estate, chased, then rammed a kid on an electric scooter.'

'Shit! How's the kid?'

'Alive and in Glangwili Hospital. Obviously we're not going to mention this outside the office until his family have been informed and your officers have been extracted.'

'What do you mean, "extracted"? They aren't teeth.'

'Some residents have surrounded their car and are preventing them from driving away. We need to round up a team and get them out of there as soon as.'

'You mean you haven't sent anyone yet? How long ago did this happen?'

'Right before you were called. I can't gather enough coppers to risk going in. Carmarthen has said they will send what they've got, but…'

'Christ, this is Haverfordwest, not a massive sink estate on the edge of a city. Can't your guys on the stake-out assist?'

'I didn't want to blow their cover.'

'For fuck's sake! This can't wait. Tell me where the patrol car is and I'll sort it.'

'You can't go alone.'

'I won't be.' She glared at him. 'You better stay here, *sir*, safe behind your desk.'

Vicki stomped out and ran down to the squad room.

'You two, kit up. Where's PC Helman? We need all the bodies we can get.'

'He's in the canteen, I think,' a young officer said.

'Find him and anyone else with nothing to do. There's trouble on the estate and we're the cavalry.'

'What sort of trouble?'

'I'll fill you in on the way, we're short on time. Meet you in the van. You've got one minute.'

* * *

Vicki peeled out of the car park and switched on the blue light. The estate wasn't far away but, knowing her officers could be in serious trouble, anywhere was too far. As she drove, she updated her small team with the situation.

'When we get there, I don't want any heroics,' she said. 'We can't rush in until we understand the circumstances. We need to get our guys out, but it would be better for everyone if we could do that with as little fuss as possible.'

'How's the kid, Sarge?' someone in the back of the van asked.

'He's in hospital. OK, we're close. Check your gear and do not move until I tell you.'

Vicki slowed as she reached the edge of the estate, turned off the lights, and tucked the van into a narrow side street. She could see the patrol car fifty yards away with an angry group of mainly teenaged lads surrounding it. They yelled abuse and hammered on the vehicle. Vicki was pleased to see no windows had been broken – yet.

'Right then,' she said. 'PCSO Phillips, I want you with me. The rest of you, stay in the van. Too many cops on show could easily escalate the situation and we don't want that. Keep an eye on us and if things get lively, I'll wave you in.'

'We should be with you,' Helman said. 'We don't want to miss out on the fun.'

Vicki glared at him. 'You'll do as you're bloody told. Fun? You're a muppet and I'll deal with you later.' She caught Dai Phillips' eye. 'You ready?'

'As I'll ever be, Sarge.'

Vicki nodded, opened the door, and stepped out followed by the bulky officer. Together they walked closer, unextended batons held low by their sides. The gang surrounding the car looked up and turned to face them. A wiry youth who appeared to be the leader, his arms and neck covered with tattoos, took a few steps closer. He had a nasty grin on his face. He laughed loudly.

'Is this the best you can do?' he sneered. 'Why have you brought a hobby bobby with you?'

Vicki smiled at the kid. 'Well, not only is he the largest officer in the station, but he's also a prize-winning cage fighter – highly strung.'

She glanced at Dai Phillips, hoping he wouldn't deny the false claim, but he kept his mouth shut and worked at looking menacing. Vicki glanced at the ringleader.

'Feel free to have a go if you fancy it, although little fellas like you won't stand much of a chance.' She pulled a mobile from her pocket and waved it in the air. 'I'll just wait here ready to ring an ambulance for you.'

'This isn't right,' the kid said. 'That bastard in the car rammed our mate and he's had to go to hospital. For all we know, you lot have killed him.'

'Last I heard he wasn't dead and I promise you there will be a full investigation. All you are doing is making a bad situation much worse.'

The young man snorted. 'You buggers always look after yourselves. This will get covered up, just like always.'

'I'll personally make sure it doesn't, I give you my word, but you must disperse and move away from the car. Do that right now, or my colleague will nick all of you, so move!'

The volume of Vicki's voice made the kid flinch. He took a step back and she knew he'd lost. She marched determinedly up to the car and the gang parted. She looked through the driver's window and saw two white-faced constables.

'Go,' she said. 'Get yourselves back to the nick.'

The driver didn't need to be told twice and began to pull away. Vicki felt a hand grab her shoulder and spun around quickly – into a fist, which landed on her left eye. The tattooed man had more balls than she thought. She snatched his arm, caught the other wrist and snapped handcuffs on before he could blink.

'Dai,' she said. 'Take him away and do what you like with him. He was warned.'

'What? No!' the kid said. 'I know my rights.'

Vicki leaned in closer. 'So do we. You can't get away with smacking a copper.'

'Are you OK, Sarge?' Dai Phillips asked as he took hold of the prisoner.

'I'm fine. We'll regroup at the nick when this one is in the cells. I'll leave PC Helman and one of the paper miners here to keep an eye on things from a distance. Meanwhile, we need to get to the bottom of what happened – and update DI Hughes.' She grinned. 'I don't expect him to be overjoyed with today's events.'

Chapter ten

Vicki found Hughes in the squad room talking to Ruth England. She strode up to the pair and recognised the shock on their faces when they saw her blossoming black eye.

'Bloody hell, Sarge,' Ruth said. 'You've taken a right old smack; your eyebrow is bleeding. I'll have a word with the doc, get him to check you over.'

'There's no need. I thought you were off sick.'

'Feeling better now, well… enough for duty.'

'So,' Hughes said, 'you'd better fill me in on this monumental cock-up.'

'Hardly a cock-up. The situation has been handled and the officers have – to use your word – been extracted safely. No injuries.'

'Apart from your face.'

Vicki waved his comment away. 'Bruises fade. Have you spoken to the officers who knocked the kid off the scooter?'

'Yes, I have. They say he shot out in front of them and there was nothing they could do to avoid him.'

'So there wasn't a chase?' she asked.

'If there was, the dashcam hasn't captured it.'

'That's good. How is the injured lad?'

'OK, as far as I know. Broken leg, couple of smashed ribs and a broken wrist. He'll survive.'

'Has anyone been out to speak to the family?'

'Not yet,' Hughes said. 'I waited to see how things panned out.'

'I suggest that is done sooner rather than later. I saw small groups of residents gathering. We don't want this to kick off like it did in Cardiff earlier in the year. Has anyone arrived from Carmarthen nick?'

'A few, yes, they're in the canteen.'

'Then haul them out and get them on the street,' Vicki said. 'It wouldn't be a bad idea if you went out to assess the situation and try to calm people down. There's a lad in the cells charged with assaulting a police officer and we better hope that's the only nicking today.'

'You don't need to tell me how to do my job.'

Vicki shrugged. 'I'm knocking off now and I'll be back in the morning.'

'Your shift isn't over,' Hughes snapped.

'I've been injured in the line of duty, sir. I need some time.'

Vicki sent Ruth a wink, turned on her heel and left the room. She made a quick visit to the custody suite and spoke to the sergeant in charge. He reported that the prisoner was bouncing off the walls, and as he was only hurting himself – the CCTV footage from the cell would confirm that – the decision had been made to interview and charge him in the morning.

Vicki left the station and made the short drive to Fron-wen. Her head ached and her badly bruised eye was more painful than she'd let on. She hoped she wouldn't be called back in – that no further trouble kicked off on the estate.

* * *

A little while later, she pulled up outside the large house, turned off the engine and rested her forehead on the steering wheel. Dregs of adrenaline were still circulating in her veins, so she took deep breaths and gradually the prickling sensation abated. She left the car, let herself into the main hallway and called for Susan.

'In the library,' her friend answered.

Vicki pushed open the door.

Susan looked up as she entered. 'Oh my good God!' she said. 'How did that happen?'

'Got involved in a spot of bother on the estate. A kid was knocked off an electric scooter by one of ours.'

'Did the kid survive the encounter?'

Vicki nodded and wished she hadn't, as the movement stirred her headache.

'Well then, we can be grateful for small mercies. Knowing you, the doc won't have looked at your eye, so let's go to the kitchen and I'll clean it up a little.'

'There's no need.'

'Maybe not, but it will make me feel better – and useful.'

Susan levered herself upright with help from her stick and made her way towards the kitchen. Vicki put the kettle on then dragged the first-aid kit from an overhead cupboard.

'Sit at the table,' Susan said.

Vicki did as she asked and the older woman gently prodded the injury, which made Vicki flinch.

'Has your sight been affected?' Susan asked.

'No, nothing like that; it's just bloody sore.'

Susan nodded, rummaged in the kit and used a sterile wipe to clean the blood away from Vicki's split eyebrow.

'It's going to need a couple of Steri-Strips and a dab of iodine. Who knows where your attacker has been.'

'How is it,' Vicki said, 'that I'm never allowed to fuss over you, but you're doing a great impression of a mother hen?'

'Just hush, here comes the iodine.'

Vicki sucked in air as Susan applied an orange-stained cotton bud to the cut. That done, Susan fiddled with the strips and pulled the edge of the wound together. Then, she examined her handiwork.

'That's all done, you're good to go.'

'Thanks. Any chance I can pinch one of your decent painkillers?'

'Yes, just one. Cupboard by the sink.'

Vicki helped herself to the bottle, then poured boiling water into the hideous teapot and placed it on the table next to the mugs.

'So, what is the situation on the estate now?' Susan asked.

'Quiet, as far as I know. I'm hoping things don't kick off later. There was a similar incident in Cardiff a while back, and that escalated into a full-on riot, burning cars – the lot.'

'I remember. I'm surprised to see you home, even with the injury.'

'Me too actually, but Hughes isn't handling the mess very well and, to be honest, I couldn't bear to look at him any longer. I'm on call though.'

'Well, fingers crossed your phone doesn't ring.'

'Yeah, fingers crossed.' Vicki poured the tea. 'What have you been up to today?'

'Been dipping my toe into Emma Hardwick's case.'

'Really? Why are you doing that?'

'Because it's bothering you and my desk is clear. As you know, I don't do boredom.'

'Find anything?'

Susan chuckled 'Hardly, I've only been at it for a couple of hours, but I did have a chat with an old colleague of mine. Seems he was underwhelmed by Hughes's handling of the original investigation.'

'Who did you speak to?'

Susan tapped the side of her nose. 'Need-to-know basis only.'

'Fair enough.'

'My initial assessment is not enough work was put in. Emma was an easy nick and we know DI Hughes is a lazy bugger.'

'Anything I can do?'

'Not sure yet. I need more time, but I'd be inclined to visit the witness – the neighbour who gave evidence in court and changed that evidence at the last moment.'

'Because Hughes slept with her,' said Vicki.

'How do you know that?'

'Gossip was rife at the nick for weeks after Emma was sent down.'

'You'll need more than gossip, which is why we should call in for a chat when you're off duty.'

'We?' Vicki asked.

'I haven't been out for a while and I'm suffering from cabin fever.'

Vicki smiled. 'Point taken, but I'm not sure she'll own up.'

'Neither am I, but it's got to be worth a try.' Susan zipped up the first-aid kit and washed her hands at the sink. 'In the meantime, go upstairs and get your head down for an hour or so. The painkiller will make you drowsy. Come back down at five and we'll have supper. Gwen has dropped off another meal – casserole, this time, so neither of us has to slave over the Aga.'

'Yeah, I'll do that, thanks – and for patching me up.'

'No problem, now scoot.'

* * *

Vicki woke nearly two hours later. She stretched beneath the duvet, then went to her small bathroom and splashed water on her face. She looked in the mirror above the sink and was shocked to see the bruise had spread alarmingly to cover her eye, temple, the top of her cheek and the side of her nose. The paper stitches made her look like a boxer. She dabbed her skin dry, dressed in baggy around-the-house clothes, then wandered downstairs to the hall. Hearing voices coming from the kitchen, she tapped on the door before letting herself into the warm room.

Susan was sitting at the table chatting with Billy Marsden and they both looked up as Vicki entered.

'Shit!' Billy said. 'I heard on the grapevine you took a whack this morning, but you look terrible.'

'Thanks for that then,' Vicki said and poured herself a cuppa.

'No, I didn't mean... He hit you hard though, didn't he?'

Vicki smiled. 'I certainly felt it, but it'll heal. What are you doing here?'

'I just wanted to see how you were,' Billy said.

Susan chuckled. 'How sweet. You should stay for supper, there's plenty to go around. Make yourself useful and fetch a bottle of red from the larder. You'll find a corkscrew in the cutlery drawer.'

Billy didn't need telling twice. He dug out the wine and began peeling the covering from the cork. He poured three glasses and sat back at the table.

'Is everything still quiet on the estate?' Vicki asked as she took a sip from her glass.

'So far,' Billy said. 'There's been some rumbling from the residents, but the chief super put in an appearance with Hughes in tow; that seems to have convinced the locals the accident won't be whitewashed away. The kid's doing OK and his family have been to visit him, so that's helped too.'

'Good to know. I really don't want to be dragged back in tonight. I feel a little wobbly now I've had a kip.'

'You'll feel worse when the wine mixes with the pain medication,' Susan said. 'Don't worry, if the nick rings I'll tell them you're not fit for duty. They'll listen to me.' She snorted. 'They are more than likely worrying themselves stupid that you'll land them with a claim. From what you've told me, you were seriously understaffed.'

'I didn't have to go, no one made me, but I couldn't leave two of my troops out there without any backup. It might have all gone tits up.'

Susan nodded. 'Yes, these things can turn on the head of a pin. Look how I copped it.'

Two years ago, Susan had been on duty at a protest outside a country hotel not far from town. The locals had heard the place was scheduled to house what the government called "asylum seekers". The plan had been badly drawn up. The influx of outsiders was nearly double the number of residents, and double the amount the place had been built to accommodate. A camp appeared outside the gates and the population ebbed and flowed. When the protest hit media outlets, numbers swelled as reporters joined the mass of people by the gates, and trouble occasionally broke out. Sometimes pushing and shouting escalated into something else and injuries were more or less inevitable.

The day of Susan's injury, the far right were out in force and the regular, local protestors didn't want them there. Two very different groups of people, who ironically wanted the same thing – for asylum seekers not to be housed in the hotel – but for very different reasons. The yelling turned nasty and when the first punch was thrown, the police moved in. Susan tackled a large, angry skinhead, intending to arrest him, but he caught her off balance and spun her away from him. She landed badly, her lower back connecting with the top of a low stone wall. The result was a swollen spinal cord, two broken vertebrae, and restricted mobility became her new normal.

'Yes, I agree,' Vicki said, 'escalation happens easily, and people get hurt.' She reached across the table and squeezed Susan's hand. 'I'm just glad the kid didn't whack me in the nose. I've always been proud of my beautifully straight nose. My best feature, I think.'

'It's not just your nose,' Billy muttered, then blushed when he realised he'd spoken out loud.

The women shared a look before Vicki removed the casserole from the Aga and dished up. She added a warm, crusty roll to each plate and carried the meals to the table. Billy leapt up to help and nearly caused a disaster in his haste, so he sat down again when Vicki frowned at him. They shared a few minutes of comfortable silence as they savoured the rich, meaty gravy and baby carrots, fresh from Gwen's polytunnel.

Billy wiped his lips on a piece of kitchen roll. 'There was another reason I called round,' he said.

'Gonna tell us what that is?' Vicki asked and grinned at him.

'The DF guy, Eli Barnes, has been in touch again. He's done some more work on the OBC from Christina Page's car and is fairly sure it was hacked remotely, as opposed to someone actually being inside the car.'

'I'm not sure exactly what that means, but how on earth would that be possible? Someone propped a laptop up on the bonnet?'

'More like someone used a phone and connected to the car via Bluetooth.'

'That only picks up phones around ten metres away, surely?'

'Not if you buy a booster which can increase that by ten times. In theory, it means that someone could stand on a motorway bridge, hack an OBC at random and cut the engine.'

'Would that really be feasible?' Susan asked.

'A month or so ago, a top-of-the-range electric car disobeyed the driver on a motorway in England. It sped up to over one hundred miles an hour, and the owner couldn't turn it off or use the brakes. He made a panicked call to the cops, who formed a rolling cordon around him until the battery went flat. No cause has been identified yet, but it is possible it was hacked.'

'Gosh, that poor bloke. He must have been terrified.'

'All computers have firewalls, don't they?' Vicki asked.

'OBCs don't,' he said. 'There have been proposals about adding them but the manufacturers – who don't want their costs to increase – insist the likelihood of anyone hacking a car is too small to worry about it.'

'Did Eli convince you that is what happened to Christina's car?'

Billy topped up the glasses. 'I'm afraid he did, and the idea scares the pants off me.'

* * *

An hour after slipping beneath the duvet, Vicki was still wide awake. She turned onto her back and stared at the silhouette of the window frame on the sloping ceiling, cast by the light of a full moon. The window was open and a gentle breeze crept inside, bringing with it the sound of a distant flock of sheep murmuring into the darkness, and a not-so-distant tawny owl. Vicki replayed the events of the day and consequently her mind was too busy to close down. Eventually, she got up to use the bathroom.

As she passed the window, she heard a different sound, the crunch of tyres on gravel, but no engine grumble. She peered through the glass and saw a white electric car pulled up outside the gate. The driver's door opened and a man stepped out. Vicki squinted into the dark, but the glow from a dim bulb above the front door didn't reach far enough for her to see anything useful, other than he was wearing a suit. He shut the car door quietly and stepped through the gate, then Vicki lost sight of him as he drew closer to the house. She heard him knock, and a few minutes later, Susan welcomed him inside.

Vicki used the toilet, got back into bed and wondered who the late-night caller was. Susan hadn't said anything about expecting a visitor, but then they didn't live in each other's pocket. Vicki burrowed into the quilt and tried to put the sighting out of her mind, but she couldn't help conjuring up wild identities for the man, including spy, lover, criminal, cad. She smiled to herself. It was more likely that the caller was the "contact" Susan often spoke about.

She rather liked the idea of Susan having a fella, even if she couldn't really picture it. Just as she couldn't see herself getting together with Billy, no matter how persistent he was. As far as she knew, Susan had divorced nearly twenty years ago in her forties, then concentrated on her career. She had only retired because of the injury she suffered on duty. If that hadn't happened, Vicki was sure Susan would have made superintendent – at least.

She wondered about popping downstairs to make sure everything was OK, but wisely decided not to. Whoever he was, it was Susan's business and she wouldn't be pleased to be checked up on. Vicki plumped her pillow for the umpteenth time and tried to settle while her mind continued to run amok, constructing mental images of what might be happening downstairs, until at last she finally managed to drop off.

Chapter eleven

The next morning, following the daily briefing, Vicki and Dai Phillips walked downstairs to the custody suite and into interview room one. The heavily tattooed man they had arrested yesterday was already waiting at the table. A custody officer leaned against the wall next to the door and kept an eye on him. Vicki was pleased to see the prisoner was quieter. A night in the cells had obviously been a good idea. She took her seat next to Dai Phillips, who stretched out a long arm and switched on the recording device. He verbally logged on with the date and time, and listed those present in the room. Vicki took a breath and began the interview.

'You are Rhys Griffiths of Fforest View, Haverfordwest?'

The lad smirked. 'No. I'm John Smith from Cardiff.'

Vicki sighed, this was not going to be an easy session.

'Don't mess about,' she said. 'Just confirm your name, address and date of birth. The quicker we get through this, the quicker you'll get to court, and if you're lucky, the quicker you'll get released.'

Griffiths shrugged and muttered his details for the tape.

'Thank you,' Vicki said. 'You have been offered legal representation and you declined the offer, is that right?'

'Yeah, I can handle this myself.'

Vicki shrugged and opened a file on the table in front of her. She flipped the paper, then looked up at Griffiths.

'I see you've not only been charged with the assault of a police officer, but possession of a class A drug. Three wraps of cocaine were found in the pocket of your jeans. Where did you get the drugs?'

'From a bloke in a pub.' Griffiths leaned back on the chair; the front legs left the floor and Vicki had an urge to push him over.

'Come on, Rhys,' she said. 'That won't hold water. Tell me where you really got them, from someone on the estate maybe?'

'I told you – bloke in a pub.'

'Which pub?'

Griffiths shook his head and began to rock the chair.

'OK,' Vicki said, 'have it your way, but three grams is – in my opinion – too much for personal use, so I think we should amend the charge to "intent to supply".'

Griffiths frowned. 'Nope. It's all mine. I'm not a dealer so you can't do me for that.'

'In the absence of a named source, that's exactly what I can do. I know someone is dealing on the estate, so tell me who you bought the coke from and I'll make sure the judge knows you were cooperative. Maybe he'll go easy on you at sentencing.'

'I'm not a fucking grass and, for the third time, I bought it from a bloke in a pub.'

Vicki smiled. 'Yeah, Rhys, I believe you.' She took another look inside the file and said, 'OK then, moving on – not that there's much more to say.'

'Is that it?' Rhys asked and got to his feet.

'Hardly. There's the little matter of assaulting a police officer, not that we need to talk about that, really. Three body-worn cameras recorded the incident from three different angles, and you, Rhys Griffiths, don't have a leg to stand on.'

Dai Phillips cleared his throat. 'To be clear,' he said, 'you attacked a police officer, her head to be exact. A case could be made for a charge of GBH; maximum sentence: life!'

Rhys blinked. 'What are you talking about? Life? You can't be serious.'

Vicki grinned. 'My officer is right. The bodycam footage is convincing, we could up the charge. Either way, you'll be held on remand while the CPS thinks about it – that might take a week – and then… who knows?'

Vicki leaned back in her own chair and folded her arms. No one liked silences and she knew, given enough time, the prisoner would feel compelled to speak.

Rhys sat back down. 'So, what you're saying is,' he eventually asked, 'if I give you a name, you won't up the charges?'

Dai Phillips smiled. 'Gotta be worth a try, considering the position you find yourself in.'

'If I do give you a name,' Rhys said, 'you have to keep it quiet. You can't tell anyone that I've told you anything. If you do, I'll get my head kicked in. If I'm lucky. Something worse if I'm not.'

'We're listening,' Vicki said.

Rhys took a deep breath. 'Well,' he said, 'I have heard there is a dealer on the estate, but I've never met him. I got the coke from a third party.'

'OK, now we're making progress, so give us some names. This is your last chance, Rhys. We're busy and can't waste much more time on you, so spit it out.'

Rhys scrubbed at his face. 'I don't know an actual name. The dealer has a nickname – Pit Bull.'

'Like the dog?' Dai asked.

'Yes, like the dog.'

'Do you have an address?' Vicki asked.

'No, I've already said I got the coke from a runner, and before you ask, I don't know the kid's name, but he was young, not a teenager.'

'So a schoolkid?'

'Yeah, eleven or twelve maybe.'

'OK, that's useful.' Vicki leaned over the table. 'Interview suspended at 11.04.' She switched off the machine. 'Right then, Rhys. You will be returned to your cell and will appear at magistrates in the morning. Too late for today's session, I'm afraid.'

'You mean I've got to spend another night in there? You said you'd go easy on me if I cooperated.'

'That's not what I said. I said we wouldn't look at increasing the charges. Unfortunately, you'll probably get a walk-out. If I had my way, you'd be on your way to prison.'

Rhys's face lost all colour. The custody officer peeled himself off the wall, clicked handcuffs on the prisoner and took him away.

Vicki smiled at Dai.

'You're good in an interview, well done. Didn't say much, but what you did say landed hard. I'll make sure the higher-ups know and maybe, this time next year you might be a proper copper.'

Dai grinned. 'Thanks.'

'Right then, coffee before we tackle anything else. I think we've earned it.'

The officers got to their feet. Dai removed the tape from the machine and they headed towards the squad room. As they passed the back door of the station, Billy Marsden walked in.

'Perfect timing,' he said when he spotted Vicki.

'Bloody hell, Billy, you again?' said Vicki. 'People will talk.'

Billy chuckled. 'They already are. Got a couple of minutes?'

'I guess.'

'Good, come with me and meet the IT guy. He's managed to get into Christina's laptop and what he's found isn't pretty.'

'In what way?'

'He reckons Christina had a cyber-stalker, as well as a particularly vicious troll. Thought you might like a peek at what's been found before it's handed over to Horrible Hughes. Might help with your investigation.'

'It isn't my investigation; it's his, remember?'

'Nevertheless…'

Vicki sighed. 'Go on then. Dai?'

'Yes, Sarge?'

'Cover for me, I won't be long.'

'No sweat.'

Dai Phillips turned away and walked up to the squad room, while Vicki followed Billy into the bowels of the station, where the digital forensic lab was based. He held the door open for her and she walked into the quiet room. Several members of staff sat at desks, eyes focused on their screen. The only sounds were the clattery taps of fingers on keyboards and the whirr of computer fans.

Billy raised his hand and a skinny, pale-looking young man, glanced up from the back of the room. He wore a black T-shirt and black jeans. His long, dark hair had been tied into a ponytail with a leather band.

'Hey, Billy,' the man said. 'Is this the sergeant you were telling me about?'

'What did he tell you about me?' Vicki asked.

'Nothing bad, so keep your knickers on. I'm Eli. Pull up a chair and let me show you what I've discovered.'

Vicki did as he suggested and squinted at the screen. 'Let's see it then,' she said.

Eli nodded, he tapped the keyboard and the screen changed. A list of emails was displayed. He clicked on one and opened the message. Vicki leaned closer and read from the screen.

> You know I can ruin you, bitch, and will destroy your life. If you don't do what I ask, everything I've gathered from your social media accounts will be sent to every one of your contacts. Your family won't speak to you, the school will sack you and, who knows, maybe even the press will pick this up. Think of the shame, Christina. It is now time to deliver the goods.

'Do we know what the sender is talking about?' Vicki asked.

'I have an idea. I found these photographs as attachments.'

Eli tapped the screen again and Vicki gasped when she saw the first image: Christina, naked, and engaged in a sexual act. She was easy to identify and Vicki swallowed hard. From what she had discovered by talking to the victim's friends and her mother, this seemed very out of character.

'There are more,' Eli said, 'all along similar lines – some are worse – but they aren't real.'

'Not real? I'm looking at them, so how can they not be real?'

'They've been altered. Basically, the victim's face has been superimposed on an existing image. It's a fake, quite a clever one, but if you know what you're looking for, you can spot that the pixels have been manipulated.' He chuckled. 'Look at the mess the royal family got into recently when the Princess of Wales did exactly that.'

'Bloody hell. So, whoever did this is the cyber-stalker?'

'I think he might also be the troll, but I'm still checking.'

'Do you know what he wanted?'

'The usual thing in circumstances like this, more photographs or video, taken by the victim and sent to her tormentor – money sometimes. I won't go into details, but this woman's stalker asked for some very explicit stuff.'

'So she was being blackmailed?'

'Looks like it and it's been going on for months.'

'Do you know if she complied with the requests?'

'I haven't been able to find that she did, but I'm still looking.'

'Maybe it was suicide then,' Vicki said.

'You know it wasn't,' Billy said. 'The tampering with her car is evidence of that. Perhaps the stalker killed her because he couldn't make her play ball.'

'How would he entice her out to the middle of nowhere?' she said.

Billy shrugged. 'No idea, I can't think like him.'

'Are the emails still coming in?' Vicki asked. 'Or did they stop after Christina died?'

Eli glanced up and grinned. 'Indeed they did. Billy might be right.'

'So who is this man? Can you discover who sent the emails?'

Eli shook his head. 'No, not yet. Whoever this is, has good computer skills and managed to hide not only his identity, but the IP address of the computer he used to post this shit. I'll keep working on it though, and let you know if I get lucky.'

'Thanks, Eli, and well done.' Vicki got to her feet. 'Right, I'd better get upstairs before anyone who matters misses me.' She patted the man on his shoulder. 'Keep at it.'

Billy led the way out of the office and they parted company by the back door.

'Fancy a drink this weekend?' he asked. 'Dinner somewhere maybe?'

'Actually, I might take you up on that.'

'Well, you have my number.' He chuckled. 'If you don't give me enough notice to book somewhere though, we'll end up at McDonald's, so don't forget to call.'

Billy left the station and Vicki made her way up to the squad room. DI Hughes followed her in.

'How did the interview go?' he asked.

'Not bad, considering. Griffiths has confirmed there is a dealer somewhere on the estate, but he couldn't give us an address or a real name. The dealer is known as "Pit Bull", like the dog, and it seems he uses children for runners. For all we know, he might control an entire county line. How is the stake-out going?'

'Slowly, we're still collecting photographs, a rogue's gallery to work from. Some of the individuals could be runners, bearing in mind what Griffiths told you.'

'Any shots of the householder?'

'Not yet, we'll give it another couple of days.'

'Who is registered as living there?'

'Pam Davis and her twenty-two-year-old son, Michael.'

'I think he might be the lad the Williams sisters talked about, but the only woman they mentioned, other than an older woman, possibly his mother, was someone young and small, and they haven't seen her very often. They told me the lad leaves the house every evening to go and play with the petrolheads. Seems they gather in the car park behind the pub at closing time, so that location might be worth checking out.'

Hughes nodded and rubbed his stubbly chin. 'I've received a preliminary report from Digital Forensics. They've taken a look at Christina's laptop and found some nasty stuff.'

Vicki frowned and allowed Hughes to tell her what had been found, without admitting she had already seen the emails.

He continued. 'No IP address, so no chance of catching the bastard until we have more information.'

'Let's hope we find some soon.'

'Yeah. What have you got on today?'

'Full shift in the station, lots of paperwork to catch up with. I want to make sure the court papers for Griffiths are in order. He's in front of the magistrate tomorrow morning.'

'At least there's something we can cross off the list, and the estate was quiet last night so maybe we dodged a bullet.' He looked up at Vicki and sniggered. 'Shame you didn't dodge, or duck even. Christ, your face looks disgusting. Good job you're not going out today, you'd frighten the locals.'

Vicki ignored his comment. 'The internal investigation needs to be dealt with as quickly as possible,' she said, 'and we have to hope the residents will accept the outcome.'

Hughes nodded. 'I'll make noises in the right direction.' He turned and strode from the room, heading for his office.

Vicki breathed a sigh of relief, then made herself comfortable at her desk and began collating documents to send to the court.

Chapter twelve

Just as the sun was beginning to rise on Friday morning, Vicki's mobile buzzed loudly on the bedside table. Her spine shuddered in protest at the aggressive sound, so she snatched up the phone and, with fumbling fingers, finally managed to answer the call.

'Yes.'

'DI Hughes. We've had a report of a woman found unconscious in a car. Very similar circumstances to our existing case. As you found the first, I want you out there with me.'

'Where was she found?'

'Not far from you. Wiston Castle – in the car park. I'll see you there.'

Hughes cut the line and Vicki scrambled out of bed and pulled on her uniform. She checked her kit, laced up her boots and crept down the stairs into the main hallway. In the kitchen, she scribbled a note for Susan on a Post-it and stuck it to the kettle, then left the house and went out to the car.

Wiston Castle – officially known as a "tiny castle" – was a motte-and-bailey affair. The sparse ruins were balanced on top of a grassy mound; a flight of fifty steps crawled up the side. The historic site was on the edge of a small village and fairly isolated. Vicki sometimes took Susan to the spot for a picnic, but they had never attempted the steps for obvious reasons.

Vicki wound her way through the lanes as the dawn began. She met no traffic at all and a little while later, pulled into the car park. The blue lights strobed across the area in the low light, and the first thing she saw was a small, black Toyota Yaris. The second thing was a woman lying on her back in the mud, a man in Lycra standing over her. Vicki leapt out of her vehicle, extended her baton simultaneously, and charged towards the man.

'Police!' she yelled. 'Stand still!' She shone her torch at the man's face and he blinked. 'Step away from the woman. Do it slowly and do it right now!'

The man held up his hands and took a couple of steps back. 'This isn't what it looks like,' he said.

'Just stay where you are.' Vicki glanced down and saw a pretty young woman, in her twenties maybe, who was deathly pale. Her eyes were closed. Vicki bent to check for a pulse.

'She's alive,' the man said, 'but she won't be if you don't let me help her.'

Vicki glared at him. 'Who are you?'

'I'm the local doctor and the person who called 999.' He looked up towards the entrance of the car park. 'Where the hell is that ambulance?'

'Have you got ID on you?' Vicki asked.

'I don't bring anything with me when I'm out running. Now, please let me care for her. Why don't you check where the ambulance is?'

Partially convinced, Vicki nodded and put in a call as she kept a careful eye on him. A few minutes later, DI Hughes arrived with an ambulance on his tail. The vehicle skidded to a halt and two guys jumped out. One paramedic carried a large black case, the other an oxygen tank and mask. They knelt by the fallen woman, fitted the mask over her mouth and nose, and turned on the bottle.

Vicki walked towards the jogger.

'Right then,' she said, 'what's your name and address?'

'David Luckett. I live in the surgery not far from here.'

'OK, so tell me how you found her.'

'I was running down from the castle to the car park – I run this way every morning – spotted the car and heard the engine running. I waved a hand but the occupant didn't return the gesture, so I ran closer and saw her face resting against the side window. She looked to be unconscious.' He ran a hand over his short hair.

'What happened next?' Vicki asked.

'I used a large stone to smash one of the back windows, but I couldn't open the doors, so I wriggled inside to bring her out. The car was thick with fumes. I thought perhaps she was trying to kill herself.'

'Did you touch anything in the car?'

'Just the locking button on the back door, the door handle on the driver's side and the ignition key, but I couldn't turn the engine off.'

'OK. Now, take a seat in my car until we see what's what.'

'I have a surgery to run.'

'Well, today you might be a little late.'

Vicki watched him get into the car, then walked closer to Hughes as the paramedics loaded the woman onto a stretcher and carried her to the ambulance.

One looked up. 'We'll take her to Withybush Hospital,' he said.

'Will she be OK?' Vicki asked.

'I think so, she was found before she inhaled too much of the exhaust gases.'

He turned away and slid the stretcher into the back of the vehicle, then with blue lights flashing, tore out of the car park.

Vicki examined the scene.

'No note, no hosepipe either,' she said. 'Looks as though we have another. The witness wasn't able to unlock the doors or cut the engine.'

'I agree,' Hughes said, 'but another what? Who would trap women in their cars and gas them?' He took a breath. 'Do you think he watches them die?'

'Dr Luckett didn't mention another car, but I'll have another chat before he leaves the scene. Is SOCO on the way?'

'Yes, Sian Jenkins is coming out, but she has further to travel, being based at Carmarthen.' Hughes scrubbed at his unshaven chin and Vicki cringed. The rasping sound was loud in the quiet of the morning. 'I'm going to go to the hospital with her,' he said. 'I'll have some of your team come out to help secure the scene, but no one touches anything until SOCO has had a look.'

'Of course. Let me know how the victim is.'

Hughes didn't reply. He just strode back to his car, cranked the engine and left the car park. Vicki fumed. Bloody idiot, she thought, leaving a female officer alone with a male witness miles from anywhere. She turned back to her own vehicle just as the Toyota's engine spluttered then died. Vicki breathed a sigh of relief and opened the back door of her car. Dr Luckett sat on the seat looking distressed and she noticed his hands were trembling slightly.

'Are you OK, sir?' she asked.

'Getting there, a touch of shock, but nothing hot sweet tea won't fix. I just didn't expect to find a woman dying in her car. I'd been trying to get some air into her lungs for what seemed like hours.'

'Did you see another vehicle? Hear one, maybe?'

'No, it's rare I bump into anyone so early in the morning.'

'No one else in the car park or close to it?'

'I didn't see anyone.'

Vicki nodded. 'I need to take some details from you before you leave.'

'We can do that later in the day, surely. You know where I live. I really need to take a hot shower and drink some tea. Screw myself together ready for my patients.'

'Just give me a moment.'

Vicki stepped back out of the car, walked a few steps away then contacted the station using her radio. She asked the controller to find out the name and address of the doctor in Wiston. A few minutes later, the operator confirmed Luckett had been telling the truth. Vicki thanked her, cut the connection and returned to the car.

'Everything checks out,' she said, 'so you can get off now. I'm sorry I can't give you a lift home. I need to wait for reinforcements and protect the scene.'

'I understand. Will someone call on me?'

'It'll probably be me. Here's my card.'

The doctor looked at the card and nodded. 'OK, thanks.'

'I'm also sorry I misread the situation and jumped to conclusions,' she said.

He grinned. 'No problem. In your shoes, I'd probably have done the same thing, but I might have waded straight in and thumped the guy, so I'm grateful for small mercies. A whack around the head with your baton would have ruined more than my day.'

Vicki smiled. 'I stay away from heads, try to stick to knees.'

Dr Luckett chuckled. 'Good to know.'

'Thanks for ringing this in and trying to help the victim.'

'It's what I do, help people. We'll speak soon.'

Dr Luckett left the car, stretched his cooling muscles, then jogged away along a footpath in the direction of the village. Vicki walked slowly towards the Toyota. She noted down the registration number then made a slow circuit staring at the ground, but found nothing of interest. She pulled out her mobile and dialled Billy Marsden's number.

'Yeah,' he mumbled when he answered.

'Sorry, did I wake you?'

'Vicki. Yes, actually. Strange time to ring to take me up on my offer of dinner.'

'That's not why I called. There's been another car found with a woman inside, the vehicle full of exhaust fumes.'

'Shit! Is it the same thing, do you think?'

'Bloody strange if it isn't. She was discovered at Wiston Castle. I'm here now waiting for SOCO. Hughes has buggered off to the hospital. The woman was unconscious but thankfully still alive.'

'Are you there alone?'

'At the moment. Hughes has promised reinforcements, they just haven't arrived yet.'

'OK, I'm on my way. The scumbag who did this might still be around.'

'Kind of you, but I reckon he's long gone. Get another hour's kip then come out to recover the car.'

'I'm awake now. I'll see you soon. If I was you, I'd lock myself in your car, just in case.' Billy put the phone down and Vicki tucked her mobile away, wondering about the wiseness of his advice.

The sun was higher in the sky now and even though it was early in the year, there was some welcome warmth in it. A wren, tucked away in a bramble thicket, puffed out its chest and sang to the new day, accompanied by a glossy blackbird perched on top of a hawthorn bush. Movement to Vicki's right caught her eye, and she smiled when she saw a small group of rabbits cropping the dewy grass a few feet away. She widened her search and frowned when she saw how many tyre imprints were left in the mud. There was a lot of work ahead. She heard an engine and turned to see a squad car in the lane. She ran over to the entrance and held up both hands.

The driver, PCSO Dai Phillips, stuck his head out of the window. 'What's up, Sarge?'

'There are tyre tracks everywhere so I don't want any other vehicles adding to the mess.'

'I'll park across the entrance,' he said. 'That'll stop any traffic.'

He backed up and after a seven-point turn in the narrow lane, managed to achieve his objective. He left the engine and lights running and walked closer to Vicki.

PC Kurt Helman got out of the passenger seat and followed. 'Have we got another dead bird?' he asked.

'Are you fucking kidding me, Constable?' Vicki growled dangerously. 'Have you ever heard the word "respect"? I'm telling you now, rein in your unacceptable behaviour or I'll find someone who can do it for you.'

'Aw, Sarge,' Helman said, 'it's just a bit of black humour. It's what gets us coppers through the day.'

'Un-bloody-believable!' Vicki looked away.

'How is the victim, Sarge?' Dai asked.

'Should be at Withybush by now. Luckily for her, an early-morning jogger saw something was wrong, smashed the window and got her out. The medics say she should be OK.'

'That's good,' he said, 'and maybe she'll be able to tell us who did this to her.'

'Yeah, maybe.' Vicki spotted a white van close to the entrance. 'That's SOCO. Show her to the scene, Dai, and, Constable Helman, go and close the lane in both directions. Apart from cops and locals, nobody gets through.'

Helman opened his mouth to complain, then wisely shut it, walked back to the squad car and began unloading temporary road signs and police tape.

'Nasty little runt,' Dai grumbled under his breath. 'He's like some spoilt kid and drives me nuts.'

'I agree, not that I'm supposed to comment on fellow officers.'

Dai chuckled and went to the lane to guide Sian Jenkins around the edge of the muddy car park.

'Hi, Vicki,' Sian said when she drew closer. 'Like to point me in the right direction?'

'There are a fair few tyre tracks, might be best to document those before we look at the car.'

Sian put her hands on her hips and sighed heavily. 'This will take some time, but I agree it's worth doing.' She glanced at the lane. 'Recovery is here, better warn him we'll be a while.'

Vicki nodded, then she skirted the edge of the car park and headed towards Billy's truck.

Chapter thirteen

Swollen clouds were creeping in from the west coast just after lunchtime, and as rain would compromise any potential evidence, the decision was made to move the car and get it undercover. Billy reversed his truck across the mud and backed up close to the Toyota. He attached a wire to the tow bar and slowly winched the vehicle onto the bed of the truck. Once the car had been secured, and a protective cover tied over it, Billy drove out to the lane and headed for the police garage. Sian had agreed to the move as she knew the car would be waiting for her back at base, and that no one else would touch it until she arrived.

With Vicki close by, Sian spent a couple of hours examining the tracks, taking photographs, and hunting for anything that might provide a clue as to who had been there in the hours before dawn. The little car park was obviously cared for, probably by locals, so consequently there was very little rubbish to be found, and certainly nothing that had been discarded a few hours ago.

'Let's hope there's more to find on the car,' Sian said and poured black coffee from a flask.

'Yeah, let's hope.' Vicki sipped from a plastic mug. 'That's good, just what I needed, thanks.' She drank some more. 'We didn't find much on the first car – no fingerprints, no stray hairs, so no DNA. Nothing to find on Christine's body either, other than the bruises and the bump on the head. The pathologist said it looks as though the attacker wore woolly gloves. Under the scope, he could see the imprint of wool on the bruised area on her arms.'

'Well, I'll do my best,' said Sian. 'Billy will check for anything mechanical, then give Eli a call. I want him to take a look before we go anywhere near the OBC.'

'Good plan.' Vicki drained the coffee and handed back the mug. 'I'm going to see Emma again on Sunday. You said you'd be up for coming with me one day. Short notice, I know, but have you got anything on?'

'No, nothing other than housework and bickering with Da. Yeah, I'd like to visit her. I have a few questions about the forensics collected at the time.'

'You've been looking at her case?'

'Yes, in my spare time, of course. How early do you leave on Sunday morning?'

'Bloody early. Why not come for supper on Saturday and stay over? Susan told me she remembers you from before she was invalided out.' Vicki grinned. 'Described you as a "nice girl".'

'Cool.' Sian chuckled. 'Sounds like a plan. How about seven on Saturday? I'll bring some wine and my toothbrush.'

* * *

Vicki finally managed to get back to the station late afternoon. She bypassed the squad room and went upstairs to check in with DI Hughes, but his office was empty. A young DC said he'd clocked off.

'He left this for you,' she said and handed over a manila envelope.

Vicki went back downstairs and wondered why Hughes had left so early. Having found a second victim in the car-gassing investigation, surely any proper DI would be at his desk until the case was closed. She pushed open the door of the squad room and strode inside.

Ruth England was hunched over a mound of papers and on her own. She glanced up as Vicki entered.

'Where is everyone?' Vicki asked as she opened the envelope and tipped out a bundle of photographs.

'Dai and Helman are still at the scene keeping the rubbernecks away. Most of the others are conducting a fingertip search in the immediate area and house-to-house in the village. Any news on the victim?'

'Nothing yet.'

Vicki spread the photos out on a nearby desk. Hughes had attached a scribbled note that informed her the pictures had been generated by the stake-out of the house on Ash Grove. He wanted her team to put names to the faces. He also wrote that the woman in hospital had been identified as Jenny Hopkins from Pembroke, twenty-four years old. She was in a bad way but the doctor was hopeful. No interview would be possible until at least Monday and Vicki should go to the hospital then to find out if Jenny was well enough.

Vicki groaned and wondered why Horrible Hughes wouldn't do anything more than issue orders and act like an arse.

Ruth joined her by the desk and handed over a mug of coffee.

'Thanks,' Vicki said. 'The end of my nose is so cold I'm tempted to dunk it in the cup.'

Ruth laughed, picked up the note from Hughes and snorted. 'He wants us to identify this lot?' she asked. 'He's not as short-staffed as we are, one of his troops should do this. And the interview? He should definitely do that.'

'I know, although it's probably better he doesn't. He's not the most sympathetic individual I've met.'

'He should be here, detecting, not swanning off early.'

'I couldn't comment, Constable.'

Ruth shrugged and bent to examine the images.

'Recognise anyone?' Vicki asked.

'Only by sight, although…' Ruth picked up a photo of a group of kids and cars, presumably taken in the car park of the pub. She offered it to Vicki, who switched on a desk lamp and scrutinised the shot.

'Oh… is that Ieuan Noonan, the lad from the garage? The kid perched on the bonnet of that low-slung, dark-blue pimp wagon.'

'That was my conclusion,' Ruth said.

'What's he doing there? When I interviewed him, he told me he only knew a couple of the petrolheads, said he'd met them when they went in for MOTs.'

'Well, he looks very chummy with all of them to me – beer in his hand, laughing and sprawled on that car.' Ruth huffed. 'Just what is it with blokes and their bloody cars?'

Vicki chuckled. 'Making up for something that he is lacking? I'm sure you can work it out.'

Ruth began to laugh and struggled to catch her breath. Her laugh was infectious and Vicki joined in, enjoying the welcome release, until her mobile rang. She managed to swallow her giggles long enough to be able to answer.

'Vicki? Are you OK? You sound funny.'

'Hi, Billy. Just sharing a joke with Ruth. Do you have any news for me?'

'The manifold *was* hanging off the engine just like the first one, but there was a small difference. A heater hose under the bonnet had been repositioned, which meant the fumes were pumped straight into the car. That woman is lucky to be alive. I'm going to take another look at the Fiat, maybe I missed something.'

'Good idea, and have the hoses dusted for prints.'

'Will do. Anyway, Eli has examined the OBC and says it has definitely been tampered with remotely. He says he'll stay late tonight to work on it.'

'That's brilliant, thanks.'

There was an awkward pause then Billy said, 'You didn't ring so I hope you aren't busy this evening cos I've booked a table at the Hotel Mariners for seven. I thought we could both do with some downtime after today.'

'Persistent, aren't you? But you're right, we could. Make it eight and you're on, thanks. I'll see you there.' Vicki cut the call.

'Why don't you knock off, Sarge?' Ruth asked. 'You've already worked a twelve-hour shift. I'll keep studying the photos and show them to the team when they get back.

Other than that, there isn't much we can do until we have the full report from the car, and taken a witness statement from Jenny. You'll be doing that on Monday.'

'We're too short-staffed. I'll stay for another hour.'

'Up to you, but I've got this covered. If I encounter any problems, I'll talk to the DCI, he likes me.'

'Is that a good thing?'

Ruth shrugged. 'It's a useful thing.'

* * *

Following a quick scrub up at home and a cuppa with Susan, Vicki let herself out of the house and drove into town. The Hotel Mariners was a large building, painted white, with a slate roof and a grand entrance. A sign directed her to the rear of the building, where an equally large car park waited. She found a space not far from the back door then wriggled into her leather jacket, picked up her bag and walked inside. At the reception desk, she was guided to a large dining room with tables equally spaced, overhead lights catching on the glasses and silverware. Vicki hesitated in the doorway then spotted Billy on the right-hand side of the room and made her way towards him.

He didn't notice her approach as his nose was seemingly glued to the menu.

'Hi, there,' she said.

Billy looked up and smiled. 'You look nice, almost didn't recognise you with clothes on… uh… I mean, not a uniform and a bright-yellow jacket.'

Vicki sat and smiled. 'Stop digging, Billy. I know what you meant.' She looked around the room. 'This is all very posh. A pie and a pint would have done.'

'Like I said, we need some spoiling. Did Hughes really leave you out at the scene on your own?'

'Yep. I'm struggling to stop myself from slapping Horrible Hughes. He doesn't seem interested in the case and didn't deal with Christina's death properly. He convinced himself it was suicide so he didn't collect evidence from her home, and is now trying to play catch-up.'

'Maybe he's being difficult because of the beef he has with you.'

'I'm not going to apologise for any of that. He tampered with witnesses on the Emma Hardwick case, physical evidence too, probably. The first witness, a young copper – Sally, who has since left the force – was pressurised into backing up his story. The only other witness changed her evidence in court, and I believe Hughes was screwing her.' She sipped from a water glass. 'Anyway, let's not talk about him. Let's have a relaxing evening. Not a school day tomorrow, so we can stay up late.'

'OK, but just one more thing. Eli got in touch. The hacks made to the last victim's car computer were exactly the same as the first. He said that might be useful because he now has double the amount of digital evidence to track the hacker with.'

'Does he think he can find this monster?'

Billy shrugged. 'He's bloody good at what he does and says he can do anything – if he has enough time.'

'That's the problem. We've had two attacks now, fairly close together. We have no idea when, or if, this guy will strike again. We must catch him before he has the chance.' Vicki caught Billy's eye and smiled. 'Now, I don't want to drink water all evening so, order some wine and we can choose what we're going to eat.'

* * *

Vicki didn't crawl out of bed until ten the next morning. The meal with Billy had gone well, so well in fact they chatted non-stop over multiple cups of coffee, until tired restaurant staff politely suggested it was time to go home. In the car park, Billy had kissed her sweetly on the cheek and headed for home. She was glad there had been no suggestion of "coffee at my place" considering how much they had drunk after dinner. She had woken with a thick head so she took a long shower then went in search of Susan. She found her friend sitting in the conservatory, a Welsh wool rug over her knees and a pot of tea within reaching distance.

'Go and fetch a mug,' Susan said, 'there's plenty in the pot. I topped it up when I heard you moving about.'

Vicki returned a few moments later, poured herself a cuppa and took a sip. 'Gosh, that's strong,' she said. 'Should de-fur my tongue nicely. I've had a bit of a slow start this morning.'

'That's what comes from working a hectic twelve-hour shift, followed by a night on the tiles romancing with Billy. He's really got the hots for you.'

'Rubbish, and we did no such thing! We spent most of the evening talking.'

'Not about work, I hope.'

'A little.' Vicki chuckled. 'We slagged off Glyn Hughes for at least half an hour. Did us both the world of good.'

Susan gazed out at the spring garden while Vicki told her about the second victim, and how Hughes had not only left her alone at the early morning scene, but had also suggested she should interview Jenny at the hospital.

'Lucky for her,' Susan said. 'The woman needs to tell her story to someone compassionate who listens properly, not an oaf without an ounce of understanding in him.'

Susan added more hot water to the pot and listened as Vicki updated her with the operation to find the dealer on the estate.

'No wonder you slept in,' Susan said. 'You should have an easy weekend and spend most of it resting. I'll lend you the box set of *Line of Duty*.'

'I don't want to spend hours with a bunch of fictional cops while I'm struggling with the real thing, but thanks. Sian Jenkins, the SOCO from Carmarthen, is coming for supper this evening. I thought I'd cook us all a roast. Is it OK to use the main kitchen?'

Susan smiled. 'Of course. It'll be good to see Sian again. She always showed great promise.'

Vicki took a breath. 'She's going to stay the night too. We're both going to visit Emma tomorrow.'

Susan frowned. 'No restful weekend then?'

'Half a one.'

'Just don't overdo it. You'll burn out.'

Vicki got to her feet and kissed the top of Susan's head. 'I'll keep your warning in mind. Right, then, I'll get the washing on and change your sheets. If you need me after that, I'll be in the kitchen cooking up a storm.'

* * *

Sian arrived fifteen minutes late and was full of apologies.

'My da decided he was going to be difficult,' she said. 'He hates cooking for himself, or finding his socks, or doing anything, really. I wish he'd get a bloody job; he's wearing me out. No wonder Mam left.'

They went to the kitchen and while Sian and Susan got to know each other better, Vicki put the finishing touches to the meal and carried the roast to the table.

'Oh my God!' Sian said. 'That looks amazing, like a Christmas dinner. Feels like Christmas too not having to cook for once.'

'The least I can do is feed you,' Vicki said. 'After all, you're giving up your day off tomorrow to spend some of it inside a jail.'

'I always enjoy road trips and I'm looking forward to meeting Emma and discovering if there's anything I can do to help her.'

As soon as the first mouthfuls had been eaten and appreciative noises made, Sian opened the bottle of wine she had brought and filled their large glasses.

'I went into work for a couple of hours today,' she said.

'Did you?' Vicki asked. 'Why?'

'That mass of tyre imprints was bugging me. I'd spent hours on Friday trying to make sense of them, but eventually they all looked the same, so I went in this morning with a fresh eye and...' She sipped from her glass.

'And what?' Susan asked.

'I found tracks that match exactly with the cast I took at the first scene. Absolute proof the same vehicle was at both locations.'

'Brilliant!' Vicki said. 'Any idea what sort of vehicle we're looking for?'

'These knobbly, all-terrain tyres are commonly used on sports vehicles, small Jeep-shaped affairs. I'm sorry I can't be more precise yet, but at least you can rule out vans, small commuter cars, Land Rovers, saloons, MPVs and some SUVs. It narrows the search a smidge.'

'Any revelations from Eli?' Vicki asked.

'Not yet, but I'm meeting him on Monday. Tell you what though...'

'I'm listening.'

'You're wasted as a copper. This is a fab meal.'

Chapter fourteen

Vicki pulled away from the house in the early morning on a cold wet day, which made driving unpleasant.

Sian nattered away about her father, what a waste of a space he was, and her mother, who Sian understood had left for a reason, though she missed her. Mrs Jenkins had not only left her husband, but the country as well, and was living in America. As Sian's wage was the only one coming into the house, she couldn't afford to visit, and her mother wasn't prepared to return to the UK.

Vicki enjoyed having company and the journey seemed to pass by quicker than usual.

They also talked about Emma, her predicament, and what could be done to change her future.

Vicki pulled up outside Eastwood Park with an hour to spare, which was just as well because the check-in process seemed to take forever. When they finally entered the visits hall, Emma was waiting for them at a table and waved.

'Hi,' Emma said. 'It's really good to see you, but I didn't expect to see you again so soon.'

Vicki smiled. 'Neither did I, to be honest, but I wanted you to meet my friend Sian. She's a scenes of crime officer and she heard I was visiting you.'

'And she thought it would be a fun day out to gawk at a murderess?'

'No, that's not it! She has offered to work through the forensic evidence in your case. She might find something we can use to get you out of here.'

'Oh,' Emma said and glanced at Sian. 'I'm sorry. I'm not in a great place at the moment.'

Sian waved the apology away.

'Why, what's happening?' Vicki asked.

'Just stuff. Nothing worth bothering about. So then tell me, Sian. How do you think you can help?'

'I've been looking through the case file and noticed that either the test reports have gone missing, or they weren't requested and therefore were never carried out.'

'What sort of tests?'

'DNA is one of them. I've only found a single report that basically confirmed the blood on your clothes came from your husband. What I was expecting to see were many more samples taken from you, him, the kitchen and door handles. Those tests would have looked for *other* DNA, shed by someone else.'

'The police took a mouth swab when I was arrested,' Emma said.

'We do that to everyone we nick,' Vicki said.

'Then I'm not sure I understand. If the tests weren't done, I guess that's bad, but what can anyone do about it now?'

Sian smiled. 'We still have all the evidence, conveniently stored in the place where I work. I can carry out the tests and re-examine your clothes and shoes. I might also be able to discover samples that were taken and not tested or, better still, a third person's DNA.'

'I already know I didn't kill the bastard so… I'm not sure how that would help.'

'If Sian can cast doubt on the evidence,' Vicki said, 'at the very least the case would be reviewed. If she finds unknown DNA, that would come under the heading of "significant new evidence".'

Emma smiled for the first time. 'And would give me grounds to appeal.'

'Yes, it would.' Vicki reached out and squeezed Emma's hand. 'I don't want to get your hopes up. Sian might not find anything, but it's gotta be worth a look.'

'Don't worry,' Emma said. 'I won't be popping champagne corks in my cell tonight.'

Sian chuckled and got to her feet. 'I'll go for coffee and goodies,' she said and made her way to the hatch.

'I like her,' Emma said. 'I don't rub up against many clever people in here. Will she be able to do what she says?'

'I know she'll give it her very best shot. Sian is bloody good at her job and wasn't happy with the verdict in your case. When she returns with the biscuits, you must tell us everything that happened on the day your husband was killed, and what you know about your neighbour with the bad memory.'

* * *

Two hours later, Vicki was on the road heading back to Wales. The rain had stopped which made travelling more pleasant, and she experienced a tiny flicker of hope in her chest. Listening to Emma recount her story made Vicki realise she was right, and the young woman's conviction was unsound.

'That poor girl,' Sian said. 'Locked up in there all this time. Her skin is grey and she's so thin.'

Vicki nodded. 'Yeah, prison really doesn't agree with her.'

'I guess that is sort of the point of incarceration.'

'It is, but this prison doesn't have a great reputation. From what Emma has told me, the place is disgusting – damp cells with peeling paint, not enough toilets or showers… or staff… or time out of cells, and rats and cockroaches everywhere.' Vicki huffed loudly. 'If we are serious about turning people away from crime and aim to rehabilitate them, we should look after them properly and fairly.'

'I agree, but that's down to the government.'

'It's all about a lack of money. Pay better wages and you'll get a better quality screw. That would help.' Vicki pulled over into the lane for Wales. 'Now you've met Emma,' she said, 'do you think you can do anything to help her?'

'Actually, I'm pretty hopeful, but I didn't want to say much in front of her, in case I don't find anything after all.'

'Why are you hopeful?'

'As you know, I don't usually work with case files. I make my report, hand it over and move on, but I think more than just test results might be missing from Emma's file. For example, I can't find any unused evidence, so I can't check it, and have no idea if the defence team was even given it.'

'What you're saying is the "full disclosure" might not have been full at all.'

Sian nodded. 'It's possible. Susan told me yesterday she's been checking through the case. With her past experience, she should be able to tell us what we're looking for and where to look. I'll have a chat with her when we get back to Fron-Wen.'

* * *

Vicki clocked on the next day feeling tired and downbeat. Sian had spoken to Susan the day before and the older woman agreed that, from what she had seen, something was wrong with the file and the investigation. The knowledge confirmed Vicki's suspicions, but she knew getting Emma released wouldn't happen by waving a magic wand. There was a massive amount of work to do before she even got close.

She briefed her team in the squad room, assigned tasks – mainly paperwork generated by both cases – and handed out patrol routes. That done, she left the room, went out to the car and set off for Withybush Hospital. She wasn't looking forward to the upcoming interview with Jenny Hopkins and knew that listening to the young woman's story wouldn't be easy. Victims' stories never were.

Arriving at the hospital, she negotiated her way through many other vehicles and finally spotted a space about as far from the building's entrance as possible. She got out of the car and put on her hat, just as a dark grey cloud split open and dropped icy balls of hail. By the time Vicki reached the main doors, the tarmac was white and very slippery. Once inside, she tucked the regulation bowler beneath her arm, announced her presence at reception, and was directed to a side ward. She tapped gently on the door and cracked it open. Jenny looked up and offered a weak smile.

'Come in,' she said, her voice scratchy. A hand went to her throat.

'Thanks,' Vicki said and sat by the bed. 'I'm Sergeant Blunt. I attended on Friday when you were discovered. How are you feeling today?'

'Rough like my voice. They used a respirator to pump oxygen into my lungs. Still' – another weak smile – 'they saved my life. What's a sore throat?'

'Can I get you anything?'

'I'd kill for a cup of milky, tepid tea, with sugar please.'

'I'll see what I can do.'

Vicki nipped out to the nurses' station and when she re-entered the room, Jenny was sitting up in the bed.

'Tea's on its way,' Vicki said. 'Bearing in mind your painful throat, are you able to talk to me? I want to ask about what happened to you on Friday. I need you to tell me all the details, even if you don't think they are important, so we can catch the monster who did this to you.' Vicki took a deep breath. 'We are certain you are his second victim. Christina Page, his first, wasn't as lucky, and I reckon he'll do this dreadful thing again if we don't stop him.'

'I'll be happy to talk if you keep the tea coming.'

On cue, the door swung open and a young nurse brought in a pair of mugs that she placed on the bedside cabinet.

Vicki nodded her thanks and the nurse left. 'Shall we make a start then?' she asked.

'Yes, let's do it.'

'My first question is whether you knew your attacker, and if you did, where you met him.'

'I don't really know him.' She sighed. 'I'm a writer, not famous or anything but it pays the rent, and I have a Facebook account. We met through the platform. He didn't post a photo and called himself "Hemingway", said he was a writer too. We private-messaged, then exchanged email addresses and were in contact two or three times a week.'

'When did he first get in touch?'

'A couple of months ago.' Jenny took a deep breath and gulped tea. 'Then, out of the blue, he sent a truly disgusting photo of me. It had obviously been mocked up, but it was scarily convincing. Made me feel sick.' She turned her head and gazed out of the window at a grey sky. 'That's when it all got silly. More pictures arrived, much worse than the first, if that was possible, then the threats and demands.'

'What did he want?' Vicki placed a hand on Jenny's arm. 'Take your time, there's no rush.'

'He asked me for bad stuff. I really don't want to go into details, but everything is on my laptop. I saved all the emails and pictures he sent.'

'Well done. That might give us a chance of finding him. I'm sorry, but I have to ask, did you give him what he wanted?'

'No.' Jenny pulled a tissue from a box and wiped her eyes. 'I told him to release the pictures, that no one who knew me would believe they were real. He kept pestering though, and I wouldn't, couldn't do what he asked, so I offered him money. Five grand to make it all go away.' She blew her nose. 'It was a stupid move, but I couldn't live with those images hanging over me. He agreed to the money and said he'd delete the photos once I'd paid up.'

'Why were you at Wiston Castle?' Vicki asked as she scribbled in her notebook.

'I'd finally got the cash together. He told me we should meet and I could watch him delete the pictures.' Jenny drained her mug and sighed heavily. 'He chose the meeting place.'

'You're doing really well, *cariad*. Would you like to take a break?'

'No, I'll keep going and get it done.'

Vicki nodded. 'OK, so you drove to the castle and pulled into the car park. Did you see any vehicles?'

'Yes, a silver SUV, small, not big like a truck.'

'A sports vehicle maybe?'

'Sorry, I'm not good with cars and didn't think to take down the number plate. I was nervous, not thinking straight, and nearly drove away. I wish I had.' She took a shuddering breath and more tears slipped down her pale cheeks. 'Anyway, I stopped about six feet away and a small guy got out of the car, short and thin.'

'Do you know what his face looked like?'

'No, he wore some kind of mask. I took the money out of my bag, rolled down the window and handed it to him. He snatched it, then held out his mobile so I could see the screen.'

'Could you see what was on it?'

'Yes, but it was gibberish. He swiped and tapped and more of the same stuff scrolled by. Then my window suddenly closed and I heard the door locks clunk. I tried the doors, but couldn't open any of them. The man peered in at me and laughed.'

'So you couldn't see his face.'

'No, only his eyes. They were dark, but I think he was white.'

'Then what did he do?'

'He fiddled at the front of the car, opened the bonnet, and I heard him using tools on the engine. I have no idea what he was doing.'

'Did you try to get out of the car?'

'God yes, but the doors were still locked and I couldn't unlock them. The key didn't work and the levers on the doors wouldn't move. I tried to use my phone to call for help, but that wasn't working either. I couldn't even get it to switch on.' Jenny drank from a water bottle. 'He came back to the window a few minutes later, held up his mobile, tapped the screen and the car's engine started. I was so scared. I could smell the exhaust and couldn't get out.' She took another drink. 'He kept staring at me through the window and it wasn't long before I felt really odd. I don't remember seeing him leave, but then I can't remember anything until I woke up here.'

'Why didn't you report what was going on to the police?'

Jenny made a rude noise. 'Everyone knows the police are useless – no offence – and I didn't want to put myself through it for nothing to be done. I thought if I paid him, he'd leave me alone' – she sobbed – 'and I could get on with my life.'

Chapter fifteen

Vicki returned to the car, slipped behind the wheel and rubbed her face. She was tired; interviewing victims always took it out of her and never seemed to get any easier, but maybe that was a good thing, she thought. If she wasn't empathetic, how could she be effective at her job? After a few moments, she turned on the engine and left the crowded car park. She was due at the station, but decided to pop in to check on Jill Page first, as she had promised. Apart from anything else, she could do with a cuppa before she spoke to Hughes.

The Welsh spring had really gathered some momentum – if you ignored the odd hailstorm. Bright-green leaves had appeared on the top of the hedges and masses of primroses and daffodils crowded the verges. Vicki spotted a pair of kites sailing high in the blue sky, and the odd blackbird zipped across the lanes kamikaze fashion as she drove by. She parked outside the detached house, walked up the path and rang the bell. A few moments later, she heard the chain being removed and the door opened.

'Morning, Mrs Page,' Vicki said. 'I was passing and thought I'd call in, find out how you are.'

'It's Jill, you know it is. Do you have any news for me?'

'Not really, but there has been another incident.'

'Surely not? You'd better come in and tell me about it. Go to the kitchen and I'll put the kettle on.'

While Jill made tea, Vicki told her about the second victim.

'That's dreadful,' Jill said when Vicki stopped speaking. 'For something like this to happen once is bad enough, but twice? Dear God.' She sipped from her mug, her hand shaking. 'You said the poor woman is in hospital. How is she?'

'She'll be fine. Luckily she was found in time, by a doctor out jogging.'

Jill sniffed and pulled a tissue from her pocket. 'Such a tragedy my girl wasn't found sooner.'

Vicki nodded and placed a hand on Jill's arm. 'I know this is hard and I'm very sorry for your loss.'

Jill smiled weakly and patted Vicki's hand. 'I know you are.' She sighed heavily. 'I do miss her though. After she moved to her own place she rang me every morning before she left for work, and again in the evenings. I suddenly feel very lonely, rattling about in this place.' She wiped her eyes again. 'A neighbour told me to get a cat – as though that would fill the gap. People don't think!'

'I reckon they do, but they overthink because they don't know what to say, and then get it wrong.'

'I suppose. If only one of them would come and talk to me about Christina. That's all I want to do, talk about her.'

'Tell your neighbours that, they might surprise you.' Vicki removed her notebook from her jacket. 'When we spoke last, you told me the headmaster at the school was a bit of a pest.'

'He sniffed around Christina like an alley cat. His poor wife. I've thought about calling her, but so far sense has prevailed and I've kept out of it.'

'Wise decision. Did Martin Llewellyn ever visit Christina here or at her place?'

She nodded. 'Following the break-up of her marriage, Christina lived with me for a while and Martin went through a phase of popping in. He used to say he was "just passing", which was a lie. Llangwm isn't really on the way to anywhere.'

'Did he give a reason for his visits?'

'Usual rubbish about checking on his best member of staff. He told her to take as much time as she needed and if she ever wanted any help or a shoulder to cry on, to call him.' Jill shuddered. 'I didn't like him, neither did my girl, but she'd taught at the school for years and didn't want to leave because of him. Eventually he stopped calling.'

'Do you know why?'

'Oh yes.' An almost invisible smile curled Jill's lips. 'There was a bust-up in the garden a couple of months after she moved here. There was a lot of shouting and a fair bit of swearing. He left in a huff and thankfully never returned.' Jill wiped her nose. 'My girl was brought up to be able to look after herself.'

'Do you know what the row was about?'

'Not really. I stayed in the kitchen so I didn't hear much, but I assumed she was telling him where to go.'

'You previously said she was thinking of reporting him for his behaviour.'

'Yes, but she didn't get the chance, did she?' Jill took a breath. 'Do you think he killed her to stop her making the report?'

'I honestly don't know, I'm sorry, but we should consider the possibility. People kill other people for many reasons – sometimes for much less. One more thing, there were some messages found on your daughter's answering machine. Did Martin Llewellyn ever call Christina "doll"?'

Again, Jill almost smiled although her eyes remained sad.

'The thought of Martin calling anyone "doll" is very funny, not his style. More "pompous arse" than "gangster". Gareth Sinclair used to call her that; a sort of nickname. It irritated me a little, such a stupid moniker, but Christina didn't seem to have a problem with it.

Gareth is a lovely boy but could go over the top sometimes.'

* * *

Back at the station, Vicki had just settled at her desk when DI Hughes stomped into the squad room and made a beeline for her.

'You took long enough,' he said. 'I expected you back before now.'

'I called in for a chat with Jill Page on the way back. I wanted to ask her about one of the messages on Christina's answerphone.'

'And?'

'Nothing to worry about. It was left by one of her friends. She did tell me about a row between the victim and the headmaster though, thought her daughter was telling him where to get off. She also confirmed Christina was seriously considering reporting him for being a pest. I plan to have another word with Gareth Sinclair about the extent of the harassment.'

Hughes nodded. 'How about the woman at the hospital? What did she have to tell you?'

Vicki recounted the interview and told Hughes what had taken place in the car park before Jenny was found.

'So,' he said, when she reached the end of her verbal report, 'the stalker didn't need access to the vehicle previously.'

'Seems not. Once his victim was trapped in the car, he could take his time. That early in the morning, in such a remote location, he was unlikely to be seen.'

'Did you speak to the mechanic at High Road Garage?'

'He's taken a couple of days off, but I'll catch up with him. Interestingly, your guys on the stake-out captured a picture of him in the pub's car park. He seemed to be part of the petrolheads, even though he told me he didn't really know any of them. I'd like to know why he bent the truth. Have your lot turned up anything new on the drugs case?'

'Not much. Work in progress. However, I'm convinced drugs are being sold from number twenty-seven.'

'Are you planning to raid the property?'

'Not yet. I want the suppliers, the kingpins. If we don't get them, the problem will only resurface.'

'So what's the plan?'

'I'm wondering about an undercover op, but that will have to be agreed by the brass. I'll let you know if we decide to go that way. Just make sure your lot are keeping their eyes and ears open.'

'They always do, sir.' She took a breath. 'Do you think now's the time to issue a statement, warning the public about this guy?'

'Again, not my decision to make.'

'Surely it would be a good idea, though. We have two victims and ought to consider he might do this again. The MO seems the same; snag a woman online, mock up some nasty photos and use them to threaten her with. So far, he's got away with it twice.'

'We need more evidence or a third-party witness.'

'Of course, but I don't think we should leave it too long. This could easily happen again.'

Hughes smirked. 'Good job thinking is above your pay grade then.'

Vicki swallowed down her anger and continued as though he hadn't spoken. 'I collected Jenny Hopkins' laptop and it's with Digital Forensics,' she said. 'Eli seems to know what he's doing so maybe he can trace the individual concerned, or at least find an IP address. Do you know if he found anything useful on the second car's OBC?'

'He hasn't been in touch. I guess he's still working through it.'

'How about checking ANPR in the area? Any available CCTV too maybe? SOCO told us we are more than likely looking for a small jeep, a sports vehicle rather than anything else. Jenny also mentioned a small silver SUV in the car park when she pulled in, so that would chime with what Sian discovered. No cameras in the lanes, of course, but he had to get to the locations using main roads.'

'Not a bad idea. Get one of your team onto that and let me know if you find anything.' Hughes turned away and left the office.

Vicki fumed. Checking hundreds of ANPR images would take hours and CID had the staff, she didn't. She got to her feet, helped herself to a coffee from the machine, then sat back at her desk, logged onto the database and began the search herself.

* * *

By five o'clock, Vicki had had enough. The hours she'd spent scouring ANPR images had been productive – but not very useful. It seemed to her that silver or grey sports vehicles were almost as common as the ubiquitous white van, and wondered whether the perpetrator had purposely chosen what he drove for that reason. Unfortunately, the cameras could not pick up images of the distinctive tyres. So far, no DNA or fingerprints had been found at either scene or inside the cars either. She groaned. A careful killer would be hard to catch. She shut down the computer, got to her feet and, after changing in the locker room, went out to the car.

The weather was dry and warmer than it had been, so she opened the window and let the sharp outdoor scent blow inside the car, happy to be on her way home. She loved her apartment in Fron-Wen, appreciated not having to live in town and put up with the noise and the traffic fumes. Her rooms at the top of the house felt like an eyrie, quiet and cosy. She knew how kind Susan had been offering her somewhere to live and, even though it had been only a couple of years, Vicki couldn't really remember living anywhere else.

Vicki let herself into the hall. A note on the banister informed her that Susan was in the summer house and asked her to make a fresh pot of tea and fill a hot water bottle. Vicki did as instructed, then set off across the lawn to the wooden shed.

The converted shed had quickly become Susan's favourite place. She had always been an outdoor person, but with her mobility issues, achieving that wasn't always easy. Vicki had carried out most of the internal changes. A local lad built a porch with a roof and sides which sheltered anyone sitting there from the wind. A small wood burner had also been installed, but to Vicki's knowledge hadn't yet been lit. Probably a good thing as even with the fireboard Vicki wasn't entirely convinced it was safe.

'Hi, Suzy,' she called. 'You must be having a better day to be out here.'

The older woman was sitting on a wooden chair filled with brightly coloured, feather cushions, a rug draped over her knees. On a table by her elbow was an open laptop, next to that, a small stack of scribbled notes.

'Hi, you,' Susan said. 'Yes, one of my better days. It's so lovely to sit out here and listen to the birds. They're all making a right old racket while they get ready for breeding.' She took the offered hot water bottle and tucked it behind her back. 'How did the interview go this morning?'

'Difficult as I expected, but we've got some new leads now. I'll let you read my report if you're interested. What are you up to?'

'Working on Emma's case file, making phone calls and appointments.'

'Doctor-type appointments?'

'Not this time. As I said, we should visit the flip-flopping neighbour, and it would be good if we could manage to talk to the probationer who backed up Hughes. I got her name from my contact, together with a phone number.' Susan removed her half-moon glasses and smiled at Vicki.

'Did either agree to meet us?' Vicki asked and poured the tea.

'Both, surprisingly, at the end of the week.'

'That is surprising. How did you manage to convince them to speak to us?'

'Sally Groves, the young ex-probationer, didn't seem to be concerned to hear from me. I got the impression that the verdict at Emma's trial has been playing on her mind. I think she could be useful.'

'And the neighbour with the bad memory?'

'Not so keen, but I'm sure I'll be able to win her round. I can be very persuasive.'

'Yes, I know you can. I see you've been working, have you come to any conclusions regarding the case file?'

'A few, and it seems young Sian was right. This was either half a case – hence half a file – or stuff has been removed.'

'Do you know what stuff?' Vicki asked.

'I'm making a list. I also managed to speak to Emma's solicitor earlier and he's agreed to pop in tomorrow for a cuppa and a chat.' Susan smiled. 'Someone else who is keen to talk.' She glanced up at her friend. 'I'm starting to believe there might be something we can do to help Emma, after all.'

Chapter sixteen

Following the briefing the next morning, Vicki headed out to the estate and took Dai Phillips with her. Both investigations were now generating serious amounts of paperwork and more officers were required to remain at the station to deal with it. Cases were solved by paying attention to detail so Vicki left Ruth England in charge and asked her to continue the search of ANPR records for the silver SUV.

Hughes had informed her that CID officers were no longer embedded with the Williams sisters, so she decided a visit was top of the list. Dai Phillips drove from the station, parked outside number twenty-eight, and they walked up the path. Vicki rang the bell and the door was soon opened.

'Morning, Ena,' she said. 'Can you spare a moment?'

The elderly woman chuckled. 'I'm Awel. Ena is in the living room watching some rubbish on telly.'

'Oh, I'm sorry, I–'

'Not to worry, *cariad*. I'm never quite sure who I'm looking at in the mirror.' She tilted her head and looked up at Dai. 'Gosh, you're a big lad, aren't you?'

'He's my bodyguard,' Vicki said. 'Useful chap to have at your back.'

'I should think so. Now, go on in and I'll bring the tea. Don't suppose you called in at the baker's on your way past?'

Dai held up a carrier bag. 'Half a dozen doughnuts any use to you?'

'There's a good boy. Go and find Ena and I'll be there now in a minute.'

Dai held the living-room door open for Vicki and she stepped inside.

'Morning, Ena,' she said. 'How are you today?'

'I'm Awel.' The elderly woman grinned. 'She's at it again, isn't she?'

Vicki chuckled. 'Looks like it. I wondered how you'd got on with the CID team, whether they behaved themselves.'

'Most of the time, but the man didn't lift the seat on the toilet. We didn't like that.'

The door opened and Dai jumped up to take the tray from Ena. He placed it on the coffee table next the bag from the bakers.

'So,' Ena said, 'to what do we owe the pleasure?'

'Just passing.'

'Checking up on us, you mean?'

'Yeah, pretty much.'

Dai handed out doughnuts and mugs then perched on a dining chair in the window.

'So,' Vicki said, 'how are things?'

'Nothing has really changed,' Awel said. 'The kids are still racing about at night and whatever is going on across the road is still going on. True, there are a couple of police patrols overnight, but the kids wait until they've left, then get back to what they were doing.'

'So, business as usual at number twenty-seven?'

'Yes, we were hoping you would raid the place.' She smiled. 'There's nothing much on the telly these days.'

'I'm sure a raid is being considered, but the bosses want to catch as many individuals as possible, not just a couple of small-time dealers.'

'I can see that. The officers who were here left a notebook for us to write in.' Ena picked up a pad from the dresser. 'We're recording vehicle numbers and noting down the times people go to the house.' She giggled. 'We keep customer score cards of how many visits they make, and gave them nicknames.'

'Oh, that reminds me,' Vicki said. 'Have you ever heard of anyone with the nickname Pit Bull?'

'Like the dogs?'

Vicki nodded.

'Can't say I have. How about you, sis?'

'No, that's a new one to me.'

'OK, well, keep up the good work, ladies. I'll just take a picture of your notes.' Vicki removed her mobile from a pocket and took a couple of shots. 'We'll pop back in a few days, but give me a call if you need anything.' She smiled. 'We have to be somewhere else now, which means you get to eat all the doughnuts. Thanks for the tea, we'll let ourselves out.'

Back in the car, Dai asked, 'Where to, Sarge?'

'Just drive around a bit; see who's out on the street. I'd also like a peek at the car park behind the pub and the lock-up garages. It's not raining so the petrolheads might be out working on their rides.'

Dai put the car in gear and set off. The sunny weather had encouraged a few locals out of their houses. Vicki saw dog walkers, mams with strollers and toddlers, a group of younger children kicking a ball around, and a couple of teenagers snogging on a bench outside the local shop. After a few minutes, Dai indicated and turned into the pub's car park. The area was nearly empty so he steered in a circle and back out to the road. As he waited to pull out of the entrance, a grey vehicle drove past.

'Turn right,' Vicki said. 'Follow that SUV.'

Dai made the turn and tucked in behind the vehicle.

'Why are we following this guy, Sarge?' Dai asked.

'Cos I recognised the driver. That's Ieuan Noonan from the garage. Let's see where he goes.'

'Probably nowhere, with a squad car behind him.'

'That's OK. I want him to see us. His vehicle matches the description given by the second victim.'

A couple of miles further on, a large petrol station appeared over a crest in the road. Ieuan indicated and pulled in, Dai followed and parked a little way from the pumps.

Vicki left the car and walked towards Ieuan. 'I thought that was you,' she said. 'I've been to the garage wanting a word, but Mr Simpson said you were having a few days off. Bit of luck bumping into you.'

'What do you want to talk about?' Ieuan asked as he pumped diesel into the truck.

'Won't take long. Tell you what, I'll wait for you in the café. Tea or coffee?'

'What?'

'I'll get us a drink.'

'Uh, builder's then, but I don't have much time.'

'I've said I'll be quick.' Vicki turned away, walked towards the squad car and bent down to the driver's window. 'Keep an eye on him and follow us into the café.' She grinned. 'Don't frighten him off, he's already twitchy.'

She walked across the forecourt and into the café. She bought three mugs of tea at the counter, took a seat at a table for four in the window, and watched Ieuan finish filling his tank.

He moved the SUV to a parking area, Dai followed him, and together they made their way into the café and sat at Vicki's table.

'So, Ieuan,' she said, 'enjoying your time off?'

'I like the lie-ins,' he said and slurped loudly from his mug.

Vicki gritted her teeth, her neck hair rising.

'When are you back at work?' she asked.

'Next week, Monday.'

'Got any plans for the rest of your break?'

'Look, what is this? I told you I'm pushed for time. Just ask me what you want to know and I'll get going.'

'To where?'

'Just shopping in Carmarthen, that's all. Meeting a friend.'

Vicki nodded. 'I wanted to ask if you know a woman called Jenny Hopkins.'

'Name doesn't ring a bell. Who is she?'

'She was found trapped in her car with exhaust fumes being pumped inside.'

'Shit! Like Christina?'

'Yes, exactly like her.'

'Is she dead?'

'Thankfully not.' Vicki reached into her pocket, removed a photograph of the second victim and showed it to Ieuan. 'This is Jenny. Are you sure you don't know her?'

'Never seen her before.' Ieuan checked the time on his phone. 'Is that it?'

'One more question. Where were you during the early hours of last Friday?'

He grinned. 'At my girlfriend's place in Milford Haven, all night, didn't get a wink of sleep. Whoever you're looking for, it ain't me. I was… busy.' He got to his feet.

'Name and address of your lady friend and then you can go.'

Ieuan scribbled on a serviette and left the café.

'Do you think he's our man?' Dai asked.

'Gotta check everything in a murder inquiry. Now, get us back to the station. We've lots to do.'

* * *

When Vicki walked into the squad room, she was pleased to see her team had their noses down – even Kurt Helman looked busy. She made her way to Ruth's desk and the young officer glanced up as she approached.

'Hi, Sarge, I'm glad you're here. I've made some progress with the ANPR data and have compiled a list of vehicles we should follow up.' She sighed. 'Quite a long list though.'

'Is this one on your list?' Vicki asked and held out a scrap of paper.

Ruth took the scrap and checked with the printed list. She shook her head.

'No, sorry. Where did this number come from?'

'An SUV belonging to Ieuan Noonan, who works at the garage.' Vicki handed over the paper serviette. 'This is his alibi, says he was there all Thursday night and didn't leave until mid-morning Friday. Check it out, will you?'

'Of course.'

'Anything else come in?'

'Eli from Digital Forensics has asked if you'd nip down, he's been working on Jenny's laptop. I've also been having a look at something else.' Ruth tapped at her keyboard and a block of text appeared. 'I've been wondering about who would do this to women, and I've made up a list of pointers.'

'Like a profile?'

'Bit like. I studied psychology before I joined the force. Take a look.'

Vicki pulled a chair closer and peered at the list.

> Young. Thin. Short. Dark eyes. Probably white.
>
> Knowledge of car mechanics.
> Excellent IT skills.
> Loner rather than a team player.
> Under thirty-five.
> Single.
> Meticulous.
> Local.
> Woman hater?
> Narcissist?

'Wow,' Vicki said, 'you have been thinking about it. How much of this is guesswork?'

Ruth chuckled. 'I prefer to call it "reasoned thinking". At least two are educated guesses, but if the rest is correct, those suggestions would be valid. The brief description at the top is what we do know.'

'Yes, I can see that.' Vicki groaned. 'Shame we don't have a decent list of suspects to compare it with. No one I've spoken to matches your profile, but I'll keep it in mind. Useful work.' She got to her feet. 'Right, I'll go downstairs and have a word with Eli, then we'll work through those reg numbers.'

* * *

Vicki found Eli at his desk, eyes fixed on the screen, fingers blurring above the keyboard. He glanced up as she drew near.

'Have you got something to show me?' she asked.

'I have.' He cleared his screen and new images flashed up. 'I found this on the latest victim's laptop.'

Vicki winced at the naked flesh on display.

'Not pleasant, are they?' Eli asked. 'Again, they've been digitally altered.' He changed the screen. 'By reading through the emails both victims received, I have been able to confirm they were sent by the same person. No doubt about it.'

'How do you know that?'

'By matching commonly used words and phrases.'

'Good to know we're only looking for one scumbag. Any idea where the emails were sent from? Location of the device used, maybe?'

'No, he's hiding. Not difficult to do for your amateur geek, same for hacking the OBC. Without any firewall, it's easy to wriggle inside if you know what you are doing.'

'How would anyone learn this stuff?' Vicki asked.

'Online. The internet shows you how to do just about anything.' Eli leaned back in his chair. 'I'll keep at it, but if you ask me, the killer plans these crimes and knows how to be careful.' Eli chuckled. 'I blame *CSI* for a lot of our problems.'

'Yeah, me too. Keep in touch, OK?'

'Will do.'

Chapter seventeen

Vicki pulled up outside the house in Fron-Wen and was surprised to see a small pink car, with a row of stuffed animals propped on the parcel shelf, parked next to the gate. She grabbed her bags, slipped out of the car and let herself in through the front door. She paused in the hall and heard voices in the kitchen so she tapped on the door and pushed it open. Susan was sitting by the Aga and a younger woman with a dark ponytail sat opposite.

Susan looked up. 'Hey, Vicki,' she said. 'I'm glad you're not too late. Do you remember Sally Groves? She worked with you for a little while.'

'I do, yes.' Vicki stepped closer and smiled. 'How are you, Sally?'

'Same as everyone else, I guess, getting on with it. And you?'

'Busy and knackered as always. It's good to see you. Susan mentioned you two had spoken.'

'It was a shock to hear from her, but I'm really glad she phoned.' Sally took a deep breath. 'I owe you an apology, Sarge. I've always felt bad about what happened to you and the main reason I resigned. I should have stood up for you – and Emma Hardwick. I was weak and stupid.'

'Hush,' Vicki said. 'You're here now.' She pulled a dining chair closer to the Aga. 'Tell me, why did you back up Hughes?'

'This sounds crap, I know, but because he told me to. I'd only been on the job a few months and everything was new to me, so when a senior officer told me to do something, I did it.' She took a huge, shuddering breath. 'Anyway, it's worse than that.'

'How is it?'

'Christ, I don't know where to start.'

'Take your time, we've got all night.'

'OK, so…' Sally gulped. 'During the investigation into the murder of Oliver Hardwick, DI Hughes…' She paused and shook her head. 'I can't believe I'm saying this… He had a relationship with a defence witness.' Her shoulders slumped.

Susan reached out and took hold of one of Sally's hands. 'How do you know that, *cariad*?'

'I acted as his driver and he often asked me to drop him outside the Hardwicks' place. A couple of times, I watched in the mirror and saw him cross to the witness's house and go inside.'

'That doesn't mean—'

'Every now and again, he'd get me to pick him up in the morning and I saw him leaving her place, kissing her goodbye on the doorstep.' Sally finally broke down and Vicki handed over a box of tissues. Sally wiped her nose and continued, 'I know I should have reported it at the time, so when Susan rang me I was *grateful*. I finally had the chance to own up to what I'd done – or hadn't done.'

Vicki let out a deep breath. 'That bastard! I always knew I was right. Thanks for telling us, Sally. Is there any chance you'd be happy to make a statement and, if there's a court case, give evidence? I know that's a big ask, but a woman younger than you is in jail with a monster sentence in front of her. She'll be ten years older than I am now when she gets out.'

'I'll be happy to help however I can,' Sally said. 'I didn't speak out when I should have because I was frightened of what would happen to me. I'm not a copper now though, am I? DI Hughes can't touch me.'

Vicki wasn't sure that was entirely true, but once the news broke and he was hopefully under investigation, she would monitor the situation closely. She got to her feet, went to the larder and returned with a bottle of wine, which she handed to Sally together with a corkscrew.

'You get that open and I'll ring for a takeaway. Indian OK with you?'

'You don't have to feed me,' Sally said. 'I've said what I have to. I should go and let you get on with your evening.'

'Nonsense,' Susan said. 'We should mark this moment and wine and a takeaway does it for me. We must also get what you've told us on paper. Horrible Hughes should be held to account for what he's done, and I'm going to make sure he does.'

'Do you think this will mean they'll let Emma Hardwick out?'

'She certainly has a better chance now, but the more information we can gather to cast doubt on her conviction, the more likely she will be given back her freedom.' Susan hauled herself upright. 'I'll go and fetch the laptop and we can make a start while we're waiting for the food.'

* * *

Sally didn't leave until after ten. Vicki walked her out to the car, delighted she had come forward and given such a detailed statement. She watched her pull away then went back indoors and opened another bottle of wine. Susan had moved into the library where they could sit in front of the fire. Spring might be busy, but the nights were still chilly.

'That went better than I thought,' Susan said. 'I like it when people find the gumption not only to admit their mistakes, but try to put things right. I always knew Glyn Hughes was a bully, but couldn't convince any of the junior officers to report him, no matter how hard I tried.'

'Do you think it will be enough to make a difference for Emma?' Vicki asked.

'It's a good start, but it'll take time. I'm seeing Emma's solicitor tomorrow afternoon so I'll show him the statement we've just collected. It was his witness that was turned due to an incident of gross misconduct in a public office so I'm sure he'll have something to say about this.'

'The witness was Alison somebody, if my memory serves me.'

'Alison Hale. She lives opposite the house where Oliver Hardwick was murdered.'

'Know anything about her?'

Susan grinned with a twinkle in her eye. 'She's thirty-four, and the good news for us is she's married. The couple have a four-year-old son. I'd be surprised if Mr Hale knows what was going on and, for all we know, might still be going on. Leverage is always useful.'

Vicki chuckled. 'When did you say we were going to visit her?'

'Thursday evening.'

'How did you convince her to meet with us?'

Susan held out her glass for a top-up. 'No idea, I haven't really tried yet. I'll work something out when we get there, but now I have some ammunition. It will be more difficult for her to refuse to talk to us.'

Vicki smiled, she was delighted Susan was now fully behind her efforts to overturn the bad verdict and see justice done. As a chief inspector, she had always been a force to be reckoned with, one of the reasons Vicki enjoyed her company so much. Few said no to Susan Thomas when she had the wind in her sails. Vicki reached out and took her friend's hand.

'Thank you so much for this,' she said. 'With you on board, I can't see how we can fail.'

'Many a slip twixt cup and lip, *cariad*, so don't jump the gun. British justice grinds slowly and we need more than this. If Alison Hale can be persuaded to come clean, and the murder weapon or a new DNA sample comes to light, we might be getting somewhere. An accusation made against a senior officer will have to be more than that. You need hard evidence, and as much of it as possible.'

'Yes, I get it – this time.'

'As I said, no one is going to thank you for dragging Emma's case back to court, or overturned. As for the complaint against Hughes? The shit that flies from that fan will bury you, so best be prepared.'

'Are you telling me to leave him alone?' Vicki said. 'Cos I won't do that.'

'I'm glad to hear it, bad coppers should be rooted out. All I'm saying is once this gathers momentum, you'll need to watch your back.' Susan emptied her glass and struggled to her feet. 'That's me done,' she said. 'I'm tired, achy and more than a little pissed. At least I'll sleep tonight. Don't mention any of this to anyone at the nick, not even Billy

Boy. Much too sensitive for delicate ears.' Susan blew Vicki a kiss and headed for her bedroom.

Chapter eighteen

Hughes was hovering in the squad room when Vicki clocked on the next morning. He was leaning over Ruth, who was showing him what had been uncovered by the team, and looked up as Vicki entered.

'I've been waiting for you, Sergeant,' he said.

'Can I help you with something, sir?'

'Constable England has provided a full update,' he said and rested a hand on the young officer's shoulder. Vicki noted Ruth's discomfort. 'It doesn't seem to me,' Hughes continued, 'as though you've made any significant progress and you need to up your game.'

'Given we're so short of staff, we're doing as much as we can, and it isn't like we're snowed under with evidence and witnesses. Without those things, suspects are difficult to come up with. How is CID progressing with the drugs case?'

Hughes smirked. 'Better than you. We reckon the drugs are coming in from South Wales and, following the stake-out, we have a few suspects we think are acting as mules. We're monitoring those individuals and building the case.'

'Anyone I know?'

'We're particularly interested in Rhys Griffiths, the kid who walloped you. As you're aware, he received a community service order, but he's been a regular visitor to the house in Ash Grove. We've been tracking his vehicle and he's made numerous trips to Bridgend.'

'What does that prove?' Vicki asked.

'The address he visits is known to us. The local CID have been watching the place for a while now and are fairly certain it's a distribution centre for the wider area.'

'Why hasn't the address been raided?'

'They're information gathering, same as us, but it makes sense to me. The supplies have to come from somewhere and we've proved there's a link.'

'What do you want us to do?'

'Keep out of my officers' way. As I said, there's a tail on Griffiths. We're working closely with Bridgend to crack open the case and nick the lot of them.'

Vicki thought he sounded too gung-ho and asked, 'Anything relating to the Pit Bull character he mentioned in interview?'

'Nothing.' Hughes snorted. 'I don't reckon he exists. The kid was spinning you a line to keep the charges down and you fell for it.'

'I can't say I'm convinced.'

'Just ensure your lot don't mess up my plans. What's on your list today?'

'I have a few visits lined up in connection with the car-gassing case. I've spoken again with Mrs Page and she's convinced me we need another word with Martin Llewellyn.'

'I reckon you're wasting your time. Why would someone like that, a respected man in a position of authority, attack young women? Just get on and find the vehicle the second victim told you about. Find that and we'll find the killer.'

Hughes glared at her before marching out of the room and Vicki took a deep, calming breath. Ruth left her desk and walked closer.

'He's such an arse,' she said. 'He shouldn't talk to you like that.'

Vicki grinned. 'And if you value your job, you shouldn't refer to a senior officer as an arse – even if he is,' she said. 'Go and lay claim to a squad car and I'll meet you out the back. You've spent too long behind a desk and need some fresh air.'

Vicki stood at the end of the room and addressed the rest of her team. 'You all heard what the inspector said, make sure you keep away from his op. Most of you should stay here and work through what little evidence we do have. I want you to look for a link between the car hacker's victims. Everything we've seen proves he must plan his crimes carefully so he must have stalked Christina and Jenny. We need to find out where their paths crossed and why our man chose them. I'm certain it wasn't random.'

'Where do you suggest we look?' Helman asked.

'Everywhere. For example, did the women use the same gym, the same café, were they in touch online, members of the same Facebook groups? They must have something in common other than running foul of the killer.'

'You haven't got a fucking clue,' Helman muttered.

Vicki rounded on him. 'What did you say?'

'That we don't have many clues.'

'Which is your purpose in life, your reason for being here, to find some. So get on with it.'

Vicki left the room and went to the car park where Ruth was waiting for her.

'You OK, Sarge?' she asked.

'That boy drives me to distraction, he's about as useful as holey socks.'

Ruth chuckled. 'Where to then?' she asked.

'The primary school to lean on Llewellyn. We need to find out if he was aware that Christina planned to report him.'

'Ah, you think he might have killed her to keep her quiet. If he'd been found guilty of harassment he'd have lost his job, his wife and his kids probably.'

'Yes, he would've, and he's undoubtedly a sleazy guy, but I'm not sure that makes him a killer. Let's just listen to what he has to say for himself. I'd also like another word with Gareth Sinclair so we should get on.'

Ruth nodded, put the car in gear and set off for the school. They arrived just after the morning drop-off so she drove onto the grounds and parked close to the entrance. The officers left the car and walked inside to reception.

Chapter nineteen

As the officers approached the desk, Gareth Sinclair walked through the main entrance doors and moved closer.

'Mr Sinclair,' Vicki said. 'Good morning. Could you spare us a couple of minutes?'

He glanced at his watch. 'Be happy to, but I don't have long. My class is waiting for me.'

'I'll be as quick as I can. Is there somewhere we can talk?'

'There's an empty room just along the corridor, follow me.'

Ruth and Vicki fell in behind Gareth, who pushed open a door and ushered them inside. He perched on the corner of a desk and smiled.

'Now, how can I help you? I hope you're here to tell me you've caught Christina's killer?'

'Unfortunately not, but you might have heard another woman has been found in very similar circumstances.' Vicki removed a photograph from her pocket and handed it to the man. 'Do you know her?' she asked.

Gareth studied the picture. 'I don't think so, sorry.' He took the image to the window and had another look. 'As far as I know, I haven't met her.'

'Did you ever see her out with Christina?'

'I don't remember her.' He handed back the photo. 'I heard she was still alive when she was found.'

'Yes, she was, thankfully. I interviewed her in hospital and she has been able to provide some useful information. Among other things she reported seeing a small SUV, either grey or silver. Does that ring any bells with you? Do you know anyone who owns a vehicle like that?'

'Not off the top of my head. Cars don't do anything for me, so I don't pay much attention to what people drive.'

Ruth chuckled. 'I'm with you on that. Cars just get you places, a necessary evil.'

'Exactly, I've never owned one.'

'While we're here,' Vicki said and lowered her voice. 'Can you tell me anything about the complaint Christina was planning to make about Martin Llewellyn? How much of a pest was the man?'

'He drove her nuts,' Gareth said. 'After her divorce she lived with her mother Jill for a few months. Chris told me Martin regularly called on her.' He snorted. 'As if she'd be interested in him! He's married, you know, with a lovely wife and two little ones. In the end, Chris had enough and told him to do one, but he was like a cold you couldn't shake off; it was difficult for her to avoid him in school.'

'When did she tell you of her intentions to make an official complaint?'

'A couple of months ago, something like that. Obviously, I told her she could count on my support.'

'Did you ever witness any of Llewellyn's bad behaviour?'

'I was aware of it. He was overly clingy, stood too close, always touching her every chance he got.'

'Inappropriately?' Ruth asked.

'Not that I saw; lots of covert stuff though, brushing past, patting her shoulder, things like that.' He rubbed his eyes. 'Christ, I miss her so much. I feel as though I've lost my right arm. She was a beautiful spirit, inside and out. You should have heard her laugh.' He checked his watch again.

'I've really gotta go, sorry, but keep looking, OK? Find whoever took my friend away from me.' He paused. 'Do you think Llewellyn had something to do with her death?'

'Too soon to tell, but I promise you we'll keep at it,' Vicki said. 'Thanks for your help, and if you think of anything that might help, please get in touch.'

'Yes, I will. Would you like me to show you out?'

'We're fine, thanks. Need a chat with your boss before we go.'

'He'll be in his office. Do you know where that is?'

'Yes, thanks. You can get off to your class.'

Gareth nodded and left the room and the officers followed him out. They walked the corridors, walls covered with brightly painted children's artwork, and it didn't take long to reach the headmaster's office. Vicki tapped on the door and pushed it open without waiting for a reply. Martin Llewellyn looked up from behind his desk and frowned when he recognised Vicki.

'Sergeant Blunt. If you want to talk to me, you really should have made an appointment. I have a lot on today.'

'No need for the police to make appointments, sir. Don't fret, we shouldn't take up much of your time.'

Vicki took a seat facing the desk and Ruth sat beside her. Martin put down his pen.

'So,' he said, 'what can I do for you?'

Vicki had already made the decision to be firm with the man so she got right to the point.

'During our investigation, we have discovered that Ms Page was planning to make an official complaint about your behaviour towards her. Can you tell me what she might have been complaining about?'

Clearly not expecting the question, Martin blinked and laughed nervously. 'This is the first I've heard,' he said. 'I have no idea what you're talking about.'

'Several people we have spoken to have told us that you were' – she turned to Ruth – 'how did they put it, Constable?'

Ruth opened her notebook. 'A bit of a pest, like a cold you can't shake off.'

Martin laughed. 'What rubbish! Who have you been talking to?'

'We're not at liberty to say,' Vicki said, 'however, we have heard similar comments from different sources. Were you aware Ms Page intended to report you to the authorities?'

'No, of course not. Why would she?'

'That's what we're asking you. Had you argued with her prior to her death?'

'If we did, it couldn't have been about anything serious or I would have remembered.'

Ruth took notes and Vicki changed direction.

'Can you account for your movements last Thursday night and the early hours of Friday morning?'

'I was babysitting the girls as my wife had gone away for a couple of days with a friend of hers. You can't leave children alone, so I was at home all night. Why are you asking this? You surely don't think I had anything to do with this business with the cars?'

'At this stage we can't rule anything out,' Vicki said. 'So, you were babysitting. Can anyone confirm that?'

'The girls, obviously, but they are probably too young to be considered witnesses.' He rubbed his face. 'I suppose you could ask my wife. She rang to check on the girls around nine after they were in bed.'

'Did you leave the house after they were asleep, after the call?'

'I've already said I didn't.'

'Did your wife call the landline?'

'I can't remember, probably, but she might have rung my mobile.'

Vicki smiled. 'Not what we call a cast-iron alibi, sir.'

'I don't need a bloody alibi! If I thought I'd need one, I'd have worked harder constructing one.' He sighed heavily. 'Quite frankly, this is ridiculous and I'm losing my patience. As if I'd kill anyone! You're barking up the wrong tree.'

'Am I?' Vicki asked. 'If Ms Page had put in a complaint about you, it would have made things difficult.'

'Yes it would, but how do you expect me to answer questions relating to things I know nothing about?'

'Maybe you did know,' Ruth said, 'and needed to prevent her making that complaint?'

'No, no, no! My conduct has always been exemplary.' Martin angrily surged to his feet. 'I've had enough of this. I don't have to talk to you and I have a school to run. I'd like you to leave now.'

Vicki stood. 'Fair enough. Just make sure we can find you if we need to.'

'Why would I be anywhere else?'

Vicki shrugged. 'We'll see ourselves out.'

The women walked out of the office and left the headmaster behind his desk, red-faced and clammy. They made their way back to the car and got in.

'I think he did it, Sarge,' Ruth said. 'He really didn't like you asking him questions about Christina, and his alibi is rubbish.'

'I agree with your assessment of his alibi, but I'm still not convinced he's a killer.'

'OK, I can't see him battering someone to death, but that isn't what happened. Gassing someone isn't like hitting them over the head with a baseball bat or sticking a knife in them.'

'Doesn't fit your profile though, does he?'

'No, but if he knew Christina was going to make a report, that would give him a motive, which is more useful than any profile. His comfortable life would have been blown out of the water by the internal investigation, even if he wasn't found guilty of anything. Mud sticks.'

'More work needed,' Vicki said, 'so let's get back to the nick and dig into his background. Might as well as there's nothing else we can do. If only there had been some fingerprints on the cars, or Eli the IT wizard could actually work out where the emails were sent from. Without more evidence, we're not likely to make much progress.'

'So, we work with what we've got until more comes in. We still have that list of vehicles picked up on the ANPR to work through and now we have some time to get on with it. There are a couple of SUVs that stand out – right time, right place.'

'Yes, I noticed that. OK, we'll pick up the file then track down the drivers and ask what they were doing out in the early hours of Friday.'

* * *

As Ruth pulled into the car park, Vicki spotted a SOCO van parked in one of the corners. She got out of the car, sent Ruth to the squad room for the file she had compiled, and walked towards the van. The driver's door opened and Sian Jenkins stepped out.

'Vicki,' she called. 'Have you got a mo?'

'Yeah, I was just going to grab a coffee. Want one?'

'No. Come and sit in the van. I'm not really supposed to be here and don't want anyone to see me.'

'That sounds serious.'

'Fucking right it is! Get in.'

Vicki slid into the passenger seat, slammed the door and turned to look at her friend.

'What's up?' she asked.

Sian took a deep breath. 'I've found a third party's DNA on Oliver Hardwick's clothes, and to a lesser extent on Emma's too.'

'Oh my good God!' Vicki said. 'No doubt about it?'

'None. Some of the blood on Oliver wasn't his. There was a fair quantity belonging to someone else, enough to think that maybe the killer cut themselves, maybe there was a struggle, maybe a lot of things. The sample recovered from Emma's clothes was a trace, probably transferred from her husband when she was trying to help him.' Sian suddenly thumped the steering wheel and made Vicki jump.

'Take a breath, *cariad*, you're changing colour in front of my eyes.' She grabbed Sian's hand and held it tightly. 'This is momentous; you know that, don't you? Bloody well done!'

'Yeah, I get it, but now we have a whole new crop of problems, the first being why was I messing about with evidence in storage?' She snorted. 'Never mind slipping an extra DNA test into the system.'

'There is that, but it shouldn't be unsurmountable. We just need to give the matter some thought, we'll work it out. I'll have a chat with Susan this evening, she's a wily old fox when she puts her mind to it.' Vicki wiped her eyes, a rush of tears catching her by surprise. 'I can't wait to tell Emma.'

'You can't do that until we know where we're going with this. The second problem is that the DNA matches a sample we have on record. An exact match.'

'That's not a problem, it's a bloody gift! Who does it belong to?'

'Rhys Griffiths from the estate. The kid who whacked you.'

'Oh… him again. He keeps popping up. What the hell was he doing at the Hardwicks's?'

Sian shrugged. 'No idea.'

'I'll have to take another look at him. This does make things more complicated though. CID have put a tail on him hoping to crack a case based in Bridgend.'

'Complicated?' Sian laughed. 'It is a bit more than that.'

A couple of minutes passed before Vicki asked, 'Are you busy this evening? Come over for supper and we'll talk to the oracle about this.'

'That's a good idea. Sitting out here in full view isn't.'

'Great. Do me a favour though, bring three cod lots with you from town, to save anyone having to cook.'

'No problem. I'll see you later.'

Vicki nodded, left the van and walked inside the station. She found Ruth loitering in the corridor, a cardboard folder tucked beneath her arm.

'Everything OK, Sarge?'

'Yeah, all good. Where are the SUVs we're interested in registered? Any chance we get to do both today?'

'Should be able to. One is in Broad Haven on the coast, the other at Pelcomb Bridge just off the A487 outside town.'

'OK. Broad Haven first then, to blow the cobwebs away.'

Ruth grinned. 'Can we get ice cream?'

'Of course, if you're buying. Now, let's get on.'

Chapter twenty

Sian arrived at the house shortly before seven, a carrier bag from the chippy dangling from one hand. Vicki directed her to the kitchen where Susan was sitting at the table, then unpacked the food and put it on plates.

'So, Sian,' Susan said. 'Vicki tells me you've pulled off a miracle?'

'Hardly. All the evidence was there, someone just had to look for it.'

'I still think we should call it a miracle.' Susan wiped her mouth on a piece of kitchen towel. 'Trouble is, how to admit we have this evidence, and who to tell? Once this is in the public domain, all kinds of things will happen. Hughes will be questioned about his handling of the original case, the bosses will want to know how you had access to the sample, whether you did this on company time, why you were looking in the first place, and on and on…'

'Yes, we understand,' Vicki said, 'which is why we're asking you how to solve the conundrum so we can get Emma out of Eastwood Park and bring her home.'

'Not asking for much then?' Susan pushed her half-eaten meal away, took a sip from her wine glass and folded her arms. 'My main advice would be to hold fire and keep your powder dry. You can't mention what you've uncovered to anyone outside this room.'

'We came to the same conclusion,' Vicki said.

Susan continued. 'You have some compelling evidence now, a written statement by an ex-copper, and a DNA sample which was, admittedly, tested unofficially, but it's not enough. You should keep searching for things that were missed in the original investigation. The more you find, the better the chance I'll have to get someone who matters to actually listen.'

'You?' Vicki asked.

Susan grinned. 'How many honest, high-ranking officers do you know personally?'

Vicki chuckled. 'Yeah, you got me. It would be bloody useful if we could find the murder weapon.'

'We should have a sniff around the estate,' Sian said, 'now we know Griffiths was in the Hardwick house at the time of the killing. The original investigation decided the killer took the knife with him. What if Griffiths dropped it somewhere closer to home?'

'Christ, Sian, that's an awfully long shot,' Vicki said. 'How would we even begin?'

'By checking knives recovered last year during the weapon amnesty.'

Susan chuckled. 'You're a clever one, aren't you?'

Sian smiled. 'I like to think so. There are other knives too in the stores, collected during other investigations. I'll also take a look at those.'

'However will you find the time?' Vicki asked.

'I'll make it, I know what I'm looking for after all. Shame we can't search where Griffiths rests his head.'

'No chance of that. He's involved with the drugs case Hughes is working on. I've been ordered to keep my lot out of his way.'

'What connection did Oliver Hardwick have with Griffiths, I wonder?' Susan asked. 'They're hardly likely to move in the same social circles.'

'We wondered the same thing,' Sian said. 'Perhaps Oliver was a cokehead who racked up one too many debts, and Griffiths was sent to collect. I'll check the toxicology report, find out what was detected in the victim's system.'

'What did he do for work?' Susan asked.

'A banker, I believe.'

Susan laughed. 'Obviously not a proper one if he was having to buy his own coke. OK, I'll have another dig into his background. The information I've been able to glean so far is scarce, to say the least, considering the man was the victim of a murder.'

'Don't get caught sniffing around, Sian,' Vicki said. 'We really must keep a lid on what we're up to. If we screw this up, we won't get another chance.'

'I'll be careful. Like everywhere else, we're short-staffed, which makes any sniffing around I do easier.'

Vicki carried the dirty pates to the sink and shared out the last of the wine, then returned to sit at the table.

'Well,' she said, 'it's good to have a plan at least, and so far it seems our luck might be on a bit of a roll.'

'Fingers crossed then,' Susan said, 'that Alison Hale rolls over with little fuss when we speak to her tomorrow. We need her cooperation, and a statement.'

* * *

After Sian had left, Vicki did the washing-up then headed towards her flat. She was about to push open the door to the library to say goodnight when she heard Susan say her name and hesitated.

'Yes, I agree,' Susan said. 'Vicki's obsession with the Hardwick case could be useful.' There was a pause then, 'Yes, of course. I can't stop thinking about Jasmine. She never leaves my mind even after all this time.' Another pause. 'That goes without saying. I'll keep in touch, and if there is anything I need to know, please ring me. You have my number.'

Vicki heard Susan hang up. She moved away from the door and let herself into the stairwell leading to the first floor, where she made tea, sat at the table and gazed through the window at the night garden. Questions flooded her mind. Who had Susan been speaking to? Her anonymous contact, perhaps? If so, what was the name of that person and why were they talking about her? What "went without saying"? And who the hell was Jasmine? Vicki had known Susan for years, ever since she had moved from Cardiff in search of a slower life in Pembrokeshire, and in all that time, her friend had never mentioned anyone called Jasmine.

Vicki topped up her mug and tried to work out what she ought to do. She had always believed she could talk to Susan about anything, but suddenly she wasn't so sure. Why might her "obsession" – if that was what is was – with Emma Hardwick be useful? Vicki wondered whether she should go back downstairs and ask Susan directly, but then wasn't sure that was the best idea. She might not like what her friend had to say.

She gave herself a mental shake and went to the bedroom, switched on the radio and stretched out on the bedspread. She tried to concentrate on one issue at a time and failed miserably. Her busy mind tangled the cases together and only produced more questions than answers. Why was Rhys Griffiths at the Hardwick house? Had Rhys really been responsible for Oliver's death? Why would he kill the man? She drank some more. Did Rhys have anything to do with the attacks on the women? Was he the stalker? And if he was, how could she prove that?

She must have dozed off because Big Ben's gongs preceding the midnight news shook her awake. She changed into pyjamas, filled a hot water bottle in the kitchen, then crept beneath the duvet and settled down. Tomorrow would be difficult, so she turned off the radio and eventually managed to drift off.

* * *

Vicki arrived at the station a few minutes late the next morning, with a thick tongue, a touch of hangover, and little enthusiasm for the day ahead. As she made her way past the front desk, she heard her name called and looked back.

'Sergeant Blunt, do you have a moment?' Julie, the civilian receptionist asked.

'I'm chasing my tail a little. Can it wait until after the morning briefing?'

'I'm not sure it can.' Julie leaned closer and lowered her voice. 'I've got a young woman in an interview room. She's been here for twenty minutes and wants to talk to someone. She appears to be distressed.'

'Surely someone else could have spoken to her. Did you ask DI Hughes?'

'He's not in yet and our guest will only speak to a woman. I offered my services, but she wants to be seen by "an actual police officer".'

'OK. Pass me a phone.' Vicki rang upstairs and spoke to Ruth. 'I've got caught up,' she said, 'but we still need to track down the SUV in Pelcomb Bridge.'

'Yeah, shame we didn't catch him yesterday. Just our luck he was out.'

'It's a loose end. Have Helman and Dai go and make the call while you hold the fort until I get there.' Vicki hung up and turned to Julie. 'Any idea what has rattled the woman?'

'All I know is her name is Laura Matthews and she's in interview room one.'

Vicki nodded, slipped off her yellow jacket and walked along the corridor. She pushed open the door and a pretty woman with long, dark hair looked up from behind the table. Julie had been right; the woman did look distressed and her eyes were red and puffy as though she had been crying for hours.

'Hello, Laura. My name is Sergeant Blunt – Vicki. How can I help you?'

'I thought I'd been forgotten,' Laura said. 'I've been in here for ages.'

'I'm sorry you had to wait,' Vicki said and took a seat. 'Not many officers available and the staff member on the desk said you only wanted to talk to a woman. Would you like a coffee or anything before we get started?'

'No, thanks. I want you to look at something.'

Laura bent down, removed a laptop from a bag at her feet and switched it on. Vicki watched, and a bad feeling settled heavily in her stomach.

'What do you want to show me?' she asked.

'I'm being terrorised and blackmailed online. I've been sent some…' Laura hesitated, searching for the right words '…sensitive and intimate pictures, which is why I wanted to speak to a woman.' She tapped at the screen, then spun the device to face Vicki. 'There are quite a few so just keep scrolling. I don't want to see them again.'

Vicki had anticipated the type of images she would see, but still experienced a wave of nausea as they passed before her eyes.

'They're not real,' Laura said. 'I'd never do anything like that, never mind take bloody selfies. They are so disgusting and I can't describe how I felt when they arrived.'

She wiped her eyes with her fingers and smeared mascara across her pale cheeks. Vicki offered a tissue and Laura snatched it gratefully.

'When did you receive these?' Vicki asked.

'Middle of the night, attached to an email. I've come in on my way to work.'

'Do you know who sent them?'

'Not really, no.' She sighed heavily. 'I'm a freelance photographer and a guy calling himself Gary Edwards got in touch a while ago via my website. Let me show you the emails he sent.'

Laura swivelled the laptop around, called up the list of messages, then turned the screen back towards Vicki who leaned closer and began reading.

'The first of these is dated six weeks ago,' she said.

Laura nodded. 'In the beginning, it sounded as though he was looking for some corporate shots to go in brochures that he said he was producing for his company. Obviously I was interested, I mean, who can turn work down these days? No one, right? Anyway, he faffed around, frequently changed his mind, but was very sweet about it and apologised for taking up so much of my time. I felt a bit sorry for him because he was so bumbling and untogether. It was kinda cute. Anyway, we messaged a couple of times a week. I didn't push, just gave him enough space to make up his mind and, like I said, the work would have been good.'

'Yes, I can see what you mean,' Vicki said. 'He's all over the place, or putting it on. The last email telling you what he wants you to do came in last night, is that right?'

'Yes, with the photos. I'd have come in earlier but I struggled to pull myself together. I was shocked, you know, and, I'll be honest, pretty scared.'

'A completely reasonable reaction, and I understand why you wanted to talk to a female officer, however there's a little problem.'

'Oh? What sort of problem?' Laura said and turned another shade paler.

'There's an IT guy who works here, a real geek-genius and he needs to see this.'

'No, I can't talk to him. You can't make me.'

'I know this is really difficult, Laura, but you'll have heard about the death of Christina Page and the attack on Jenny Hopkins. They were found in cars parked in remote areas.'

'Yes, it's all my mum talks about. Shit! You don't think *this* guy is *that* guy, do you?'

'Both women had been contacted by a stalker in much the same manner as you have, so it is a possibility and something we must look at.'

'I don't know. I don't think I'm strong enough. He'll look at the pictures while I'm sitting here, literally in the room with him.'

Vicki took her hand. 'And he'll know they are fakes and will want to help you. You *are* strong enough, Laura. After all you're here, aren't you? It was brave coming to the station.'

Laura nodded and Vicki squeezed her hand.

'My guy's name is Eli and he's a gentle soul, utterly non-threatening, and I won't leave your side. All you need to do is show him what has been sent to you, answer any questions he might have, and allow him to copy everything on your laptop. It won't take long, then we'll have a cuppa in the canteen.' She smiled. 'The stuff they serve here will either kill you or cure you. I always bank on the second option.'

'OK, I guess, but you really must stay with me. I can't do this on my own.'

'I will. You're doing the right thing, Laura. If this is the same guy who targeted the other women, he needs to be stopped. The evidence you have brought in will be invaluable. Now, sit tight, and I'll give Eli a shout. Don't worry, you'll be fine.'

Vicki nipped out to the front desk and made the call. Within a few minutes, she returned to the interview room and introduced Eli. Laura glanced up from her seat like a mouse caught out in daylight. Vicki rested a steadying hand on her shoulder and bent to talk quietly into her ear.

'I promise you,' she said, 'if Eli does anything to upset you, I'll taser him.'

Laura smiled and Eli pretended to look fearful as he moved his chair six inches further away from Vicki.

* * *

A little over two hours later, Vicki walked Laura out to her car and promised to keep in touch. She handed the young woman her card with her personal numbers, then walked back inside and headed for Digital Forensics. Eli was in his usual seat, eyes fixed to the screen. Vicki walked closer.

'Thanks for that, Eli,' she said. 'Laura really didn't want to talk to a guy, but you handled her brilliantly.'

'She reminds me of my sister,' he said and sighed. 'That poor kid having to go through something like that.'

'Can you tell me anything yet?'

'I've taken a quick look and I'd say this is the same cockroach, but he's getting better at modifying the images and more... inventive.'

'Can you see where these messages came from?' she asked.

'Nope, he's still being careful. What happens now?'

'I go upstairs and talk to DI Hughes, he'll make the decision. What I think we should do is string the stalker along, arrange a meet, nick him, and chuck him down the nearest mineshaft, but as I said, not my decision.'

'I'd back you all the way. OK, let me know if and when you need me on this. In the meantime, I'll keep trying to track him down.'

'Yeah, will do.'

Chapter twenty-one

Vicki made her way upstairs to CID and found DI Hughes slumped behind his desk, staring at his computer screen. He saw her approach and quickly cleared the screen. He waved her to a seat.

'Where were you for the briefing?' he asked. 'That young Constable England seemed to be conducting ceremonies this morning. It should be a sergeant.'

'She's more than capable, sir. I got caught up on the way in. A young woman wanted to report a crime. She only wanted to talk to a female so, as I was on the spot…'

'God, why are girls so twitchy these days?'

Knowing it was a rhetorical question, Vicki ignored the comment and summarized Laura Matthews' complaint.

'You said Eli in DF has the emails?' Hughes asked.

'Yes, he made a copy of everything on her laptop. It's his opinion the sender is the same person who targeted the other victims.'

Hughes rubbed his chin. 'This is a bit of luck,' he said. 'We could pose as his victim, try to convince the stalker to meet up, and we'll be waiting for him.'

'My thoughts were similar, but we can't rush in until we're sure everything is in place. We can't tip him off. If he smells a rat we'll lose him.'

'I agree.' Hughes laughed. 'That's a first, me actually agreeing with you.'

'Yes, sir.'

'OK. I'll leave it to you to arrange the sting, with Eli's help, of course.'

'We did have a quick chat about it and he's on board. Would you like to talk to him before we start?'

'No need. I'm up to my eyes in it with the ongoing drugs investigation, so I'll leave it to you as I said, but I'll want twice daily updates. Don't mention the sting around the nick either. Treat this as an undercover op. The least people know about it the better. We can't risk missing out on the opportunity to catch this guy red-handed. Keep it between the three of us for now.'

'Yes, sir. How is your case progressing?'

'Slowly. Operations like this take time, and with Bridgend nick involved, there's even more paperwork. We're fairly sure the Griffiths boy is a mule ferrying supplies around Wales, but so far no clues about who is running the show.'

He frowned and began tapping a pen on the edge of his desk. Vicki forced herself to ignore the sound and gazed out of the window.

'I want that bastard like a fox wants a chicken,' Hughes said.

Vicki nodded. 'I've reminded my lot about your op so they won't get in the way.' She got to her feet. 'If that's all, I need to pop into the squad room, then I'll probably spend the rest of the day in Digital Forensics.'

'Just make sure you keep me up to speed.'

'I will.'

Vicki shut the door behind her and went to the squad room. She was pleased to see Ruth had been cracking the whip and everyone was working hard.

'Ruth,' Vicki called. 'Can I have a word?'

'Course, Sarge. What's up?'

'I'll be in DF with Eli most of the day,' Vicki said. 'We're working on the second victim's laptop trying to discover where the emails were sent from. Any problems, you know where to find me,' she said and made her way downstairs.

Entering the quiet environment, she was surprised to see Eli's workstation empty and gazed around. One of his colleagues pointed towards a small glass office in a corner of the large space, so Vicki walked through the desks and pushed open the door.

'DI Hughes has agreed to our plan,' she said and took a seat next to him.

'That's good news,' Eli said. 'I anticipated a green light, so I moved in here where it's quieter.'

Vicki chuckled. 'Your main office isn't noisy. You should try working upstairs.'

'No, thanks. I don't do my best work with too much background noise.' He leaned back in his chair. 'I've been studying the emails to and from Laura Matthews so I can get a feel for the way she writes. That way, when I compose replies, I should be able to "sound" like her. So, tell me, how do you want to proceed?'

'Extremely cautiously,' Vicki said. 'We want to catch this guy, not scare him off.'

'Makes sense. How about I send a reply from Laura querying the creep's email, something like…' He began to type.

> Hi Gary,
> I've had a very odd email which says it's from you. Don't get me wrong, I don't think you did send it, but maybe you've been hacked and someone has taken over your account. Let me know, will you? Hope you're OK.
> LM.

Vicki read from the screen. 'Yeah, that's good, sounds natural. We need to slow him down so I have a few days to plan the rest of the op – as Hughes has basically passed me the case,' she huffed. 'I'm not a DS these days.'

'You never stopped being a DS,' Eli muttered.

Vicki smiled. 'OK, send the email, but don't arrange any meeting without speaking to me.'

'I won't, but I don't think we'll have a problem. The emails exchanged between the stalker and Jenny Hopkins were over a span of a couple of months. The last email, with the photos attached, was sent two weeks before she was found at Wiston Castle. You should have plenty of time.'

'Good. I don't want to rush this and make mistakes. So, as I said, send the email, then monitor the account. If you receive a reply, call me. Oh, and Hughes said we should keep this between ourselves for now.'

'Not a problem. Meanwhile, I'll keep digging around to find a location for this twisted bugger.'

'Yeah, do that and we'll speak soon.'

* * *

Vicki successfully managed to keep out of DI Hughes' way and was relieved when she could clock off. On the way home, she nipped into the supermarket for supplies, then drove on to Fron-Wen. She found Susan in the kitchen and a large indoor picnic set out on the table, consisting of sandwiches, hard-boiled eggs, a bowl of mixed salad, and a loaf of bara brith.

'I hope this is OK,' Susan said as Vicki walked in. 'We won't have time for a proper supper before we go to speak with Alison Hale.'

'Are you still up for that?' Vicki asked.

'Of course, while we're on that roll you talked about.'

'Does she know we're visiting?'

'No, but she will.'

'What happens if she doesn't let us in? Slams the door in our faces?'

'You really can be a dreadful worrier, *cariad*. Go with the flow, that's what I do.' Susan smiled. 'Although, not so much flowing goes on these days.'

They ate quickly, then walked out to the car and half an hour later, they pulled up outside the Hale household. Vicki glanced across the road at the house where Oliver Hardwick had died, and shuddered, recalling how he had been found there surrounded by so much blood.

'You ready then?' Susan asked.

'Yep.'

Susan refused Vicki's arm and relied on her stick as they walked up the path. Susan rang the doorbell and removed an identity card from her pocket.

'What are you doing?' Vicki hissed. 'This isn't official.'

'Maybe not, but I'm still Detective Chief Inspector on my library card.'

Vicki was about to speak when the door opened and a blonde woman in her early thirties looked out. Susan raised her card and held it a little too close to Mrs Hale's face, then tucked it away.

'DCI Susan Thomas,' she said. 'I wonder if you have a moment, Mrs Hale.'

'You're a police inspector?' The woman's eyebrows raised. 'How do you chase bad guys on a stick?'

Vicki's hackles twitched at Alison's rudeness, but Susan smiled.

'*Chief* inspector, actually,' she said, 'and I'm employed for my brain. I leave any chasing to the others. I'd be grateful if I could sit down though.'

'Uh, yes, you'd better come in then.' She stood to one side and waved her guests into a small living room at the front of the house. 'Is everything OK? Whenever you see police on the door they bring bad news.'

'Not always.'

Susan lowered herself onto a dining chair pushed up against a wall.

'Is your husband in, Mrs Hale?' Susan asked.

'No, he's working away this week. Is he OK? He hasn't had an accident or anything?'

Susan smiled. 'As far as I know, Mr Hale is hearty.'

Vicki tried not to laugh and covered her mouth.

'Why did you ask about him then?' Mrs Hale asked.

'Because you probably wouldn't want him overhearing what we are about to talk about.'

Alison looked wary and blustered. 'So talk then,' she said. 'I have to go upstairs to check on my boy in a little while.'

'You were a witness in the Hardwick murder case, weren't you?' Susan asked.

'I was, yes, but that was ages ago. Why are you asking about that?'

'An internal case review,' Susan lied. 'During the process I saw the statement you gave to police a few hours after Mr Hardwick's body was found, wasn't the same as the evidence you gave in court.'

Alison's cheeks flushed red. 'This was gone into at the time. I got it wrong, that was all. Mixed up the days.'

'What did you get wrong? The statement or the evidence?'

'The statement. It was very disturbing for someone living so close to you to be murdered. I said I'd seen a man, dressed in black, leaving the house shortly before Emma came home, but it was a different day entirely.' She smiled and held out her hands, as though asking for forgiveness. 'We all make mistakes, don't we?'

'I wonder if you class your affair with the investigation's officer a mistake?'

Vicki blinked, stunned by the question. Susan had obviously lost none of her interview techniques, but she was surprised by her bluntness.

'What are you talking about?' Alison said. 'I haven't had an affair with anyone. I'm happily married.' She surged upright. 'I want you both to leave.'

Susan didn't move and glanced up at the angry woman. 'Thing is, Alison, I know you were sleeping with DI Glyn Hughes and have a witness who confirms the fact.' Susan took a deep breath. 'I also know he more than likely influenced you to change your evidence. Because of *your* actions, a young woman languishes in prison, found guilty of a crime she didn't commit. I have proof of all this and you and Glyn Hughes will be prosecuted. You'll be able to find out first-hand how hard prison is.'

'No, you can't!' Alison squealed. 'I can't go to prison; I have a child.'

'No problem. If his father won't care for him, I'm sure the local authority will find somewhere to place your boy.'

Alison dropped onto the sofa and hid her face in her hands. Susan reached out and rested a hand on her arm, obviously multi-tasking. Good cop, bad cop in one.

'I can help you,' Susan said. 'If you come clean and make a statement, I'll make sure Glyn Hughes is dealt with and will impress on the CPS how helpful you've been.' She squeezed the arm. 'We don't really want you, *cariad*, we want him. A serving police officer who bullies and sleeps with women he meets on the job.'

Alison wiped her eyes. 'He did bully me.'

'Then tell us how things went and we can use your evidence to help free Emma Hardwick.'

'Will you tell my husband?'

'I won't make a point of it, but he'll probably find out. Your biggest worry really should be the perjury you committed at the trial. A serious matter.'

Alison flushed again and her eyes filled with fresh tears. 'But you said–'

'That I'll do everything I can to keep you out of prison and at home here with your child, but you have to own this, Alison. Take some control and I promise I'll do my best for you. Now, tell me, when did the affair start?'

Alison closed her eyes. 'The day Oliver was discovered. Glyn came to take my statement that evening.' Alison took a deep breath and looked down at the carpet. 'Andy, my husband, was away and I told Glyn I was scared being in the house on my own with a child.' She snatched up a cushion and clamped it to her chest as though it was a breast plate. 'I was really freaked out, to be honest.'

'Did he stay the night?' Susan asked quietly.

Alison nodded miserably.

'OK, *cariad*, take your time. You're doing well, and when you've told us everything, you'll feel much better. Really you will.'

* * *

Susan and Vicki arrived home just before nine. Susan settled in the easy chair by the Aga and Vicki filled the kettle.

'Tea or coffee?' she asked.

'Whisky to help me sleep. Pour a couple.'

Vicki poured two generous measures, handed one to Susan, then sat the opposite side of the stove and sipped from her glass. Susan frowned at her.

'You shouldn't look so pleased with yourself,' she said. 'I did all the work.'

'I enjoyed watching you in action – always did – but yes, I am extremely satisfied I was right about Hughes.'

'You ought to focus your attention on the man Alison saw at the house, a couple of hours before Emma came home to find her husband on the kitchen floor.'

'I don't know how,' Vicki grouched. 'No one will remember seeing him after all this time. "Thin man, maybe young, dressed in black" is a near useless description.' She topped up the glasses. 'Anyway, I'm convinced we have enough. You should talk to your contact, get the ball rolling.'

'No, not yet. True, you have two statements in hand now, but any half-decent barrister would be able to tear them to shreds.'

'Emma can't wait forever. We both know it'll be months before anything starts to happen,' Vicki said.

'Give it a few weeks at least, how can that hurt? Remember, you'll get one shot at this and, if it goes the wrong way, you will be sacked this time.'

'It's not me I'm worried about.'

'I know, but it should be. You're a good copper. Don't wreck your career by allowing your heart to rule your head.' Susan put her glass down and got to her feet. 'I'm worn out and need to get flat. Think carefully about what I've said though.'

Chapter twenty-two

Vicki's mobile woke her shortly after four the next morning. She scrabbled around on the bedside table to find the device and switched on the lamp. She peered at the screen and saw the number was withheld. She answered cautiously.

'Hello?'

'Am I speaking to Vicki Blunt?' a female voice asked.

'You are. Who is this?'

'Ms Green, governor of HMP Eastwood Park. I apologise for ringing so early in the morning, but I'm sorry to tell you Emma Hardwick has been taken to Gloucester Hospital. You are named as her next of kin.'

'Am I?' Vicki rubbed her eyes and sat up in bed. 'Tell me what's happened. Is Emma OK?' She snorted. 'Daft question. If she was, she'd still be in your prison.'

'She was found an hour ago in her cell. She had cut her wrists using a razor blade removed from a disposable razor. She has lost a lot of blood and, as soon as she'd been assessed, was taken to the hospital.'

'How did she get hold of a razor?'

'We issue disposables to the prisoners when requested and for some reason this one was not collected after use.'

'For "some reason"? I sincerely hope you're intending to investigate this to find out what actually took place?'

'Of course.' The woman sounded irritated.

'Do you know what prompted her to self-harm? Was this a suicide attempt, or a call for help?'

'At this point, I have no idea. She wasn't conscious when she was discovered.'

'Did she ring for help in her cell?'

'That will all be looked at in due course as part of our investigation. My main duty in cases like this is to inform the next of kin at the earliest opportunity if an injury occurs on the estate, hence my call to you. In accordance with the rules, you may visit Emma. I have alerted the officers at the hospital that you will be allowed an hour's visit, at ten o'clock this morning. Shall I confirm your intention to visit?'

'Yes, I'll be there. I'm assuming you will be at your desk tomorrow?'

'I'm in all day.'

'Good, because after I've seen Emma, I'll be coming for a word.'

Vicki cut the call and stared into the dark. She hadn't known Emma had recorded her as next of kin and wasn't sure how to feel about it. Knowing she would never be able to get back to sleep, she got out of bed and put the kettle on. She wondered again what had happened. Why had Emma suddenly taken a blade to her wrists in a bid to end her life?

She carried the tea and her laptop to the bedroom, slipped beneath the quilt and began surfing the net to find out exactly where the hospital was, and how long the journey might take. She was on shift in a few hours, but knew she wouldn't be going in. Emma needed her. Haverfordwest nick would cope. She decided to leave at half past five, so she finished her tea, took a hot shower and got dressed. In the kitchen, she made a couple of cheese sandwiches and filled a flask with coffee to keep her going during the drive. At a quarter past five, she went downstairs to the main hall and tapped lightly on Susan's bedroom door.

'Susan,' she called quietly, 'are you awake?'

'Yes, come in. What's up?'

'I've had a call from Eastwood Park. I was told Emma has made an attempt on her life so I'm going to visit her in hospital.'

'Shit! Who rang you?'

'The governor. Emma put me down as next of kin.'

'Did she? Why not someone from her family?'

'No idea, but I must go to Gloucester.'

'Of course. I'll ring in sick for you, tell them you're feeling the after effects of the whack in the face.'

'Thanks. I'll be back as soon as I can, but I want a word at the jail before I head for home.'

'Just make sure you drive safely. Gloucester is a long trip and you can't be fretting all the way. I'll see you later.'

Vicki nodded and went out to the car.

Knowing Susan was right and she should concentrate on the drive, Vicki turned on Radio 4 and listened to the news and an episode of *In Our Time*. The weather was kind, not raining, and the roads were quiet, so she made good time to England. Following directions gleaned from the internet, she found her way to the hospital and battled with other vehicles in the car park, before finally finding a space. As promised, she sent Susan a text and checked her watch. She had time to kill before heading to the ward where Emma was held, so she went to the canteen and bought a bacon sandwich. Sitting at a small table surrounded by staff and other visitors, she tried to settle her thoughts with little success. The sandwich wasn't the best, so she drank the tea, carried the tray to the rack and went in search of her friend. After a few wrong turns, she spotted a pair of prison officers sitting on chairs either side of a door. They looked up as Vicki approached.

'Morning,' she said. 'I'm here to visit Emma Hardwick. My name is Vicki Blunt. I'm expected.'

The officers got to their feet and the taller of the two asked, 'Can I see some ID?'

Vicki offered her warrant card and the man twitched. 'You're early,' he said.

'The traffic was light. Can I go in?'

'Doctor's with her. That's why we are out here. If he says Hardwick is up for a visitor, you can have an hour.'

'Fair enough.' Vicki leaned against the wall. 'How is she now?'

The man frowned. 'I'm a prison officer, not a doctor.'

'Not overly friendly either, are you?'

He looked away. Five minutes later, the door to the side ward opened and a young doctor in a white coat stepped out. He saw Vicki and walked towards her.

'Hi,' he said. 'Are you Ms Blunt?'

'That's me. How is she?'

'Better than when she arrived. We've given her four units of blood and she is improving steadily. She's suffering from extreme fatigue and is also very underweight, which isn't helping the situation.'

'Is she well enough for a visitor?'

'I'm sure she'll be pleased to see a friendly face. Don't overdo it though, and be warned, she may well fall asleep, but that isn't anything to be worried about.'

'Thanks, Doctor. How long will she be kept in?'

'At least another night. I want a member of the mental health team to assess her before she is released.'

'Hardly released,' Vicki said. 'You mean sent back to prison.'

The man blinked. 'Yes, of course, I do mean that, crass of me. Please be assured, Emma won't be going anywhere until I'm happy.'

Vicki held out one of her cards and saw his eyes widen.

'You're a police officer? I thought you were Emma's next of kin.'

'I'm both. I know it's irregular, but… any chance you could give me your number?'

He nodded, took her phone, tapped the screen and handed back the device.

'Thanks again for taking care of her,' she said.

He smiled and strode away.

Vicki received a nod from the tall prison officer, so she pushed open the door and walked inside the room. Emma glanced up from the bed.

'Vicki,' she mumbled. 'Why are you here?'

'The governor rang and told me what happened. I didn't know you'd listed me as your next of kin.'

'Sorry, I meant to tell you. I couldn't think of anyone else.'

'No worries.'

Vicki pulled a chair up to the bed and took a good look at the patient. Dressed in a hospital gown, not the baggy sweatshirt and joggers she usually wore, Vicki noticed just how thin she was. Emma's skin was loose and had a pale-yellow tinge. Her deep brown eyes had lost their shine and seemed too large for her head, and her shaved scalp emphasised the shocking image. Vicki took hold of Emma's hand.

'Now then, *cariad*, tell me why you've done this.'

Emma took a deep breath, turned her head towards the small window. She stared through the glass, then eventually said, 'I couldn't do it anymore,' she said. 'I just couldn't keep living in that madhouse for another second, never mind twenty-odd years.'

'You really wanted to kill yourself?'

'Yeah, I wanted out.'

Tears slipped from Emma's eyes and ran down her cheeks, leaving wet, shiny trails. Vicki sat on the bed and gathered the young woman into her arms and held on while she sobbed.

'I'm sorry, Vicki, but I can't spend my life there. I'd rather not carry on living than have to live in that place.'

Vicki passed over a box of tissues and watched as she cried. Vicki felt her heart tighten and worked hard at not joining in with the tears. Shockingly, her friend felt angular, bony, no flesh anywhere, like a skeleton wrapped in skin – nothing more. The tears kept falling and Vicki gave her time to cry.

'You won't be there for years,' she said after a while. 'You know Sian and I are working at proving your innocence. We believe in you. All you have to do is hang in there and don't give up. We're not going to.'

'I know you mean well, and I am very grateful you're my friend, but I don't believe you'll be able to do that. No one listened to me in court. Why would anyone listen now? The jury heard me say I didn't kill him, even though they knew what he had done to me. I bared my soul in that courtroom and it made no difference at all.'

'We're making progress, good progress,' Vicki said.

'It won't be enough,' Emma sobbed. 'Whatever you do, it will never be enough.'

Vicki held on tighter. 'I promise you it will be, trust me. We have help.' She lowered her voice. 'Sian has found a new sample of DNA, and we have two witness statements now which back your version of events that day. Every day we're getting closer to having the case reopened, or overturned entirely.' She released Emma and stared into her eyes. 'Promise me you won't do anything like this again, give our new investigation a chance. Please, Emma, you're young, you have your life in front of you. Don't let the system rob you twice.'

'I don't think I can. I've lost everything, even my family won't talk to me. You're the only one who visits, the only one who has *ever* visited.' She closed her eyes. 'I've got nothing left to fight with.'

'Yes, you have! I've spoken to the doctor and he's referring you to the mental health team. You're seriously underweight and might be suffering from anorexia. The prison must take care of you, and I'll make sure they do.'

'How can you do that?'

'When I leave here, I'm off to have a word with Ms Green, the governor. I'll make her listen. What you need to do is start eating, build yourself up, and do *not* try to harm yourself again. When I'm back in Wales, I'll start banging heads together and make the authorities listen. Please believe me, we can do this.'

Emma closed her eyes and slumped back onto the pillows. 'I want to believe you, really I do, but–'

'Then believe me! I can do this.'

The door opened and a prison officer looked in. 'Your time's up, you must leave.'

'I've come a long way, just give me a little longer.'

'You were lucky to have even been granted a visit and I must insist you leave now.'

Vicki turned back to Emma and gave her another hug. 'I'll have to go. I'll see you again soon, *cariad*. Stay strong, get well, and don't mention what we've talked about – to anyone.'

She kissed Emma's forehead, got to her feet and without looking back, strode from the room.

Chapter twenty-three

Vicki arrived home late that afternoon, and felt utterly shattered. The driving, the stress, and an incredibly unsatisfying and frustrating conversation with the governor of Eastwood Park, had sapped every spark of energy she had. Hauling herself out of the car, she let herself into the hall and found Susan sitting at the kitchen table.

'How did you get on today?' Susan asked.

Vicki dropped on a leather easy chair and groaned. 'I'm wiped out,' she said. 'The driving was easy enough, but everything else in the middle was tough.'

Vicki accepted a glass of whisky from Susan, then shared everything the doctor had told her. 'We have got to get her out of jail,' she said. 'If we don't… well, I'm not convinced she won't try this again.'

'Did you speak to the governor?'

Vicki nodded. 'I'm sure that was a waste of time – apart from being able to vent my spleen. I asked why Emma was so underweight and Ms Green told me she couldn't force-feed prisoners these days. Uncaring cow!' Vicki got to her feet and began to pace.

'Don't do that, *cariad*, you'll make me cross-eyed.'

'Sorry, I've been sitting down most of the day.'

'Then make yourself useful. There's a chilli in the fridge that could do with heating up, and open a bottle of wine. You look like you could do with a glass.'

'That good, huh?' Vicki chuckled.

* * *

They were about to start eating when the front doorbell rang.

'Bugger,' Vicki said and put down her fork. 'I'll go.' She got to her feet, walked along the hall and opened the door.

'Billy. I wasn't expecting you, was I?'

He smiled. 'No, but I heard you were off sick so thought I'd nip in, see how you are and if there's anything I can do.'

'You certainly timed your visit perfectly. We're about to eat.'

'Oh God, sorry.'

'Don't be. There's plenty to go around so come and have supper with us.'

'Are you sure? I don't want to be a nuisance.'

'You're not. Go through to the kitchen.'

'Thanks.'

Billy stepped inside and walked along the hall and into the warm room.

'Evening, Susan,' he said. 'I've been invited to supper. I hope I'm not disturbing you.'

'Not at all, it's good to see you. Grab a plate from the drainer and help yourself to food and wine. Don't be shy.'

'Great, thanks. I haven't eaten today, been busy at the garage.'

Susan winked at Vicki who responded by sticking her tongue out. Billy spooned casserole from the pot, poured wine, then walked to the table and took a seat at one end.

'So, how are you, Vicki?' he asked. 'Someone said you were suffering after-effects of the punch in the face. I've never known you to be off sick, so I was worried.'

Susan smiled at him. 'You're very sweet, Billy Marsden, but as you can see, she's fine. Bad headache, that's all. It was me who convinced her to take a day.'

'I did try to ring,' Billy said around a mouthful of food.

'Sorry,' Vicki said. 'I turned the phone off and spent the day in a darkened room. I'm feeling more like myself now though.'

Vicki hated lying to Billy, but she didn't want to tell him how she had spent her day. A quicksilver memory zipped behind her eyes. She swallowed hard, recalled what she had told Emma, and hoped the woman wouldn't share their conversation. Vicki knew she should have kept quiet and not told her friend about the progress the unofficial investigation had made. It was good to see Billy, but she wished he hadn't called. She needed to talk to Susan and confess how unwise she'd been.

'Just a headache then?' Billy asked, shaking Vicki from her worries.

'What? Oh yes, like a migraine, it began to lift a couple of hours ago. It's kind of you to drop by.'

'Back in tomorrow then?'

'Yes, I'll be there,' Vicki said. 'Did I miss anything today?'

'Not much.' Billy gulped from his glass. 'I had another look at the heater hoses on the first car and they had been rerouted exactly like the second. I have no idea how I missed it the first time I looked.'

'Any prints?'

'None. SOCO found some smears, but said that only proved whoever messed around beneath the bonnets wore gloves.'

Billy scraped his plate enthusiastically with his knife, the nails-on-blackboard sound made Vicki want to scream. To stop him, she gathered up the dirty plates and carried them to the large, stone sink.

'Coffee anyone?' she asked.

'Oh yes, please,' Susan said. 'Make them Irish, there's some cream in the fridge and plenty of whisky in the cupboard.'

'Good plan, the booze can counteract the caffeine.' Vicki put the kettle on and lined up three glass mugs. 'Nothing else from the cars, Billy?' she asked.

'Nothing. Eli from forensics confirmed the hacks were made using a burner phone on each occasion, both have since dropped off the radar. He also confirmed that the Bluetooth connection had been the way in.' He grinned. 'Bluetooth was named after a Norwegian pirate, I believe.'

'Christ, Billy,' Susan said. 'You do have some shit in your head.'

'I thought it was interesting.'

'It sort of is,' Vicki said, 'if you compete in pub quizzes. What would be more interesting is something we can use to track and nick this killer.'

She handed out the coffee glasses. Half an inch of cream floated on the dark brew. Susan took a sip and nodded her approval.

'So,' Billy said. 'Vicki, I was wondering if you fancied a trip to the coast on your next day off. Lunch maybe? One of my mates runs a brilliant little pub in the harbour at Solva. Beautiful spot if the weather's right.'

'Yeah, I reckon I'd like that, but let's get this case closed first. I'm really up to my eyes in it at the moment, and being off today didn't help much. Now I'll be playing catch-up.'

'OK, give me a shout when you're up for it and I'll let my mate know. We'll need to book, his place is very popular.'

'Sounds like a plan, thanks.'

Billy smiled. 'Cool, I'll look forward to it.' He finished his coffee and got to his feet. 'I better get off, I'm on early tomorrow. Thanks for supper, that was a great meal.'

'Watch yourself on the way home, Billy,' Susan said. 'Wine *and* whisky puts you over the limit in my book. You wouldn't want to get nicked.'

'I'll stick to the lanes, but thanks for the warning.'

'You could stay over,' Susan said. 'The sofa in the library is really very comfortable.'

'Nice offer, but I'll get on home.'

Vicki showed him to the door and, as at their previous meeting, Billy leaned closer, brushed a kiss on her cheek and went out to his car. Vicki watched him leave then returned to the kitchen.

'He's a nice boy,' Susan said. 'Don't let the grass grow or someone else will snap him up.'

'He's a friend and colleague, nothing more.'

'Not yet. He's very keen on you, I can tell.'

Vicki didn't answer and began filling the sink with hot water. She loaded the dirty dishes in the bowl, then walked back to the table and sat opposite her friend.

'I think I've made a dreadful mistake,' she said.

'Then you'd better tell me what you think you've done.'

Vicki groaned and took a deep breath. 'I mentioned the new evidence we've found to Emma today. I hope she won't mention it to anyone.'

'Bloody hell, *cariad*, you better hope she doesn't. I told you to keep it quiet, so why on earth did you say anything?'

'To give her some hope, try to prevent her from hurting herself again. You should have seen her, Suzy. She looked more dead than alive.'

'You're too involved,' Susan said and finished her wine. 'OK then, I'll test the waters and try to discover if the evidence you have will be enough. For your sake, I hope it is. In the meantime, watch your back. You may be right and Emma will keep quiet, but you know there's no guarantee of that.'

'Yeah, I get it.'

'I was hoping for a more controlled release of the information, but never mind. I'll do what I can.'

Susan hauled herself upright and Vicki watched as she limped out of the kitchen and headed towards her bedroom. She knew Susan was right and the next couple of weeks would be difficult. She finished the clearing up, then left the room and went upstairs to her apartment, hoping sleep would not be a stranger.

* * *

Vicki strode into the squad room the next morning and was pleased to see everyone in attendance.

'Morning, you lot,' she said. 'Settle down and listen up.' She gazed around the room until all faces were turned in her direction. 'Does anyone have any updates for me?' No one spoke but heads were shaken. 'Right then, we need to make much more progress on the stalker case.'

Kurt Helman asked, 'Why are *we* doing that, Sarge? Surely it's a job for CID?'

'Because, Constable Helman, CID are working the drugs case and we've been tasked with this.'

'I reckon the scumbag's given up.'

Vicki sighed. 'You should know by now that we can't relax until we've caught him.'

'How do we do that without any real evidence?'

'We work with what we've got. Constable England.'

Ruth got to her feet, a bundle of printed sheets in her hand. She gave it to Dai Phillips. 'Pass them on, would you? OK, this is what we know. The suspect is short, thin, young and male. He wore a mask but our second victim is fairly certain he's white with dark eyes. He obviously has IT skills and knows his way around under a vehicle's bonnet. He more than likely drives a grey or silver, older SUV.'

'Not much to go on, is it?' Dai asked.

'No, which is why we need more,' Vicki said. 'I'm certain he lives locally and knows the area well. He chooses his meeting places carefully. Even though Christina Page sadly couldn't give us a statement, we know he was at the first scene. SOCO matched tyre tracks to both locations, the distinctive type used on SUVs. There's a photo in your bundles.'

'So what do you want us to look for, Sarge?' an officer at the back of the room asked.

'It's obvious he plans these attacks and spends time grooming his victims online. I don't believe he picks them at random so their paths must have crossed and we need to find out where. There will be a link so get out there and find it. Talk to anyone and everyone who knew either victim. Ask in every shop, pub and café in town, as well as on the outskirts.' Vicki saw heads nodding. 'I also want some of you to stay in the office and work through what we've already collected with a nit comb.' She tried to meet as many of her officers' eyes as possible. 'The other thing we need to determine is – and this is a biggie – his motive. There will be one, and if we can work out what it is, he should be easier to catch, so let's get on with it.'

The room emptied quickly. Ruth, Dai and a couple of younger officers remained behind. Vicki fetched coffee for them all, then settled behind her own desk and began trawling the evidence already collected, looking for the link she knew must be there.

Chapter twenty-four

Just before lunch, Vicki's phone rang. She recognised Sian Jenkins' number and answered the call.

'Hey, you,' she said. 'How's tricks?'

'Fine, I guess. I spoke to Susan earlier and she told me what happened in Gloucester, how you'd made a trip to the hospital. I wondered if you'd like to meet up for lunch at the café in town so we can talk it over. Are you OK?'

'Yeah, just tired and rough around the edges. Be good to get together though.'

'Any chance we could do that now? I'm in town and on my break.'

'I can be there in ten minutes if that's good.'

'I'm already here', Sian said. 'Can I order for you? Cut down on the waiting time.'

'Ham and cheese toasty would go down well.'

'Not a problem. See you soon.'

Vicki made sure Ruth knew what the team should be doing then went to the locker room, swapped her bright-yellow jacket for her own, and left the station. The streets were busy. The usual influx of tourists had begun, encouraged by the good weather, and she dodged around them as she headed for the café. A bell on the door tinkled as she walked in, and she spotted Sian tucked in a dark corner near the door to the toilets. The woman looked up and smiled when she saw her friend approach.

'Food's on the way,' she said as Vicki removed her coat and sat at the small table. 'Now, tell me about yesterday.'

Vicki shared the details of her day, told her how ill Emma had looked, and how the governor didn't seem to be too bothered about the suicide attempt.

'That prison doesn't have a great record,' Sian said.

'I'm not sure any of them do these days,' Vicki muttered. 'Inexperienced staff paid shit wages and, ironically, not enough of them. All UK jails are unsafe, especially for those who suffer from mental illness. We must get that girl out of there, as soon as possible.'

Vicki didn't mention she had told Emma about the new evidence and, not for the first time, wished she had kept her mouth shut. Susan was right, trouble was bound to follow.

A waitress wearing a red apron approached the table and delivered two toasties oozing with cheese, a side salad on each plate, cutlery wrapped in paper serviettes, and two steaming mugs of coffee.

'Can I get you anything else?' she asked.

'No, we're fine, thanks,' Sian said. She spread brown sauce on her sandwich and got stuck in. 'God, I needed this,' she said. 'I've been on the go since first light and missed out on breakfast. As usual, Da was being a pain in the arse.'

They ate in silence for a few minutes before Sian asked, 'How is Susan getting on with the case? Does she think we have enough without the murder weapon?'

'Not sure, really,' Vicki said. 'She still wants us to find the knife, but how we do that after so much time has passed, I don't know.'

'Shame I couldn't discover anything in the store.'

'Yeah, it was. Anyway, the statements will go a long way and the DNA match is the icing on the cake. Susan has warned it won't be easy to reopen the case and, as soon as she raises doubt on the original investigation, Hughes will hear what we've been up to.' Vicki sipped her coffee. 'She says we should watch our backs – well, me in particular. I've been down this path before and look where it got me. I promise to do my very best, though, to keep you out of it.'

'Kind of you, but we both know that won't be possible. It was me who slipped the extra DNA test into the system, no getting away from that.'

'About that test. Are you absolutely certain it was Rhys Griffiths' blood on Oliver Hardwick?'

'No doubt at all. You need to get that boy into an interview room. I'm convinced he was responsible for killing Oliver, even if we don't know why. Could be all kinds of reasons, not just because the man might have had a drug debt.'

'Did you manage to take a look at the original toxicology report?'

'I did and cocaine was detected, lots of it. His hair was also tested and results proved he had a long-standing habit.' She snorted loudly. 'Not that anything was mentioned in court. It doesn't seem as though the test results were shared with the defence.'

'At least that proves there's a possible link between the pair, but there's no way we can haul Rhys in while Hughes is working the drugs case.'

'You know,' Sian said, 'I'm beginning to wonder if Rhys is the man who is attacking the women. He fits the description, albeit vague.'

'Short, thin and young with dark eyes, not much to go on. I don't know why Jenny said he was young; after all, he didn't speak and his face was covered. She could be wrong and, let's be honest, that description fits every other lad around here.'

'Maybe she said young because he was so tech savvy, that thing he did with her car, hacking in while she watched.'

Vicki snorted. 'My gran is tech savvy, so we can't bank on the killer being young – or being Rhys Griffiths.'

'We should keep it in mind though.' Sian finished her lunch and pushed her plate away. 'How is the drug investigation going? Is Hughes getting any closer to nicking anyone?'

'No idea. I haven't spoken to him for a while; just as well while we're sneaking around behind his back. I'm actively trying to keep out of his way.'

'Good plan.' Sian got to her feet. 'Sorry, I'd better get off. Unexplained death scene waiting for me in Milford Haven. Keep in touch, OK?'

'Will do, and take care.'

Vicki finished her coffee, paid the bill then walked back to the station. She left her coat in the locker room and headed for Digital Forensics. Eli was working in the corner office so she tapped on the door and entered.

'Hey, Eli,' she said. 'Thought we were overdue a catch-up. How's it going?'

'Like an odd game of tennis, lots of batting emails back and forth while I play hard to get and the killer gets increasingly threatening.'

'Do you know yet where he sends them from?'

'No, and it's driving me nuts. He's using an onion network.'

'What's that?'

'In layman's terms it is a multi-layered system – Tor – that deals with encryption.'

Vicki looked puzzled.

'Tor can be downloaded for free and is an acronym for The Onion Router. Basically it directs all internet traffic – searches, messages, all of it – via an overlay network of more than 7,000 relays. Internet anonymity.'

'Does that mean you'll never be able to obtain an IP address?'

'It will certainly make things difficult if not impossible, but I'll keep at it.'

'Can you give me a flavour of his emails?'

Eli nodded, tapped the keyboard and called up the last message received. Vicki peered at the screen to read.

> You ain't got no choice, bitch. I got you good and proper so you better send me those special selfies or I swear, every single contact in your address book will get a surprise. Your family, friends, business contacts, hell, even your fucking dentist!! You shouldn't piss me off cos I'm not a patient guy, you need to get on with it. You've got till the end of the week, bitch, then I start lighting up social media with photos of you!!

'Does Laura Matthews get to see these emails and your replies?' Vicki asked.

'No. I've set up what you could call a "diversion" and blocked this guy's account from everyone in Laura's contact lists. None of them can physically receive anything from him even if he carries out his threat.'

'Will he be able to tell he's been blocked?'

'Nope, he won't be aware anything has changed. How's it going at your end? Got your ducks in a row ready for when we move to the real world?'

'To be candid, not really. Been a bit hectic and I took a sick day.'

'Are you better now?'

Vicki waved away his concern. 'Yeah, I'm fine. OK then, I'll get something in place over the next couple of days and let you know when we're ready to go.' She got to her feet. 'The next reply you send, offer money and we'll see where that takes us. Make sure you keep me in the loop.'

'Yeah, no sweat.'

Vicki left the department and groaned. She would have to clear any proposed operation with Hughes, long before she started planning a take-down. She walked up to CID and found him laughing with a group of officers gathered by the coffee machine. Hughes turned, noticed Vicki and beckoned her into his office.

'All better now, are you?' he asked sarcastically.

'We need to talk about the sting operation,' she said. 'I've just spoken with Eli and he's told me the killer is getting agitated and angry. He's repeatedly demanding the victim supplies the goods. I've told Eli to try offering money so, I reckon, if we're lucky, we might have a couple of days to set things up.'

'Bit short notice and you know all my time is spoken for. Do you have something in mind?'

Vicki sat on a plastic chair facing the desk.

'The way I see it,' she said, 'we have to set a trap to catch this bloke. To do that, we'll need to send him a young woman in a car.'

'He'll be expecting Laura Matthews. I won't sanction the use of a civilian as bait.'

'I'm not asking you to, sir. Ruth England is the right age and stature. If she wore a long wig, I'm sure we'd fool him; after all, it will be dark and he'll see her through the glass of the window. As he approaches her, we'll nick him.'

Hughes scrubbed at his chin. 'Hmm, should be straightforward enough if he does take the bait. If you have enough time to mobilise, you could embed officers at the scene and tail Ruth's car.'

'Exactly, manage and control the situation. We can also fit a GPS device so, even if we lose contact with her, or he changes the venue, we'll still know her location.'

'Is Ruth up for it?'

'I haven't spoken to her yet, but I'll let you know. I reckon we should still keep all this as quiet as possible.' Vicki saw Hughes nod and continued, 'I can have officers on standby and inform them of what's happening just before the off.' She paused and looked Hughes in the eye. 'Are you sure you can't take this on? It's really beyond my remit as a uniformed sergeant and should be handled by CID. You know it should.'

'And you know we're busy,' he snapped. 'It'll be good for your lot to get stuck in with some real police work.' He shrugged. 'We're understaffed. It can't be helped and you are capable.'

'Just make sure you're available in case we need you. I'll provide regular reports so you'll know where we are.' Vicki got to her feet. 'I really don't get you.'

'Like I give a rat's arse, but tell me, what don't you get?'

'This is a huge case for Pembrokeshire; murder, blackmailing, stalking – all the good stuff – and it's in the public eye. Surely, you want to be involved to take the credit when my team nicks this guy?'

Hughes chuckled. 'Oh, I'll get the credit, that's a given, but if you cock this up, you'll get the credit for that.'

Vicki turned away in disgust, left the room and headed to the squad room. She found Ruth bent over forensic reports and the statements already generated by the investigation.

'Ruth, got a minute?' she asked.

'Yeah, of course.'

'Could you fetch us some coffee and bring it to the office?'

'Is everything all right, Sarge?'

'Fine, I just need a quick chat.'

Vicki settled herself behind the desk and a couple of minutes later, Ruth walked in juggling two mugs of coffee and the notepad and pen she always carried at work.

'Shut the door and take a seat,' Vicki said.

'That sounds serious, have I cocked up?' Ruth asked.

'No, you're good. I want to ask if you'd be up for a short undercover job.'

'Me? What sort of job?'

Vicki told her officer about Laura Matthews, the work Eli had put in, and the planned sting. She told Ruth she'd be safe, that officers would be in place for the arrest, more would tail her car, and a GPS device would be fitted.

'Gosh, Sarge,' Ruth said. 'That's not what I expected you to say. I guess I have a few questions.'

'Thought you might, I would. Go on then, ask away.'

'Why me?'

'You're about the same age as Laura and look a little like her. Not only that, but I can trust you to do a good job. We only get one go at this.'

'So, if I've got this right, I'll pretend to be Laura, drive her car to meet the killer to draw him out, then you guys pile in and nick him?'

'That's more or less it. Of course, your safety will be our number one priority. The car will be tracked, as I said; there will be a radio which shouldn't – as I understand it – be affected if the OBC is hacked, a tool to smash the glass, and – if it makes you feel better – a couple of cans of pepper spray and a taser.' Vicki grinned. 'I'd cheerfully give you a shotgun if I could, *cariad*. Oh – and you'll be wearing a wig.'

'The wig has sold it to me.' Ruth laughed. 'Sounds like you're guarding the Crown Jewels.'

'You're more important than a bunch of half-inched diamonds.'

'Oh, Sarge, you'll make me blush.'

'So, are you up for it?'

'You know? I reckon I am.'

'Good, I thought you would be. Don't chat about this in the nick though – or anywhere else. It's vital to keep ops like this quiet during the planning stages.'

'I won't say a word, Sarge. Thanks for putting me up for this.'

'As I said, you're the best for the job. Right then, crack on and I'll arrange for us to meet with Eli, let him know you are going to play our victim. We need to get you up to speed and copied in on everything. Then, when he reaches the point that locations are being suggested, he'll let you know.' Vicki got to her feet. 'Thanks for agreeing to this.'

'No need, it's my job and this sounds like a breeze. It'll be great to be involved with the arrest of this creep. I'm actually a little excited.'

'Don't be! This is serious stuff, Constable. Wary and cautious would be better than excited.'

'Yes, Sarge, of course.'

'We'll speak again when I know more.'

Chapter twenty-five

At clocking off time, Vicki walked downstairs and was about to leave the station when she heard someone call her name. She turned and was surprised to see DCI Morrison at the bottom of the stairs. She had always liked the man. He was a good copper, but he rarely ventured from his office so their paths didn't often cross.

'Evening, sir,' Vicki said. 'Can I help you?'

'I think you probably can, Sergeant Blunt. Let's go to my office.'

He turned away and began to trudge back up the stairs. Vicki followed and wondered what on earth Morrison wanted with her. She decided he probably wanted to check on her health after being injured on duty, and relaxed a little. He held open the door to his office and waved Vicki to the visitor's chair.

'How are you, Sergeant?' he asked.

'I'm good, sir, thanks.'

'You took a sick day.'

'Yes, I woke up with a dreadful headache. After the recent whack in the face I decided to err on the side of caution and stayed at home in case it got worse.'

'I was told your landlady rang in for you, ex-DCI Thomas.'

Vicki nodded and couldn't see a problem, so she waited for Morrison to continue.

'Coincidentally,' he said, 'she rang me today, anxious to talk about the pickle you've got yourself into.'

'Yes, sir,' Vicki mumbled. She hadn't realised Susan was going to make waves so soon.

'She has explained the situation fully, from DI Hughes' bad behaviour' – he paused and rubbed his eyes – 'to the unauthorised DNA testing of evidence stored in the Hardwick case.'

'Are you going to suspend me?' Vicki asked and added, 'Sir,' for good measure.

'Warned would be a better word. DCI Thomas was very persuasive, always was known for it. I will be visiting her tomorrow to look over exactly what you have uncovered.'

'You are taking this matter seriously?'

'For now I am, but I must review the evidence, then take some time to consider it carefully. If it is as good as your supporter says it is, I will set the ball rolling for an investigation into the inspector.'

Vicki hadn't expected that and could only say, 'Gosh.'

'If that does happen, I'm minded to give you leave on full pay. Bearing in mind how Hughes acted the last time we reached this point, I would be concerned if you were to remain on duty.'

'No need for that, sir. I can take care of myself. What about the Hardwick case? Can we get it back to court?'

Morrison chuckled softly. 'You know that's not down to me and anyway, no use running until we're walking.' He smiled across the desk. 'OK, you can stay where you are for now. If a report is made, I'll give you as much notice as I can and we'll reassess the situation. In the meantime, I'll keep quiet and you must do the same.'

'Yes, sir. Thank you.'

'I must admit, I admire you for not giving up. Susan spoke very highly of you, then – if I remember correctly – described you as, "bloody-minded on steroids".'

'I'm guessing that's supposed to be a compliment.'

Morrison smiled. 'Maybe.' He got to his feet. 'I'll be in touch,' he said. 'Meanwhile, keep your head down. If you encounter any problems at all, let me know immediately. We'll speak again.'

'Yes, sir.'

Vicki left the office and walked back downstairs. Her head buzzed and the concrete steps didn't feel quite as solid as they usually did. She hadn't known Susan was going to act so quickly, or in such a direct manner. Vicki had to warn Sian. She walked to her car, sat in the driver's seat, sent Susan a text to say she'd be late, and another to Sian asking to meet up.

* * *

By the time Vicki finally arrived home, she felt done in. The busy day, the pressure of planning the sting, and her conversation with the chief inspector all weighed heavily on her shoulders. She checked her watch, saw it was after nine and wondered if Susan would still be up. She could do with a chat. Vicki opened the front door and closed it quietly. There was no sign of Susan in the library or kitchen, so Vicki tapped lightly on the bedroom door.

'Come on in, *cariad*,' Susan said. 'I'm wide awake, no need to creep around.'

'Hey, Suzy,' Vicki said. 'Everything OK?'

'I'm just tired and achy and needed to get flat.'

'I know you've been busy. DCI Morrison called me into his office as I was leaving the nick. He told me you'd been on the phone.'

'What did Morrison have to say?'

Vicki related the conversation while Susan sipped whisky and listened carefully.

'He wanted me to take paid leave,' Vicki concluded, 'but I've convinced him I'll be fine.'

'Will you?' Susan asked. 'You're poking the bear for a second time and putting yourself at risk.'

'And you call *me* a worrier. What else could Hughes do to me? Anyway, when Morrison sees the strength of the evidence, I'll be fine. They're hardly likely to sack me and that's all that matters.'

'Well, if something happens don't say I didn't warn you.' Susan topped up her glass. 'Now then, tell me about the sting you're setting up. Two heads are better than one so let's make sure you've stitched up any holes in your plan.'

* * *

At seven the next morning, Vicki got into the car to drive to the station when her mobile rang.

'Hey, Vicki. It's Julie at the nick. There's been an RTA not far from you at Wolf's Castle on the A40. Sounds a bit of a mess and an extra officer would be useful.'

'OK, it's just up the road. Can you tell me anything more?'

'A tractor with a trailer load of Welsh Black cattle got into an argument with a couple of cars. That's all I know.'

'I'm on it,' Vicki said and started the car.

'Don't get too near the cattle,' Julie warned. 'Da's farmed them all his life and still won't turn his back on one.'

'Noted,' Vicki said, put the car in gear and turned toward the main road.

After a few miles, she joined the end of a traffic jam obviously caused by the accident ahead. Nothing was moving so Vicki pulled onto the verge, removed her spare yellow jacket from the boot, and walked towards the gathering of emergency vehicles parked on the carriageway. An officer noticed her approach and began to walk towards her. She frowned when she recognised Kurt Helman.

'Morning, Constable,' she said. 'What can you tell me?'

'Two injured, one already gone to hospital, the other is walking wounded and still here. There's a driver trapped in his vehicle. The fire service are cutting him out now.'

'Julie said something about cattle?'

Helman nodded. 'The vet's here. The two still in the trailer have been put down, another five are on the loose. The farmer has contacted his family to help round them up and they are on their way.'

'OK.' Vicki turned and gazed at the long line of backed-up traffic. 'Who's on the scene?' she asked.

'Dai Phillips, and two patrol cars from Traffic.'

'We need to divert the traffic and close the road until we can clear up this mess. You handle that and call the nick. Find out if there are a couple of officers going begging.'

Vicki marched past the stationary vehicles and soon reached the site of the accident. As she drew near, the fire officer in charge walked closer.

'Morning,' Vicki said. 'How are things placed?'

'We're nearly done here,' he said. 'A vehicle was crushed by the tractor and there's a lad stuck inside. He doesn't appear to be injured other than cuts and bruises and we've nearly got him out. The farmer is chasing after his cows, and the passenger of the second car is talking with one of your officers.'

'Could have been worse then?'

'Everything can always be worse,' the man muttered as he turned away.

Vicki went to check on the witness and satisfy herself a statement was being taken, then headed towards the wrecked vehicle. She kept her distance and watched as rescue personnel carefully cut away the damaged and twisted metal. She could see the back of the male driver through a hole in the roof. He moved his head to look sideways and, with a jolt, Vicki recognised Ieuan Noonan. A few minutes later the roof was completely removed and a fire officer helped Ieuan climb out of the tangled mass. Vicki walked closer.

'Ieuan,' she called. 'Are you OK?'

'Bit shook up, to tell the truth, but I don't think I'm injured.'

'We'll have a paramedic look you over. While we wait, tell me about the accident.'

'It was fucking scary. I was minding my own business and that tractor came over the hill and ploughed straight into me. He was proper shifting and there wasn't anything I could do. I had nowhere to go. The car behind clipped me, I felt that, but everything happened so fast.'

A green-clad medic appeared by Ieuan's side. 'Come over to the ambulance, mate,' he said. 'I just need to check you over.'

'I'm fine.'

'Nevertheless, we need to take a quick look. Won't take long and I'd be happier.'

Ieuan nodded and began to walk to the vehicle, Vicki at his side. He perched in the open back door and submitted to breath and blood pressure tests. The medic shone a light into the patient's eyes and asked him to count fingers.

'Well,' the man said 'I hope you know how lucky you've been. I can't find anything to cause concern so I'm happy to let you go. However, if you develop a headache or any pain anywhere, my advice would be to go straight to A & E.'

'Thanks,' Ieuan said and got to his feet as Dai Phillips called for Vicki.

'Sergeant,' Dai said. 'Can you spare a minute? There's something you should look at.'

'I'll be right there.' She turned to Ieuan. 'Go and sit in one of the patrol cars for a moment. I'll be back to take your statement.'

'Yeah, OK.'

Vicki strode towards Dai who was standing next to the remains of the disassembled SUV.

'What am I looking at?' she asked.

Dai didn't speak, he merely pointed to a section of the roof. Vicki spotted something tucked between the sheet metal and the headlining, so she pulled on latex gloves and crouched down for a closer look. She reached out and, with thumb and forefinger, took hold of what looked to be a plastic-wrapped bundle and gently winkled it out. The clear plastic enclosed a brick of something; Vicki knew it was bound to be drugs, cocaine probably, and she smiled.

'Well spotted, Dai,' she said. 'Work with one of the others and find out if there's more. Take photos of them in place, then collect everything securely and carefully and take it to the nick. Has anyone else arrived?'

'Constable England has just pulled up.'

'Good, tell her where to find me. We'll arrest Noonan and get him back to base.'

PCSO Dai Phillips nodded as Vicki made her way towards the patrol cars and spotted Ieuan sitting in the back of one with the door open. He looked up as she approached.

'Get out of the car, Ieuan,' she said.

He wriggled out and Vicki removed a set of handcuffs from her belt as Ruth joined her.

'Hold out your wrists,' Vicki said.

'Hey, wait a minute,' he said. 'What's going on?'

'Ieuan Noonan, I am arresting you on suspicion of supply and possession of illegal substances. You do not have to say anything, but it may harm your defence if you do not mention when questioned something which you later rely on in court. Anything you do say may be given in evidence.'

'No! This isn't right. I haven't done anything.'

'If that's true, we'll be able to clear everything up during interview. Now, hold out your hands.'

For a moment, it looked as though Ieuan considered legging it. He gazed around the scene as if calculating his chances of escape, but quickly realised he was outnumbered and allowed Vicki to apply the cuffs.

'Right then, come with me, lad.'

Vicki took hold of one of his arms and began to lead him past the crash scene and towards her car parked on the verge.

'Ruth,' she said. 'Let the others know we're leaving and radio the nick to tell them we're bringing in a prisoner.'

Chapter twenty-six

As soon as Vicki passed Ieuan over to the custody sergeant, she went up to the squad room. Ruth placed a mug of coffee in front of her.

'Any sign of DI Hughes?' Vicki asked.

'Haven't seen him today, Sarge.'

'Well, we need to find him. This arrest is bound to be connected to his case with Bridgend and he should be involved with the interview.'

'I'll nip up to CID and tell him what's happened.'

'Yeah, do that while I catch my breath. Have you heard anything from Eli?'

'Not yet.'

'That's good. We still have work to do before you are sent into the field. Are you still up for it?'

Ruth chuckled. 'Do bears shit in the woods?'

'OK, so pop upstairs and find Hughes, then we'll go and have a chat with Eli to find out what's happening at his end.'

Ruth left the room. Vicki took the coffee to her office, sat behind the desk and switched on the computer. She was checking her emails when there was a knock at the door. She looked up and saw a tall man in a smart suit, leaning on the door frame.

'Sergeant Blunt?' he asked.

'Yeah, that's me. Who are you?'

'DI Sam Fletcher.' He leaned across the desk and they shook hands. 'I'm based in Carmarthen and have been seconded by DCI Morrison. He said you could do with an extra pair of hands, what with DI Hughes off–'

Vicki gulped. 'Why is the inspector off?'

'The boss didn't say, but I'm fully briefed on today's arrest. The guv also mentioned an upcoming, confidential op that could do with backup.'

'Oh.'

Vicki wasn't sure what to think. Had Morrison lit the fuse on the internal investigation already? Did that explain Hughes' absence? She didn't think that could be the case as he couldn't have had time to review the evidence that Susan held. She didn't know DI Fletcher and that worried her too. Could he be trusted? She would have been happier if she knew exactly what Morrison had told the man. She saw Ruth enter the squad room and waved her over.

'Ruth, let me introduce DI Fletcher. This is Constable England. She will be involved in the op.'

Fletcher shook her hand. 'Good to meet you,' he said 'Now, are we ready to interview your prisoner, Sergeant?'

'I guess we are. Will you be sitting in, sir?'

'Thought I would. Lead the way and we'll crack on.'

Together they walked downstairs to the custody suite in the basement of the station, settled themselves in and a few minutes later, Ieuan Noonan was brought into the room. The custody officer removed the handcuffs while Vicki set up the recording device. She switched it on and verbally logged the date, time and those present. Ieuan confirmed his name and address and the interview began.

'So we're clear,' Vicki said, 'you've been arrested on suspicion of being in possession of a large quantity of white powder which was discovered hidden in the roof of your vehicle. We have reason to believe the substance is cocaine and it is being tested. Do you have anything you would like to say?'

'I haven't put anything in the roof of my vehicle,' Ieuan said. 'If you've found drugs then they aren't mine. I bought the SUV second-hand so you should ask the previous owner. Nothing to do with me.'

'I must say, I don't believe you, but the plastic wrapping is also being examined for fingerprints and DNA.' She paused for effect. 'If you did tuck those packages beneath the roof lining, we will be able to prove it.' She leaned back in her chair. 'Now's the time to come clean. This will go much better for you if you speak up.'

Ieuan snorted. 'I'm hardly gonna own up if it's not mine, am I?' He grinned. 'Not like you can beat it out of me. Those days are long gone.'

Vicki abruptly changed direction. 'Why were you on the A40 this morning?'

'On my way to see mates of mine in Fishguard.'

'Give us the name and address of your mates and we'll check.'

'I'm not doing that. They won't be happy if you lot turn up on the doorstep, especially as they haven't done anything illegal either.'

'I want to confirm what you've told me.'

Ieuan smirked. 'Yeah, and I want a solicitor.'

'We can certainly ask the duty solicitor to come in, unless you have one of your own. Might take a while to arrange that, though. Why don't you just tell me what you were up to this morning?'

'I already did. I was going to see my mates.'

'Were you delivering the drugs to them? Are you a drug mule, Ieuan?'

Ieuan sighed heavily. 'They aren't my drugs and I didn't put them in my truck.'

There was a tap on the door and DI Fletcher got to his feet. Ruth England was standing outside and passed him a cardboard file, a wide smile on her face. Fletcher closed the door, returned to his seat at the table and flipped open the file. After a moment he passed it to Vicki. She quickly reviewed the contents then looked up at Ieuan, a smile on her own face.

'Do you know Rhys Griffiths?' she asked.

'I've heard the name, but we're not mates. We don't hang out or anything.'

'Really? That surprises me. You've been seen socialising with the petrolheads on the estate, and Rhys is part of the group. When we spoke a couple of weeks ago, you told me you didn't know them, but I have photos that say different.'

Ieuan folded his arms. 'Whatever.'

Vicki removed a document from the file and slid it across the table towards the prisoner.

'What's this?' he asked.

'Details of fingerprints discovered on the packets found in your car. You've been lying to us again. Your prints, together with a few belonging to Rhys Griffiths, have been found on the plastic wrapped around' – she checked something in the file – 'all three kilos of what has proved to be cocaine. Uncut, apparently. I reckon we should start this again, don't you?'

Ieuan lowered his eyes. 'I want a solicitor,' he said. 'I'm not saying another thing until I get one.'

'If you're sure. As I said, it might take a while to arrange and you will be held in a cell.'

'Do your worst.'

'OK, have it your way.'

Vicki got to her feet. 'Interview suspended at 13.02.'

She switched off the recorder as DI Fletcher called for the custody sergeant to remove the prisoner.

'Well,' Fletcher said when the door was closed. 'Looks to me as if you've hit on something big.'

'I'm fairly certain it's connected to the case DI Hughes is working on with Bridgend nick. He should be here to deal with this.' She sighed. 'In an ideal world, I'd go out and pick up Rhys Griffiths, but the inspector ordered me and my officers to keep away.'

'Why did he say that?'

'Apparently he had a tail on him. Where is DI Hughes, do you know?'

Fletcher shrugged. 'I think we should get stuck in,' he said. 'Nick this Griffiths character and raid the Ash Grove house on the estate. We have clear evidence the lad is involved with the drugs in the SUV, and it's a significant quantity. Let's get back upstairs, grab a coffee and I'll run it past DCI Morrison before we make a move.'

'Uh, I wonder…'

'What do you wonder, Sergeant?'

'You mentioned the undercover op. Did the guv talk to you about anything else ongoing?'

'Like what?'

'It's not important.'

'Is there something you aren't telling me?'

Vicki kept her mouth shut, still not sure she could trust the man.

'I can see you're twitchy about something,' he said, 'so I suggest we both go and talk to DCI Morrison. I don't blame you for being wary. If I had an unknown boss foisted on me, I'd be twitchy too.'

They gulped down a quick coffee then walked upstairs and found DCI Morrison at his desk. He looked up and beckoned them inside his office.

'Come in and take a seat,' he said. 'Tell me, how have you got on with the Noonan lad?'

'Limited progress in interview, sir,' Vicki said, 'but we have initial fingerprint and lab results on the substance recovered from his vehicle.'

'What was found?'

'Three kilos of pure, uncut cocaine. We lifted fingerprints from the wrapping belonging to Noonan and Rhys Griffiths.'

'Interesting,' Morrison said. 'Is this the same individual whose DNA has been found at the Hardwick case?'

Vicki glanced sideways at Fletcher, unsure how to answer.

'Settle down, Sergeant. DI Fletcher and I have talked at length about all matters in hand.' Morrison smiled across the desk. 'We met a long time ago at Hendon and he's an excellent and trustworthy officer. You have no need to be concerned.' Vicki nodded and Morrison continued, 'I have spoken to Susan Thomas and examined the evidence you have collected. I'm sure we have enough to reopen the murder investigation.'

Vicki opened her mouth to speak, but he held up a hand.

'I will also be talking to the chief constable regarding the actions, or inactions, of DI Hughes. I can't begin any investigation without a senior officer involved.'

'Gosh,' Vicki said. 'I didn't think things would move so fast.'

'Best to strike while the iron is hot, and DI Hughes is otherwise engaged in Bridgend.' He chuckled. 'Seems as though by the time he returns, you'll have wrapped up the case for him. Have you planned your next course of action?'

'Yes, sir,' Fletcher said. 'We want to nick Griffiths and simultaneously raid the property on Ash Grove. I don't know why that hasn't already happened; there was enough evidence without today's efforts. Hughes has had enough to bust the place for a week at least.'

Morrison nodded and folded his arms. 'Sounds good to me. Now, moving on. Sergeant, are you any closer to obtaining a time and venue for your sting?'

'No, sir. Eli is still trying to convince the killer to accept money rather than intimate photographs. He's offered ten grand and the guy is thinking about it.'

'Is Constable England fully briefed and ready to play her part?'

'Yes, she is, but I haven't mentioned the operation to my officers yet. It's not a complicated thing to arrange so I'll leave it as late as possible to inform them.'

'I agree, good move.' He smiled across the desk. 'You have rather a lot on your plate at the moment, Sergeant, so make good use of Sam. You need to stay sharp; I don't want any mistakes because you're overdoing things.'

'Yes, sir.'

'OK then. Raid the house on Ash Grove and arrest Griffiths first thing tomorrow. Make no mention of the Hardwick case. Once you've brought him back to the station, I want you to remain at your desk. Eli could receive an email at any time, and I want you here and ready to go.'

'I understand,' she said.

Morrison got to his feet. 'Go and set it up then and keep me informed at all stages.'

Chapter twenty-seven

The team gathered in the squad room before six the next morning for the final briefing. DI Fletcher sat at the back of the room and allowed Vicki to take centre stage. He listened carefully as she assigned tasks to the officers involved in the raid, and named those who would arrest

Griffiths at the home he shared on Fforest Road with his mother.

'Any questions?' Vicki asked.

'How many individuals can we expect to encounter at the property on Ash Grove?' a constable asked.

'Definitely two. Records show that Pam and Michael Davis, mother and son, live there. Witnesses in the house opposite have reported seeing a younger woman, but no recent sightings so she might have moved on.'

'Do we know who she is?'

'Not yet. Anyone else?'

'Are we sure Griffiths is at home tucked up in his pit?'

'The last intel we have says he is.'

Vicki looked expectantly at the assembled group, but no one else spoke.

'OK, then. Check your kit and we'll head out. No heroics – any of you. We're aiming for early morning shock and awe, so I'm not expecting too much in the way of resistance, but wear your protective gear and keep your eyes open. As we know, drugs and guns often go together and, for that reason, an armed officer will be on site. A few more on standby. Hopefully they won't be called on.' She smiled encouragingly at the team. 'Stay safe and look after each other. I'll see you in the van.'

The room emptied quickly and DI Fletcher moved to stand next to Vicki.

'They seem like a good bunch,' he said.

'They are – mostly. Some less so. Watch out for Constable Helman. To be frank, he can be a prat, and he's relatively untested in the field.'

'That's useful to know. I'll keep an eye on him.'

They walked downstairs to the car park, climbed into the unmarked van and squashed on wooden slatted benches with the rest of the team. Most remained quiet as they contemplated the raid, but Kurt Helman had plenty to say.

'This is more like it,' he said rubbing his hands together, 'getting to drag scumbags out of bed. This is what I signed up for, not being stuck behind a desk all day.'

A few of the others nodded half-heartedly, but no one spoke. A short while later, the van pulled up outside number twenty-seven, the doors flew open and officers spilled onto the road. Vicki watched as Dai Phillips marched up to the door with a heavy metal device in his hands and smiled. Someone had scrawled "Knock Knock" in black marker pen on the side. Dai glanced at her. She nodded her approval and he swung the battering ram at the door. The lock burst instantly as the force ripped it out of the door frame. The sound was shockingly loud in the quiet of early morning. Dai stood back and method-of-entry officers streamed inside announcing their presence.

'Police! Down on the floor – Now!'

The shouts barrelled around the small house. Vicki and Fletcher followed the MOE squad inside as four officers in full protective gear charged up the stairs. A woman's scream knifed through the air and Vicki ran after them.

'Get down! Hands behind your back!' she heard an officer yell.

Vicki reached the narrow landing and pushed her way into a small bedroom at the rear of the property. In the room was a young woman dressed in a baggy T-shirt barely long enough to cover her underwear. She knelt on the floor, already in handcuffs, while tears poured down her face and her body trembled violently. Vicki was shocked by how young she looked and helped her up to perch on the bed.

'Allow her to get dressed,' Vicki ordered, 'then remove her and take her to the station.'

Kurt Helman stepped forward, grabbed hold of the handcuffs and yanked the young woman to her feet.

'Hey!' Vicki protested. 'No rough stuff. You can see she's no kind of threat.' She raised her voice. 'Someone fetch a female officer.' She glared at him. 'Step back and find something else to do that better suits your talents.'

Crashes and more shouts came from another room so Vicki turned quickly and hurried along the landing. In the front bedroom was a different scene. An older, overweight woman, with bottle-blonde, straggly hair, struggled furiously with an officer as he tried to force her hands behind her back and apply cuffs.

'Fucking pigs!' she screamed. 'Get your filthy hands off me.'

Vicki took a step closer. 'Calm down,' she warned. 'Keep on like this and I'll have no choice but to taser you. Who are you?'

'None of your fucking business.' The large woman kicked out angrily. 'You have no right to smash my door in. This is my bloody house.'

Vicki persisted. 'Give me your name.' She unclipped the taser from her belt and pointed it at the suspect. 'Name!' she demanded and took a step forward.

Knowing she had little choice, the woman stopped thrashing about and snapped, 'Pam Davis.'

'Anyone else in the house?'

Pam laughed nastily. 'There's enough of you to look yourselves.'

'Is your son Michael here?'

Pam shrugged and looked away.

'OK, have it your way.' Vicki formally arrested the woman, recited the caution, and fastened the cuffs on her. She stood back. 'We will now conduct a search of the premises. Once that's been completed, you will be removed to the station. Constable England, stay with her while the others search.' Vicki went to the hall. 'Anyone found Michael Davis?' she called.

'No, Sarge,' an officer said. 'No one else in residence.'

'Make sure you check everywhere; the house, the garden shed and the garage. Get this right.'

DI Fletcher stood at Vicki's side as the search began. It wasn't long before there was shout of triumph from the attic as a large stash was discovered behind the water tank. Bags of various drugs and a quantity of cash was handed down through the hatch, placed inside large evidence bags and carefully labelled.

'This is going well,' Fletcher said. 'Good collar, this one.' He chuckled softly. 'Looks like DI Hughes will miss out. Bloody good result for you, though. This will look good on your record.'

Vicki was about to answer when her mobile rang. She nodded an apology and removed it from her pocket.

'It's Eli. Where are you? I've been trying to get hold of you.'

'Out on a job. What's going on?'

'The killer has been in touch. I'm looking at an email he sent shortly after one this morning. He has agreed to take the cash and wants to meet Laura Matthews at one tomorrow morning.'

'Shit! Not great timing. Do you have a location?'

'Yep, got everything we need.'

'Did you find out where the email was sent from?'

'OK – so not everything.'

'Keep on it. I'll be back as soon as possible and will bring Ruth with me.'

Vicki hung up and told Fletcher about the development.

'You should get off,' he said. 'I can keep an eye on this, but you need to get back to base and plan the sting.'

'Are you sure?'

'Perfectly. Take Constable England with you. We can manage here. Any news from the second team?'

'I haven't heard anything.'

Fletcher nodded. 'I'll chase them and catch up with you at the nick when the search is over and this lot are in the cells. You mustn't be distracted by anything. Your op is vital as lives are at risk and it's also potentially dangerous, so leave this and go.'

'OK, thanks.'

'Make time for some rest.'

Vicki called Ruth from the room where Pam Davis sat fuming on the bed. Kurt Helman had reappeared and was placed on guard duty. Vicki reasoned that if he overstepped the mark, the prisoner would more than likely headbutt him. She smiled to herself. The experience would probably do him the world of good.

'Where are you two going?' he asked.

'Nowhere that should concern you, concentrate on what you're doing here. Any problems, speak to DI Fletcher; he will remain on site. Ruth, with me.'

The women left the house, commandeered one of the squad cars and headed to the station.

'I'm so glad to get out of there,' Ruth said. 'Not only was that the ugliest and most unpleasant woman I've ever seen, I don't reckon she's washed for weeks. Proper smelly.' She scrubbed her hands on her trousers. 'She looks like a bloody bulldog.' She paused. 'OMG! Do you reckon that's Pit Bull, as in Pit Bull Pam?'

'Now there's a thought, great lateral thinking. I'll leave a note for DI Fletcher with the custody sergeant.'

'So, where are we going?' Ruth asked.

'Eli's been in touch,' Vicki said. 'Looks like the sting is on tonight.'

'Really? Wow. I wasn't expecting that.'

'Are you still OK with it? You don't have to do this.'

'I'm fine. I know you'll keep me safe and watch my back, but I do feel a bit nervous. This is my first time.'

'Nervous is good, sharpens your instincts.' Vicki turned out of the estate and sped up. 'As soon as we've found out the where and when from Eli, you'll need to go home and get your head down.' Vicki glanced at Ruth and caught her eye. 'You have to be sharp, not half asleep.'

'Yeah, I get it.'

Vicki pulled into the car park, found a space at the rear of the building, then they made their way to Digital Forensics on the ground floor. As expected, Eli was working in the corner office. He saw the women enter, got to his feet and opened the door.

'Morning,' he said. 'I was about to fetch coffee and you both look as though you could do with some.'

'God, yes,' Vicki said. 'Black with sugar twice, thanks.'

'Will do. Go on in and take a look. Do *not* touch the keyboard.'

Ruth and Vicki sat close to the desk and saw an email from the killer displayed on the screen. They leaned forward to read his words.

> I'll take the cash and delete the images. Meet me at Talbenny Airfield at one tomorrow morning. There are rules! Break ANY of them, bitch, and I'll release the pictures. Come alone – I don't want to see anyone else in the car and I'll be watching. No police!!! If you contact them, or tell anyone about our meeting, I WILL know and all bets will be off. Don't be late and don't be early. Do as you're told and this will be over soon. Break the rules and I will make you pay. I fucking promise you!

'Where is Talbenny Airfield?' Ruth asked. 'I've never heard of it.'

Vicki grinned. 'Oddly enough, it's near Talbenny, eight miles south-west of town.'

'I didn't know there was an airport there.'

Vicki laughed. 'Airfield, not airport. It's disused now. In 1944 it was called RAF Talbenny and around 2,500 personnel were based there. It had three runways and many buildings, most of which have been demolished. A few remain, though, and part of the site has been returned to agriculture. I'm not surprised the suspect picked it for the meet, very isolated, but this is good.'

'Is it? Why?'

'We have plenty of time to tuck officers away in the derelict buildings a few hours before show time.'

Vicki looked up as Eli returned juggling three cardboard cups of vending-machine coffee.

'What do you think?' he asked. 'I reckon we've got lucky.'

'Me too,' Vicki said. 'All we need to do now is check the plan is ready for the off later.'

'You told me the car would be bugged,' Ruth said.

'Yes, we'll fit a GPS tracker, plus all the other safety equipment we talked about. When we're done here, we'll have a word with DCI Morrison, then pop down to the garage; Billy can talk you through it. Don't worry, I promise we'll keep you safe.'

'I know you will, Sarge.'

'OK then, let's crack on. After the chat with Billy, you're going home for a kip. Come back in at seven so we can run through it one last time before we spill the beans to the rest of the team.' Vicki got to her feet. 'Great job, Eli. See you later.'

Chapter twenty-eight

Despite the order she had given Ruth, Vicki didn't make it home for a rest so, with permission from the custody sergeant, she finally got her head down in one of the empty cells. After an hour, she was tempted to give up. Her brain was noisy and way too busy to switch off as she replayed the events of the morning.

She had seen Fletcher return to the station with Pam Davis and offered her services for the interview, but he'd refused. He told her the prisoner needed to settle down before anything like that was attempted and, due to the quantity of drugs and cash seized, an extension of custody would not be a problem. There was no desperate rush. He'd also informed her that Rhys Griffiths was in the wind. The team with the arrest warrant had gone to the house where his mother informed officers she hadn't seen her son for a day or two. She allowed them inside to look around. They didn't find the suspect, but took the opportunity to search his room and many items were confiscated. Vicki didn't know what had been seized but she was unhappy knowing the lad was out there and had the opportunity to run. If Sian was right, though, maybe he'd turn up at the airfield. Vicki wasn't convinced, but without a decent suspect or two, her mind flitted around out of control.

She fidgeted on the thin mattress but couldn't get comfortable enough to actually sleep. She dozed on and off as worries spun cobwebs in her foggy consciousness. She gave up at six o'clock when the new shift came on, thanked the custody sergeant and accepted a cuppa, then went up to the female locker room to shower and change. Like Ruth, she experienced a rush of nerves and gave herself a shake. This was her plan, even if she wasn't technically a detective any longer, and she cursed Horrible Hughes. He was right, if she cocked this up, she'd be lucky not to be demoted – even dismissed.

At her desk, she found a note stuck to the screen asking her to talk to DCI Morrison before informing the team about the upcoming sting, so she finished her tea and headed for his office. She tapped on the door and he waved her inside.

'Evening, sir.'

'Take a seat, Sergeant. Did you manage to get some rest?' he asked.

'Yes, sir,' she lied. 'Grabbed a couple of hours in one of the cells.'

'Any new developments I need to be aware of?'

Vicki shook her head. 'We're good to go. I'm going to send the extra officers to the site later to tuck themselves away. They should be able to see most of the airfield from inside the few buildings still standing. I'm going to brief them separately, and once they've left, I'll let the others know what's going on. I'm also intending to position a couple of cars close to the perimeter. The rest of us will follow on behind Ruth England. I'll be the first on her tail with Dai Phillips.'

Morrison raised his eyebrows. 'Phillips is a PCSO.'

'Whose ambition is to be a proper copper sometime soon. He's a good officer, sir, dependable, solid, not a flapper like some.'

He nodded. 'I won't interfere, it is your operation. How do you see the arrest panning out?'

'We'll wait until the suspect is out of his vehicle and approaching Ruth's car. She can hold the money to partially obscure her face, which is bound to focus his attention on the cash. When Ruth hands it over, we'll make our move. If he does manage to leave the airfield – which I think is unlikely – the cars parked up nearby can pursue him.'

'Looks like you have everything covered. You have my home number so I expect you to keep me in the loop. Be careful and make sure you look after your team.'

'Yes, sir.' Vicki got to her feet.

'When this is over, Sergeant, you and I will need a chat about what comes next, but for now, good luck.'

Back downstairs, Vicki sent the extra staff – seconded from Carmarthen – to Talbenny, as soon as she was satisfied they knew what they were expected to do, and how important the operation was. In the squad room, the next shift had taken over; a few she knew, some she didn't. As she had requested, Dai Phillips was still at his desk and Ruth at hers. Vicki tapped her on the shoulder and beckoned her into the office.

'Take a seat,' she said. 'Did you get some shut-eye?'

'Yes, some. I feel good.'

'Make sure you eat something before the off, and I don't mean a snack.' Ruth nodded and Vicki continued, 'The plan is we will leave the station at half midnight to arrive at the meet at one. You'll travel on the B4327 and the journey will take around twenty minutes. I'll be following at distance with Dai. You might not be able to see us, but we will be there. Arrive as close as you can to midnight.'

'I've got it. Nothing changed from this morning?'

'Nope. Nothing more from' – she waved her fingers in the air – '"Gary Edwards". Backup officers should already be on site. My next task is to brief the rest of the team. Shame I couldn't have hung on to the day shift.'

'Everything will be fine, Sarge, they're a good bunch. Let's crack on and give them the good news so they have enough time to ask questions and get their heads around it all.'

* * *

At half past midnight, Ruth started the engine of a small, red Nissan, waved a hand at Vicki, and pulled out of the car park. Dai waited a few moments then set off behind her. The night was warm and Vicki opened the passenger window. The scent of honeysuckle on the breeze blew inside the vehicle and she took deep breaths to calm her nerves.

'Do you reckon the killer will fall for this?' Dai asked.

'Can't see why not. Eli has been very careful not to tip him off and, as far as I can see, the plan is watertight.'

'Thanks for letting me in on this, for trusting me. I won't let you down.'

'I know you won't.'

Vicki called Ruth on the radio. 'Everything OK?' she asked.

'All's well, but this bloody wig is itchy. I hope it hasn't got fleas or nits.'

Vicki chuckled. 'Watch your speed. Remember, you mustn't get there early. We're behind you so don't worry and, as you know, there are officers already on the scene. Any problems just holler and we'll move in. Don't take any risks.'

'I won't. Just before I drive onto the airfield, I'll call you on your mobile and leave the line open as we arranged, so you will be able to hear what's going on.'

'Good, then if the killer hacks the OBC and cuts the communications, we'll know at the same time as you.'

Vicki used the radio again to check in with the team hidden on site, and personnel in the cars stationed close by. Convinced she had done all she could, she sat forward in her seat and focused her attention on the back lights of Ruth's car some distance ahead. As Dai drew near to the airfield, she instructed him to pull into a gateway and tuck the car behind a tall hedge. He turned off the engine and they both listened to Ruth via the open phone line.

'I'm on site,' she said. 'Can't see anything yet.'

Ruth bumped over the rough ground towards what had once been the main runway and provided a running commentary. Vicki listened intently and wished she was closer, but another car on such a flat and open area would stand out like a white cat on a slag heap.

'I'm on the runway,' Ruth said, 'or what's left of it. Can't see anyone about and no vehicles.' There was a pause, then, 'Hang on. I think I can see something… yes, an SUV maybe with the lights off and it's…'

The line died abruptly and the sudden silence was unnerving.

'Has her car been hacked?' Dai asked. 'Is the suspect with her now? Do we go in?'

'What's the mobile signal like up here?' Vicki asked.

'Don't know, Sarge.'

Vicki slapped the dashboard. 'We should have checked! If the signal has dropped and we go charging in, we'll frighten him off.'

'Radio the other cars. Tell them what we know and to keep an eye out. If the guy runs, they'll be able to nab him.'

'Can you see anything on the airfield? Any movement?'

Dai peered through a pair of binoculars and shook his head. 'No, nothing.' He wound down the window and listened. 'Can't hear anything either.'

'OK, we're going in on foot. If we work around the edge of the airfield until we're in line with the old runway, we might be able to see if something is going on. I'll let the others know what we're up to so we aren't confused with the bad guy.'

Dai and Vicki left the car and made their way slowly along the inside line of the perimeter. They moved quietly and kept to the shadows, pausing frequently to scan the surrounding land. A few minutes later, Dai stopped suddenly and held up his hand. He tapped his ear and pointed into the darkness. Vicki listened hard and heard the quiet throb of a small petrol engine.

'That has to be Ruth,' Dai whispered, 'but I can't see her car or anything else out there. What should we do?'

'I'm thinking.'

Vicki stared across the open expanse of grassland. The moon was obscured by low cloud, the night so dark she wasn't sure her eyes were open and blinked. The car's engine whirred on, but it was the only sound. Vicki couldn't detect the rumble of a second vehicle. Suddenly she spotted a weak, orange glow at the far end of the runway and pointed it out to Dai. They watched as the glow grew and intensified.

'That looks like a fire,' Dai said.

'Yes, it does,' Vicki agreed. 'We need to get over there.'

She radioed the teams, then broke cover and ran towards the fire. When they were still a hundred yards away, an explosion shook the air and both officers flinched and ducked down.

'Shit!' Dai said. 'That's a vehicle fire. Where's Ruth?'

'I don't know.'

Vicki ran faster, Dai by her side. The flames lit up the crumbling tarmac and Vicki spotted a dark shadow moving quickly towards the edge of the airfield.

'Check that out, Dai,' she yelled, 'while I go to check on Ruth.'

Without hesitation, Dai changed direction as Vicki ran towards the fire. A little away from the burning vehicle, she caught sight of the red Nissan and sped up. Ruth was in the car, fists pounding on the side window. Vicki took hold of the handle, but the door wouldn't open.

'Get me out!' Ruth screamed. 'I can't breathe! I'm choking and can't turn the engine off.'

'Use the tool for breaking the window,' Vicki yelled.

'I can't find it.'

'Shift over to the passenger seat and cover your head.'

Vicki pulled the baton from her belt and swung it at the glass with little effect.

'Hurry, get me out,' Ruth screamed again.

Vicki took another swing, and another. The glass cracked, but still didn't break.

'Ruth. Pull one of the headrests out of the seat and use the metal struts.'

Ruth scrabbled behind her, snatched a headrest, turned it around and drove it into the driver's window. After a couple of hefty blows, the toughened glass finally shattered and showered her with small chunks. Ruth dropped the headrest and wriggled her torso through the hole. Vicki tucked her hands beneath Ruth's arms, and dragged her from the car and over to a patch of scrubby grass. Ruth gasped for air, coughing and retching.

'Are you OK?' Vicki asked.

'I will be. Did you catch the guy?'

Vicki didn't know so she said, 'Don't worry about that now. I'll whistle up an ambulance.'

'No! I'm OK. Go and get him, he's got the money.'

'Are you sure?'

'Yes! Go! Don't let him escape.'

Vicki turned and ran past the Nissan, its engine still running, then dodged around the fire and headed in the direction Dai had gone. Other figures ran out of the darkness as the officers on site broke cover.

'Go and take care of Ruth,' Vicki yelled. 'She needs an ambulance. A couple of you follow me. The suspect's loose and PCSO Phillips is in pursuit. He cannot be allowed to get away.'

Vicki ran on and a minute later saw a large, bulky shape emerge out of the smoky darkness.

'Dai, is that you?' she yelled.

'Yeah and I've got him. You really won't believe this.'

Chapter twenty-nine

Dai marched closer with a small man dressed in black almost dangling from his strong arm, his feet barely touching the ground. Dai held the man tightly as he wriggled and shone a bright beam at his face. The prisoner blinked furiously and tried to turn his head away, but Dai's grip prevented much movement.

'Shit!' Vicki said. 'Is that—'

'Yep. Kurt bloody Helman.'

Dai forced the man's wrists together with his large hands and snapped on the cuffs, then he rummaged inside Helman's jacket and removed a large wad of cash as a group of other officers arrived. Vicki walked closer and got right into Helman's face.

'You, disgusting little fucker!' she spat. 'Attacking young women, one dead, one nearly dead, and now this! It's taking everything I've got not to beat you to death with my baton.'

Helman didn't look away and locked his gaze with Vicki's – then he smiled. She took another step closer, grabbed hold of his shoulders and ploughed her knee into his groin. She released him and he crumpled to the rough ground groaning loudly. Vicki glanced at the other officers. 'He tried to run,' she explained and was happy to see them nodding their heads. 'Dai, get him out of my sight.'

Dai Phillips grabbed hold of the cuffs, hauled the whimpering man to his feet and dragged him towards the squad cars.

'Anyone know how Ruth England is doing?' Vicki asked.

'She's OK, Sarge,' a nearby officer said. 'First response is pumping her full of oxygen and she's improving all the time. They want to take her to hospital, but she has refused to leave the scene.'

'I'll go and have a word. Someone get that fire out and call for a SOCO. I'm not sure there will be much to find, but we must do this by the book,' Vicki said. 'The entire country will be watching us on this one and there can't be any mistakes.'

The armed officer moved to stand next to her. 'I can deal with this,' he said. 'Not much to do now and I can see you're itching to get the suspect back to base.' He lowered his voice. 'Someone said he's a serving officer. That can't be right, is it?'

'Unfortunately it is,' Vicki growled. 'Looks as though we've got our very own rotten apple.'

'Any idea why he was doing this?'

'None at all, but trust me, I will find out if it's the last thing I ever do.' She took a mobile from her pocket, tapped in a number and moved away from the group. Her call was answered by a sleepy voice.

'Good morning, sir. I'm calling as requested to inform you that the operation was successful and we have a suspect in custody.'

'Bloody well done, Sergeant! I never doubted you. Any chance the suspect can wriggle away from this with a clever lawyer?'

'None at all. We've got him banged to rights. Caught in the act and the cash was found on him.'

'Is Constable England safe? Any injuries to anyone?'

'No, sir, apart from the suspect; he thought about running so I had to prevent him doing so. He'll live. Ruth is fine and I'll update you face to face later on today. There is a problem, though, a sizeable one you should be aware of.'

'Oh? Tell me.'

Vicki swallowed hard. 'The suspect we've arrested is Kurt Helman – a serving officer at the nick.'

* * *

Vicki marched across the airfield and dropped into the passenger seat, happy she didn't have to drive to the station. As the adrenaline began to dissipate, she felt suddenly wobbly and more tired than she could ever remember being before. She scrubbed at her face and noticed her hands were shaking so she clasped them together in her lap. She wasn't sure if they shook because things had so nearly gone wrong, because they hadn't, or because she was so full of anger she felt dangerous. She was pleased she couldn't get at Helman behind the wire grill. Given the chance, she would happily have pounded him like she would a steak – repeatedly and with a spiked mallet.

No one spoke on the journey to the station and Vicki was glad, she had lots to think about. Her main concern was how to keep Kurt Helman's identity from the press. As yet, there had been no sightings of reporters at the airfield, but she knew that wouldn't last. When the sun rose, the large police presence on the flat empty land would be obvious to the locals. Someone was bound to contact *WalesOnline*, then it was likely all hell would break loose. Had there ever been a serving police officer accused of being a potential serial killer? Would Helman be deemed fit for interview? As far as Vicki was concerned, he was barking mad. He certainly looked deranged, sitting on the back seat grinning as though he was on a day trip. Why did he attack his victims? Did he know them? More to the point, did they know him? What possible motive could he have? Vicki glanced sideways at Dai, who was concentrating on the narrow road, headlights on full beam. A muscle twitched in his jaw and she knew he was also struggling.

'Do you have any idea why he did this?' she asked quietly.

'Because he's a twisted little fuck,' Dai snarled. 'Make sure you don't leave me in a room alone with him.'

On the back seat, Helman smirked and Dai tapped the brakes so he bounced off the back of the front seats. Vicki covered her mouth to stifle a chuckle. A little while later, Dai pulled up at the back door of the station and together they escorted the prisoner inside and presented him to the custody sergeant. The man's eyes widened when he recognised Helman standing in front of his desk in handcuffs, but he passed no comment and began the booking in process. The main door to the suite opened and DCI Morrison stomped in. He shook his head and glared at Helman.

'What the hell have you been up to?' he snapped angrily. 'I can't believe any of my officers would behave in this despicable manner, you have betrayed the entire police family. What were you thinking? Why do something as disgusting as this?'

'I don't believe he was thinking, sir,' Vicki said. 'As to the why, I'm sure we'll uncover that during interview.'

Helman spoke for the first time since his arrest. 'I'm not talking to you. No interview will happen until I have a solicitor and my Federation rep.'

Morrison took a few steps closer and towered over his constable. 'You better not test me, boy,' he growled. 'You have brought shame on this station, on the force as a whole. Our organisation cannot operate without the trust of the public, and you…' He ran out of words and took a deep, shuddering breath. 'Get him banged up and watch him like a bloody hawk. When that's been done, I want you two in my office before you do anything else. Got that?'

'Yes, sir,' Vicki said. 'This won't take long.'

Morrison nodded, turned on his heel and marched angrily away. The prisoner smirked again, and Vicki stuffed both hands into her pockets. She could tell the chief inspector was furious and couldn't remember ever seeing him so angry.

Kurt Helman was searched, his belt and shoelaces were removed, his pockets emptied and a list of his possessions made. Two constables then led him to a room where they took away his clothes for testing and gave him a paper boiler suit and rubber shower shoes. The custody sergeant then escorted him to a cell, removed the handcuffs and shoved him inside. The metal door was slammed and locked and the sergeant leaned against it and rubbed his face.

'Thanks, Bob,' Vicki said. 'Make sure you keep a good eye on him like the guv said. I'll be back as soon as I can.'

'No sweat, Vicks, he's not going anywhere.' He frowned and rubbed his eyes again. 'I can't believe this,' he said, 'over thirty years I've been here and nothing like this has ever happened. The Met might have form, but not us.'

Vicki patted the man's arm. 'First time for everything, Bob, but I feel your pain.' She leaned closer and lowered her voice. 'Goes against the grain, I know, but keep him safe. No visitors, OK? No one gets in that cell until you've run their names past DCI Morrison or me.'

'Yeah, I get it.'

Vicki patted his arm again then left the suite with Dai and walked upstairs. Morrison was waiting in his office, his head in his hands. He looked up as they entered and waved them to seats.

'OK,' he said, 'let's hear it.'

Using as few words as possible, Vicki delivered a verbal report of the events at the airfield and the arrest of Kurt Helman. When she finished speaking, Morrison closed his eyes and shook his head.

'You told me he was banged to rights,' he said. 'Are you completely sure you have enough evidence to put him away?'

'Yes, sir, I'm certain. When I leave here, I'll speak to Eli in Digital Forensics. Once he's had access to Helman's computer, I know we'll find more.'

'We need everything so dig into his background, his family, his finances, service record – I said everything. When this gets out, the public will quite rightly call for blood. The very least we can do at this point is to have some answers for them.' He sighed heavily. 'Yes, you speak to DF and I'll speak to the ACC. He'll appoint a senior investigating officer. Until then, we work this as we would any crime.'

'Can we conduct an initial interview, sir?' Vicki asked.

'No reason not to until an SIO is in place, but there's no rush. Helman can stew until we get our ducks in a row.' He looked across the desk. 'Good job, both of you. Must have been hard to arrest a fellow officer in such circumstances.'

'Fellow officer, sir?' Vicki spluttered. 'You're kidding. He's nothing to do with me, or any of the other, good officers working here. He is a killer who happens to be a police officer, not a police officer who is a killer.'

'Good point, Sergeant. Now, I can see you're tired, so after you've spoken to Eli you need to go home. Nothing will need your attention for a few hours and certainly nothing that can't wait, so get some rest and return at four. We'll have a go at Helman then.' He caught Dai's gaze. 'Good arrest, son. You won't be a PCSO for too long – you have my word. We need good officers.' Morrison got to his feet. 'Goes without saying, you don't mention this outside the station, now get off and we'll reconvene at four.'

Vicki and Dai left the office and walked downstairs.

'You heard him,' Vicki said, 'you've been on for nearly twenty-four hours which included a raid and a take-down. You must be shattered.'

'I'm OK, Sarge. I grabbed a couple of hours in the canteen.'

Vicki shook her head. 'Go and rest, you're no good to this investigation if you're exhausted. Send Ruth home too. I'll have a word with Eli, then I'll get off. Back at four, don't oversleep.'

'Yeah, all right then.' He looked at Vicki. 'You know, that was a great sting, a perfect operation and arrest, so why do I feel like I've done something wrong? Dirty somehow. Why aren't I jumping up and down and cutting notches on my baton?'

Vicki chuckled. 'We don't do that these days, but I understand how you're feeling, how it was to put handcuffs on a colleague. You'll settle though. You did bloody well this morning, Dai, never forget that. I'll see you later.' She patted his arm and set off for Digital Forensics.

* * *

Vicki was pleased to see Eli at his desk. She tapped on the glass door and he waved her inside.

'Gosh,' he said, 'you've seen better days. How did it go?'

'It worked and we nicked a suspect – a serving officer as it turns out.'

Eli nodded. 'I picked up some chatter, terrible thing.'

'Yeah, isn't it? Morrison is livid and feels betrayed that one of his could behave like this. Anyway, I told him that now we have access to the computer, you'll be able to gather digital evidence to put the lid on the case. Please, tell me I'm right.'

Eli grinned. 'You're right, but you need to take me to the actual kit he used. If this guy has built in system defences, anyone unplugging anything could trigger the computer's kill switch and we'd lose everything.'

'I'll let the search team know and arrange to get you there. Top priority on this, please.'

'Of course. Who did you nick?'

'Kurt Helman.'

'Name doesn't ring a bell, but I don't meet many of your lot.'

'I think that's a good move on your part.' She got to her feet. 'I'm off for some shut-eye. Talk to DCI Morrison or DI Fletcher if there's any problems and I'll be back at four. I'll see you then.'

Eli nodded and turned back to the screen, and Vicki headed down to the locker room to change before she left the station.

Chapter thirty

Vicki took a hot shower. A strange kind of lethargy had crept up on her, an extreme tiredness that made her limbs feel heavy, and she was anxious to get home. She was hanging her police jacket in her locker when the door burst open and Hughes stormed in. She spun around and glared at him.

'Female only space, *sir*.'

'As if I give a shit about that!' he snapped. 'I've just been informed I'm under investigation, so tell me what you've done.'

'What I always do – my job.'

Hughes took a couple of steps closer and looked like he meant business, but even though his hands formed fists, they remained by his side.

'It won't work, you know,' Hughes raged. 'We've been here before and look where that got you.' He snorted and was close enough for Vicki to feel his spittle on her face. 'Well, this time you'll be demoted, kicked out of the force if I have my way.'

Vicki grinned. 'I'm sure it won't be you who makes that decision. Your actions and inactions had consequences and not just for yourself. An innocent woman was convicted of a murder she didn't commit. Did you frame Emma Hardwick, or was it just lazy coppering?'

Hughes kept quiet and Vicki continued.

'See, I think it was intentional. Why else would you remove reports from the murder file or shag Alison Hale, a defence witness?'

'So you say. Emma Hardwick was found guilty, a unanimous verdict and you can't prove anything.' He laughed nastily. 'I'll think of you, stuck here with your nose to the grindstone while I'm enjoying gardening leave on full pay. The investigation will drag on and I'll be allowed to retire early while you're still getting smacked in the face by scumbags.'

'Things will move faster than that.' Vicki looked him in the eye. 'I have plenty of proof and you are well and truly in the shit.'

'You, fucking bitch!' Hughes spat and moved closer.

Vicki backed up against the tiled wall. She had nowhere to go and raised her hands defensively, hoping he'd move back. Suddenly the door opened and Dai Phillips strode into the room.

'Everything OK, Sarge?' he asked.

'Yeah, DI Hughes was just leaving.'

'Not until I've had my say,' Hughes growled.

'From what I've heard, you've had your say and now you must get out – sir,' Dai said.

'You're gonna make me, are you? You're just a PCSO, no one gives a fuck what you think. You're expendable.'

Hughes turned to face the large man and for a moment Vicki thought things were going to get rough, but he hesitated then stormed out, slamming the door behind him. Vicki dropped onto a bench and took a deep breath. She glanced up at Dai.

'Thanks, mate,' she said. 'Thought I was in trouble there for a minute or two.'

Dai chuckled. 'You could have taken him, Sarge, I know you could.'

'I'm glad you have such faith in me. Why are you still here? You're supposed to be on your way home.'

'I was about to set off then I saw him barrelling down the corridor so I thought I'd hang about, see what he was up to.'

'Well, it's all over now; we should both get some rest, then return this afternoon to tackle Helman. God, what a mess this is. That little rat has made me feel grubby. How the hell did he get into the force?'

'We'll find out, but as you said time out first. If you're OK I'll get off, it's been a very long day.'

Dai left the room. Vicki gulped water from one of the basin taps, then grabbed her stuff and left the station.

* * *

Vicki found Susan in the kitchen drinking tea in her dressing gown.

'I thought you'd left home,' Susan said. 'Everything OK?'

'Far from it.'

Vicki told her friend about the arrest and the confrontation with Hughes in the locker room.

Susan nodded. 'I've been trying to get hold of you to warn you things were moving fast and he was being suspended, but I couldn't get your phone to ring or leave a message.' She hauled herself upright and collected a mug from the drainer. 'Thank God for Dai Phillips, eh?' she said and poured tea from the garish pot.

'Yes, things might have gone in a totally different direction without him. Good bloke is Dai, and he made a blinding arrest. That disgusting worm Helman was on his toes and might have got away – which doesn't bear thinking about. I'm due back in at four for the initial interview. By then, I'm hopeful Eli will have gathered reams of evidence from Helman's computer.'

'Have you got enough without it?'

'I'm sure we have.' Vicki groaned, slumped on the table and rested her head on her arms.

'You look done in, *cariad*. I'll rustle up an egg and bacon sandwich. After you've eaten, you must get your head down. Don't worry about oversleeping, I'll make sure you get to the station on time.'

'OK, I know when I'm beaten. What about Hughes? What happens now?'

'You can't worry about that, not until Helman is charged. Morrison won't let you down though, and with a bit of luck, you won't see Hughes again until he's in the dock.' Susan reached across the table and grasped Vicki's hand. 'You did good, Vicks. I'm certain no one will be able to touch you now. Right then, breakfast.'

* * *

Vicki's alarm buzzed aggressively on the bedside table. She snatched for it, but only succeeded in knocking it beneath the bed. She untangled herself from the duvet, fished the device out and slapped it off. She sat on the bed and rubbed her eyes, feeling battered and groggy. The events of the early morning flooded back and it took everything she had to get up and prepare to return to the station. On the way out to her car, she popped her head into the library and told Susan not to wait up, that she would keep in touch if she could.

'Don't worry,' Susan said. 'I'll assume that no news is good news, and see you when I see you.'

A little while later, Vicki walked into the station, changed into her work clothes, then wandered downstairs to the custody suite.

'Hey, Bob,' she said, 'shouldn't you have clocked off by now?'

'I wanted to stay and keep an eye on things.'

'And how are things?'

'Quiet at least. He's just sitting on the bunk, staring at the door. We offered lunch but he didn't eat it.'

'Anyone been to see him?'

Bob snorted. 'Only the curious, and they didn't get anywhere near.'

'Good job. I'm hoping we can interview him soon, I just have to round up as much evidence as I can before we begin.'

'I heard about DI Hughes,' Bob said. 'Just wanted to let you know most of us are on your side and very glad to see the back of him.'

'Thanks for that. I'll be back soon.'

Vicki left the basement and called into DF, pleased to see Eli was working at his desk in the glass office. He looked up as she entered.

'You look better,' he said, 'and, as I've got good news, you will only continue to improve.'

'So, tell me what you found?' Vicki said and sat next to him.

'I'll have to give you the highlights cos there's a lot of stuff that won't mean much to you – no offence.'

'None taken.'

'So, we have the emails Helman sent to his victims, and proof he was the one who altered the photographs. He cocked up and left a trail in the metadata. I also reckon I've been able to work out where his path crossed with the victims.'

'Have you? That is good news. Where?'

'While he was on duty wearing his uniform. All three were spoken to by him over the last six months. Random traffic stops, all of them.'

'How do you know that?'

'He kept an online diary, wrote down just about everything that happened to him each day.' Eli chuckled. 'He probably thought no one would be able to access it without the encryption key. Didn't give us hackers a moment's thought.'

'Did he happen to record his motives for what he's done?'

'Not directly, but I've discovered he's an incel.'

'That group of misogynistic creeps who think it's women's fault they don't get laid?'

'That's them, the involuntary celibate. He's a member of some very sick and twisted forums.' Eli reached over to a desk by his side and handed Vicki a stack of files. 'Everything is in there, but I will have much more by the time I've finished.'

'Any evidence someone else was involved? That he was sharing stuff around the nick?'

'Not so far. I still have to take a look at his phone and check his social media groups.'

'OK, thanks for this.' Vicki stood and smiled. 'He won't stand a chance in hell now I'm armed to the teeth.'

* * *

DCI Morrison sat in the observation room overlooking interview room one and watched as Kurt Helman was brought in by the custody sergeant. He was led to a seat and the handcuffs were removed. On the opposite side of the table sat Vicki and DI Fletcher, and Helman's Federation rep made up the numbers. Vicki started the tape, listed those in the room, the date and time, and took her seat. She opened one of the many files she had brought with her and slowly riffled through the documents inside. The silence lengthened and the prisoner began to twitch. Finally, she looked up at him.

'I don't know what to say to you,' Vicki began. 'What am I supposed to say to a man who has abused the trust he was given in the worst possible way? I always knew you were an idiot, but a killer?'

'Shouldn't judge books by their covers,' Helman said and folded his arms.

'Why did you attack those women?'

'No comment.'

'I think I know why, but I'd like to hear it from you.'

'No comment.'

'Do you have a problem with women?'

'No comment.'

Vicki sighed and leaned back in her chair. 'I'm sure your rep has told you that if you assist us with the investigation, things will be easier for you. Not much, admittedly, but in your position anything will help.'

Helman looked down at the desktop and said nothing.

'With the prisons as crowded as they are, and of course who you are – were – a single cell for the rest of your life might make a world of difference. What do you think?'

'You can't promise anything,' Helman muttered. 'I'm going "no comment" so if you want to waste your time, keep going. It's better in here than the cell so you'll be doing me a favour.'

'OK, have it your way, but let me tell you what we know so far to convince you this is not going away.' Vicki opened one of the files and slipped documents across the table. 'Digital proof it was you who blackmailed the victims with digitally altered – by you – pornographic images. We also have your digital diary and know you had contact with the women before you attacked them, so we can add stalking to your crimes. The SUV found burnt-out at the site wasn't completely destroyed and physical evidence has been obtained. We have witnesses–' she paused and grinned '–a fair few of whom are coppers, present at your arrest, and of course your second victim who, luckily for her, didn't die. You're screwed; you know that, don't you?'

Helman shook his head and began picking at a scab on his hand. The officers waited, but he said nothing further.

'OK then, back to your cell for a period of reflection.' Vicki got to her feet, called for the custody officer and turned off the tape. She leaned on the desk and glared at Helman. 'I don't care if you don't speak, it won't make any difference. We've got you, you bastard, and we'll *never* let you go. You're done! The rest of your life will be spent behind a metal door, shitting in the same place as you eat your food and keeping one eye over your shoulder.' She grinned nastily. 'Pretty boy ex-cop like you won't stand much of a chance inside. Is that single cell looking attractive now?'

Vicki stood and stormed from the room, Fletcher behind her, and Helman was returned to his cell. In the observation room, they spent a few moments with DCI Morrison. He made the point that the prisoner might be more talkative if a male officer conducted any future interviews.

'He shouldn't be allowed to choose, sir,' Vicki said.

'I know, but I want to hear him tell us why he committed these dreadful crimes,' Morrison said. 'He'll hang himself if we can get him to engage with us.'

'Leave the cell door open,' Vicki said. 'There are plenty here who would do that for real.'

Morrison chuckled. 'I'd probably be at the front of the queue. We'll leave him where he is for now. He might be a little more talkative after a few hours in solitary. Meanwhile, Pam Davis and Ieuan Noonan, the drug dealers, are still cooling their heels and I'd like to see them charged and taken to court in the morning. No doubt they will be remanded, which will give us some breathing space.'

'We're nearly there with that, sir,' Fletcher said. 'The initial interviews were interesting and have given us plenty of new leads.'

'What about the young girl arrested at the house?' Vicki asked. 'Do we know who she is?'

'She claims she's an Afghani refugee,' Fletcher said. 'Says she was taken in by the Davises when she was refused asylum, but there's much more work to do.'

'Does her story hold water?' Morrison asked.

'Difficult to answer that until we've had more time with her.' Fletcher sighed heavily. 'The doc has checked her over and puts her in her mid-teens. So far we haven't found any ID in the house, but SOCO are taking the place apart and we might get lucky. I don't reckon she had anything to do with the drugs though and I need to talk to social services. It's my opinion she is more victim than criminal.'

'I know I can trust you to sort it out,' Morrison said and turned to Vicki. 'PCSO Phillips has informed me that Hughes confronted you in the locker room. Are you OK?'

'I'm fine, sir.'

'Well, he's off site now and won't be returning. The evidence you collected regarding his conduct is good and has been passed to the appropriate department. I will personally make sure that this time the matter will be correctly handled and none of the airborne shit will stick to you.'

'Thank you, sir. What about Emma Hardwick?'

'I haven't forgotten about her, Sergeant, but as the saying goes, Rome wasn't built in a day.' He smiled. 'Getting our hands on Rhys Griffiths would help. Put pressure on the lad you nicked with the cocaine in his car. I'm sure he'll know where Griffiths is.'

Morrison turned away and headed back to the office, while Vicki and Fletcher went in search of coffee.

'You know what?' Fletcher asked.

Vicki chuckled. 'No, you haven't told me yet.'

'The guv wants Davis in court, Ieuan Noonan too. The way I see it, we have enough on both of them to have them remanded.'

'Yes, I agree with you.'

'Then let's crack on with that, pack those two off in the morning so we can focus our attention on Helman.' He grinned. 'I can see to that and you can have a lie-in.'

'Oh, I don't know, I–'

'I do, and I'm the boss. Come in at lunchtime and we'll start again then.'

Chapter thirty-one

The next morning, following a couple of extra hours in bed, Vicki and Susan shared a leisurely breakfast with plenty of coffee. While on their second cup, the letter box rattled and Vicki walked along the hall to collect the post and took it back to the kitchen.

'Anything interesting?' Susan asked.

'Bills and junk mainly,' Vicki said, 'although…' She used a butter knife to slit open a cream-coloured envelope, scanned the contents and smiled. 'Nice. A party invite, to a one hundredth birthday, no less, at the end of August, from the Williams sisters on the estate.'

'That's still some way off,' Susan said. 'I hope they aren't being premature.'

Vicki chuckled. 'Think positive, Suzy. It says "plus one". Do you fancy coming along?'

'If I'm still here.'

'Gosh, you're in a grumpy mood. What's up?'

'This awful business with Kurt Helman. Bad coppers really drag me down and he has to be the very worst. All my professional life I've worked on building trust with the community and I don't think I did too badly, but this?' She sipped from her mug. 'How do we recover from this? It will take the force years to get back to where we were – if that's even possible.'

'I understand and feel exactly the same. DCI Morrison was livid and I thought he was going to batter the man.' Vicki sighed. 'I actually had a brief go and have to admit, although I shouldn't, that it was satisfying.'

Susan grinned across the table. 'I heard he was trying to leg it.'

Vicki shrugged.

'Has anyone spoken to the CPS?' Susan asked.

'If they have, I'm not aware of it. Helman will be interviewed again today and if an SIO has been appointed, I won't take any further part, other than as a witness. I reckon DI Fletcher will keep me informed.'

'Should do. I worked with him when he started in CID; he always behaved in an exemplary manner. No wonder he rose up the ranks so quickly. Be good for you if he stays at Haverfordwest nick, he's utterly trustworthy and a joy to work with.'

'Let's hope then. Mind you, anyone is better than Horrible Hughes.' Vicki glanced at her watch. 'Davis and Noonan should be appearing in court about now, which will give us a bit of a breather. My job today is to discover the ID of the young woman found in the Davises' place, and once I've done that, I'm on the hunt. I don't like the fact that Rhys Griffiths is wandering around, especially as he is more or less bound to be involved with any retrial for Emma.'

'Sounds like a decent plan, and it will be much easier not having Hughes creeping around the nick.' She smiled. 'You and Sian make a great team and did a proper number on him. By the end of the year, he'll be fighting for

Universal Credit, a legal aid brief, and of course no pension. Bloody marvellous.' Susan poured herself yet another coffee and used it to swallow her pain medication.

'Can I ask you something?' Vicki said.

'Yes, of course.'

'Who is Jasmine?'

Susan blinked. 'Where did you hear that name?' she asked.

'From you, actually, the evening Billy came over. I did the washing-up then looked for you to say goodnight before I went up. You were in the library and I heard you talking on the phone. How did you put it? "Vicki's obsession with the Hardwick case". Who were you discussing me with?'

Susan looked alarmed. 'Have you been eavesdropping outside my door?'

'No, of course not. I heard my name, and you can't blame me for listening. You'd have done the same. What are you up to, Suzy?'

The older woman rubbed her eyes. 'Nothing bad,' she began and took a deep breath. 'I used your bloody-minded determination to free Emma to help me settle my own obsession.'

'Which has something to do with a woman called Jasmine?'

Susan nodded and wiped her eyes with her fingers.

'Who is she?'

Susan gulped from her mug and rubbed her eyes again. 'Jasmine *was* the daughter of old friends of mine. Such a beautiful girl, Indian with honey-coloured skin and the largest, almond-shaped eyes you ever saw.' Susan paused, took a breath then continued, 'Jasmine had always called me auntie, which made me feel simultaneously flattered and old. As a child she wanted to join the force, to be a police officer. It was all she talked about.' Susan sighed heavily. 'I thought I was helping by encouraging her to achieve her ambition, and her parents were incredibly proud when she signed up. She would have been a great officer – given the time.'

Unusually for Susan, a tear ran down her cheek.

Vicki reached out and covered her hand. 'What happened?' she asked gently.

'Hughes happened!' Susan snapped. 'I really don't want to go into details other than to say he attacked her. Three days after the event, alone in her room and swamped with shame, Jasmine took too many pills.' Susan swallowed hard. 'She died. I should have taken better care of her and made sure she was safe. I've hated myself for a long time, but couldn't prove what I knew he had done. And of course Jasmine couldn't make a statement.'

'Where exactly do I come into this awful tale?'

'I'll be honest, when you started your crusade to free Emma, I didn't think you had a chance. I even tried to put you off, if you remember.'

Vicki nodded. 'Yes, I do.'

'But then Sian Jenkins came on board and you became even more determined to put things right. Unable to deflect you, I decided to encourage you to enter the lion's den for the second time. I reasoned that I could help you nick Hughes for *something* and get him jail time, but I knew it was your career I was risking. I shouldn't have done that and I am truly sorry.'

Vicki took a deep breath. 'So you used me to help settle your own demons?'

'"Used" is a nasty word and I'm not proud of what I did but' – Susan glanced up at Vicki and smiled – 'we've got him! I've spoken at length with DCI Morrison and he says it's a slam dunk. Who knows, maybe the powers that be will reopen Jasmine's case.'

'OK,' Vicki said, 'I agree "used" is a bit strong. Perhaps you would prefer "manipulated"?' Vicki patted her friend's hand. 'You really should have told me what you were up to, given me the choice whether or not to wreck my own life, but… I forgive you. How could I not? We've known each other too long to fall out and I don't fancy finding somewhere else to live.'

Susan smiled. 'That's a relief. I don't fancy finding a new tenant.'

'One thing though,' Vicki said. 'Who were you talking to on the phone?'

Susan tapped her nose and drank more tea. Vicki grinned and recalled spotting Susan's gentleman caller on the front step.

'Ah, your mysterious contact,' she said. 'I wonder if he's more than that. Does he ever stay overnight?'

Susan tapped her nose again, smiled and deftly changed the subject. 'Have you booked a visit to see Emma? she asked.

'Yes, hopefully this weekend, I'm just waiting for confirmation.' Vicki rubbed her eyes. 'How long do you think it will take to have her released?'

'Almost certainly longer than it should and depends which way the Home Office want to play it. The best result would be for her to be acquitted and released, but realistically, a good result would be a mistrial. It would then be the decision of the CPS whether or not Emma would face a new trial, and that will be dependent on what happens with Hughes.'

'British justice has always moved slowly, but following the backlog built up during Covid and the barristers' strikes, the waiting list is bloody enormous with thousands of people waiting for justice.'

'I know, but as the government has concocted some early-release schemes to make room for new prisoners, you might be lucky.' She grinned. 'You can be sure Helman won't have to wait for his day in court. They'll make room for a bastard like him. Just don't over-egg Emma's chances when you speak to her, that wouldn't be fair.'

'Could her solicitor agitate on her behalf?'

'I have no doubt he will. As you know, I've talked with him about the case and he is a very vigorous and committed young man, eager to right wrongs. I'll make sure to encourage him to kick up a fuss, a little rear-guard action never goes amiss, so fingers crossed, eh?'

'Yeah, I guess there's nothing to do now but wait.'

* * *

Vicki didn't get the chance to hunt for Rhys Griffiths because helping the young girl found at number twenty-seven took all afternoon. Arranging a social worker to sit in on the interview had taken longer than it should, but the small group eventually got together in an office, rather than an austere room in the custody suite. Vicki videoed the meeting, and the girl's story had been long and harrowing. When the session finally ended, and emergency foster care had been arranged, the social worker agreed to settle her charge in and promised to contact Vicki again in the morning.

Back at her desk, Vicki drank nasty coffee, checked her emails, then reached across the desk and switched off the computer. She was about to leave the office when DI Fletcher appeared at her door and plonked himself on a chair facing her.

'Evening, sir,' she said. 'Can I help you with something?'

'No, not really, just thought I'd pop in and find out what progress you've made with the girl.'

Vicki smiled. 'Better than I thought. Once she had settled down and realised she was safe, she was happy to talk. Her English is extraordinary. No way I could speak more than a couple of words of her language, never mind fluently.'

'So who is she?'

'Mina Ghaznavi, fourteen years old and separated from her family in the camps in France.' Vicki took a deep breath. 'She's had a tough time.'

'I don't doubt it,' Fletcher huffed. 'I have a daughter about the same age who struggles to walk from her room to the fridge, never mind from Afghanistan to France. What's Mina doing in Pembrokeshire?'

'Long story. Basically, she's looking for her folks. Her father worked for the British Army – until they pulled out, of course. He had papers to allow him to come to the UK, but in the chaos didn't get the chance to hand them over at the airport.'

Fletcher nodded. 'That happened to a lot of people. One gigantic cock-up.'

'Anyway, the family managed to get to the French coast then there was trouble, heavy-handed Gendarmerie tried to clear the camp and residents fought back. In the confusion, Mina was separated and made her own way to the UK. She heard on the grapevine her family were in Wales so came to look for them.'

'Has she claimed asylum?'

'No. The Davis boy picked her up in Merthyr about ten months ago, promised her the world then didn't allow her to leave the house. It seems the asylum claim was a cover story he'd given her.' Vicki wiped her eyes with her fingers. 'I asked about what happened in the house, but she shut down on me. All she would say was that it was nice to be able to hear the rain without getting wet. That was her best memory. Poor kid, it makes me want to weep.'

'The world is a difficult place these days, but I have some news that might cheer you up.'

'Oh, what is it?'

'Rhys Griffiths was arrested an hour ago in Bridgend by the local nick. Their end of the drugs case was still ongoing and, sure enough, the kid turned up there. I'm guessing he arrived empty-handed as you'd seized the coke from Ieuan's car. CID was watching the house, just as well as it turns out.' He chuckled. 'The occupiers of the property obviously weren't best pleased about losing their stash, and a ruckus kicked off. Officers went in to prevent anyone being killed. Multiple arrests, Griffiths included, and…' He took a deep breath. 'It seems we've recovered the knife used in the Hardwick case. It was found under his bed when we tossed his room.'

'That *is* good news. Makes coppering worthwhile when we get results.'

'That and weeding out bent cops.' He sighed heavily. 'When the story about Kurt Helman hits the press, there will be righteous outrage. The SIO interviewed him this morning, but got nothing out of him – not that we need anything. Thanks to you and your sting, we have enough to keep him off the streets for the rest of his natural.' He grinned. 'Bit of luck, Glyn Hughes might keep him company for some of it.'

'Any chance you could make sure the investigation into him doesn't drag its feet, sir? Emma Hardwick has been in prison for nearly two years and I don't think she'll be able to survive much longer. Did you hear about her suicide attempt?'

'Yes, I did, and DCI Morrison is on side too. Rhys Griffiths doesn't know he's about to be charged with murder so, with careful handling, we might get enough out of him to allow a judge to rule Emma's conviction was unsafe.'

'How likely is that?'

'I'm bloody good in an interview room, it's one of my superpowers. You can trust me to get the goods.'

Vicki laughed. 'You have more than one superpower?'

Fletcher shrugged. 'So I'm told, but what I'm interested in now is what happens to you.'

'To me?'

'You're obviously wasted in uniform. You should return to CID; recent events have proved you're a great detective.'

Vicki chuckled. 'I always knew that, but I'm not sure. I quite enjoy being in uniform, change is as good as a rest and all that.'

Fletcher nodded. 'Yes it is, but don't expect me to stop asking. For now, though, once the dust has settled, there's work to do rebuilding the community's trust and I reckon you're the best person we've got for that.'

'Thank you, sir. I'm actually looking forward to getting back to what counts as normal policing. Are you staying with us, sir?'

'I am. I needed a change of scenery too.'

'That's good news. My landlady – ex-DCI Susan Thomas – remembers you from when you joined the force and speaks very highly of you.'

'Nice to know.' Fletcher got to his feet, held out his hand and grasped Vicki's tightly. 'Let's get on with it then,' he said. 'As soon as we've won back some hearts and minds, between us we'll do our best to make our county a safer one.'

* * *

Three days after being remanded, having still not said a word to the SIO in charge of his case, Kurt Helman reached out via his solicitor. It seemed he was now willing to talk to DI Fletcher, on the condition Vicki was also present at the interview. After some discussion, DCI Morrison sanctioned the visit which was quickly arranged for the following day – before Helman could change his mind.

The officers travelled to Newport the next morning and Fletcher parked close to the main entrance of Newport Remand Centre. Together they walked across the car park and after gaining entry, endured the laborious booking in process. Once all the boxes had been ticked, they were shown to a small, secure room with two doors on opposite walls, a table, and three plastic chairs. They settled themselves and waited for Helman to appear, which he did a few minutes later. A prison officer brought him in through the second door, removed the handcuffs without a word, then left the room and locked the door behind him.

Helman looked dishevelled and tired and was wearing a grey prison T-shirt and matching, baggy jogging bottoms. He sat at the table and, despite a lumpy-looking nose and an impressive black eye, he smirked at his visitors.

'Didn't think you'd come,' he said looking directly at Vicki. 'Glad you did though.'

'Why is that?' Vicki asked, but Helman looked away and shrugged.

She chuckled. 'Doesn't look as though you and the boys are playing nicely.'

Helman glared at her. 'Shut your mouth,' he hissed.

'We were told by the SIO handling your case that you wanted to talk to us,' Fletcher said, 'that you had something to say.'

'We'll get to that,' Helman said. 'I'm sure you have questions though. How about we get those out of the way first? We can save the best for last.'

'The best? What do you mean?'

Helman shook his head. 'We do it my way or I'll go back to my cell and will never speak to any of you again. This is your only chance.' He grinned. 'I'm not bothered either way. Not like anything that happens in this room will make a difference to me.'

'You're not wrong there,' Vicki muttered. 'A full life tariff for you is a given considering what you've done.'

'Only if the jury finds me guilty.' Helman folded his arms and gazed at the stained ceiling. 'I thought you wanted to know why I attacked those girls. You certainly kept banging on about it after my arrest.'

'So tell us then,' Fletcher said. 'Why did you do such a terrible thing?'

'Because they were disrespectful – and I could.'

'That makes everything clear then,' Vicki said sarcastically.

Helman looked at her. 'You'll get your turn, but for now shut the fuck up and let the men speak.'

'Cut the language,' Fletcher said, 'and just tell us how your victims disrespected you. We know you stopped all three on random traffic checks and that's how you came into contact with them, but what did they do to you?'

'Christine laughed at me,' Helman muttered and studied his bruised knuckles. 'I asked her out for a meal – after I'd promised to let her off a ticket, mind you – and she bloody laughed. Jenny told me to piss off, and Laura actually drove her car at me! Can you believe it? I could have just nicked her for the attempted murder of a police officer.'

Vicki stifled a snigger and Helman glared at her.

'What is it with girls these days?' he asked, turning his gaze back to Fletcher. 'They have so much power over us men and it isn't right, they should know their place. It's our duty to reset the system. We are the hunters, the providers, and we should be treated with respect.' He leaned back in his chair. 'I decided to teach them a lesson.'

Fletcher snorted. 'By trapping them in their cars and gassing them?' he asked.

'Yes, exactly that. A brilliant plan.'

'A crap plan,' Vicki said, 'considering you got caught and we're having this conversation.'

Helman frowned at her again. 'I've told you to shut up!'

'If you don't want me to speak, why did you insist I attended this farce?'

'I said you'll find out, when I'm ready.'

Fletcher took back control of the interview. 'How did you know how to hack the onboard computers in the cars?' he asked.

'One of my mates online was talking about it. I didn't believe it was possible at first, but I did some research and found out there are modern cars doing weird things all over the world.'

'Like what?'

'Some speed up, some just stop in the outside lane of the motorway and cause pile-ups, others trap people inside, and all that before Chinese electric cars start flooding the market. Online chatter among those who know say that will be a big problem as their government will be able to switch off every one of their cars in the country.'

'We're not talking about the Chinese,' Fletcher snapped. 'Let's keep to the point. Why did you decide to attack your victims in this manner?'

'Seemed a good way to deal with them without having to get my hands dirty, and it was clever.' He glanced at Vicki. 'You'd never have caught me if I'd been on shift that evening and heard about the sting op.' He grinned. 'Call yourself a bloody detective? You didn't suspect me for a second, didn't have a clue. I'm telling you, if I wasn't in here, I'd–'

'But you are in here,' Vicki said, 'and you'll never get out. You might think all of this was clever, but you got caught and now you'll pay for what you did.'

'I don't think so,' Helman said and began rocking his chair back and forth.

'You're planning to escape then, are you?' Vicki chuckled. 'Good luck with that.'

Helman shrugged. 'You can't make me pay for things you don't know I did, can you?'

'This is a waste of time, sir,' Vicki said. 'We have better things to do than this. He's talking rubbish.'

'No I'm not!' Helman slapped the table and made the officers jump. 'I'm making perfect sense. You're not listening.' He leaned on the desk and stared at Vicki. 'You asked why I wanted you here. Truth is I wanted to be able to see your face.' He took a deep breath. 'You've already admitted hacking the computers was clever, and it was, especially with the extra mechanical sabotage. I spent ages working everything out, months. I didn't just decide to punish Christina one day and kill her the next.' He smiled, his eyes focused elsewhere as though reliving the memory. 'It all worked perfectly.'

'I don't understand what you're trying to tell us,' Fletcher said.

Helman laughed. 'It's not difficult to work out. I had to practise. Took me a couple of goes, but I got it right in the end.' He leaned back in his chair and chuckled softly. 'Trust me, Christina wasn't the first.'

Epilogue

Four months later

The weather turned in late August, as a period of hot sunshine settled over Wales and encouraged tourists to descend on the beautiful west coast beaches. Vicki settled back into her day-to-day job, organising the squad, keeping the office running and an eye on the younger officers. She also kept a careful eye on the internal investigations into Hughes and Helman, but, anxious not to prejudice any outcome, she stayed away unless called to give statements. She had to admit, the investigations had great momentum. Both officers had been charged appropriately. Hughes entered a guilty plea and was sentenced to twelve years on multiple offences, including perverting the course of justice, and gross misconduct. Helman was languishing on remand awaiting trial, a full life tariff more or less a given. Another exciting development was that Mina Ghaznavi's family had been found living in Aberystwyth and they had been reunited.

Vicki had got so involved with her work that the Williams sisters' birthday party managed to creep up on her and, too late, she realised she was double-booked. She called Sian in a panic, bribed her with an invite and asked if she would mind taking Susan.

'I'll be there as soon as I possibly can,' Vicki said. 'There are flowers and chocolates for the twins in the hall. Thanks, mate. I owe you one.'

* * *

Sian helped Susan into the front seat of the car and made sure her seat belt was properly fastened.

'Leave off, girl,' Susan said and flapped a hand. 'I'm not a bloody cripple.'

Billy Marsden, who was sitting on the back seat, tried but failed to stifle a chuckle.

'Yeah, laugh it up,' Susan said, 'that's what I do. Better than crying. Now let's get going before all the cake is gone.'

Sian got behind the wheel and pulled away from the house. 'Vicki called earlier,' she said. 'Bit of luck she'll be there soon after we are.'

'Do you know why she was called in on her day off?' Susan asked.

'She didn't say when she phoned. Work, probably.'

Susan glanced over her shoulder. 'Do you know, Billy?'

'Nope. I thought she'd be here.' He changed the subject. 'I've never been to a hundredth birthday bash before, never mind for twins. I hope they don't kick me and Sian out. Even though Vicki invited us I still feel like a gatecrasher.'

'Seems Vicki doesn't really know what plus one means,' Susan said. 'Sian, did you collect the flowers and chocolates from the hall?'

'Yes, all safely loaded in the boot together with some bottles of champagne from Billy and me.'

'All in order then.' Susan settled back in her seat and suddenly burst into song, 'You gotta fight… for the right… to paaarty.'

'Blimey,' Billy said. 'You know about the Beastie Boys?'

* * *

Vicki was still a few miles away from Ash Grove when her phone rang and she answered using her hands-free kit.

'Yeah, yeah, I'm on my way. Keep your hair on.'

'I'm sorry?' a male voice asked. 'Is that you, Sergeant?'

'Oh, Chief Inspector Morrison, I'm sorry. I'm driving and didn't check who was calling. I'm on my day off,' she said, hoping he hadn't called with something else for her to do. 'I'm on my way to a birthday party on the estate and my plus-ones have been ringing to ask where I am. What can I do for you, sir?'

'I'll be blunt, Sergeant,' he said, not noticing the pun, 'I want you back in CID. DI Fletcher is short-handed and has specifically asked for you.'

'That's flattering, but I'm a bit busy–'

Morrison didn't seem to have heard and continued. 'You should never have been put back in uniform, it was wrong and you certainly didn't deserve it. I want you working where you belong.'

'Thank you, sir, but it would be good to have a chance to discuss this first thing on Monday maybe? As I said, I'm driving and on my way to–'

'Yes, yes of course, but if you're not in my office by nine on Monday, I'll come looking for you. Enjoy your party.'

Vicki cut the call, she navigated around the large roundabout on the edge of the estate and headed towards Ash Grove. She smiled as she pulled into the road, there was no mistaking the party's venue. The front of the sisters' house had been decorated with multi-coloured balloons, streamers and brightly coloured birthday banners dangled from the upstairs windows. The front door stood open and 1940s band music wafted out to the front garden where groups of suitably dressed guests stood around chatting with glasses in their hands. Barbeque smoke wafted around a grill set up on the lawn, where a couple of less suitably dressed teenaged lads flipped burgers and sausages, ear pods firmly in their ears.

Vicki pulled up behind Sian's car and waved at an elderly couple performing the Lindy Hop on the pavement and felt as though the day had slipped back in time. She thought they were making a much better job of it than she ever could and were probably in their late eighties. She smiled happily, then she got out of the car, walked past the bonnet and opened the passenger door.

'Right then, my lovely,' she said, 'take a deep breath. Hold my hand if you want to.'

'I might need to,' Emma said. 'I'm not feeling very brave, but this was a good idea.' She chuckled softly. 'Certainly a novel way of integrating me back into society.' She suddenly threw her arms around Vicki. 'This day wouldn't have arrived without you not giving up on me. Believing in me. I'll never be able to thank you enough. You've given me back my life.'

THE END

If you enjoyed this book, please let others know by leaving a quick review on Amazon. Also, if you spot anything untoward in the paperback, get in touch. We strive for the best quality and appreciate reader feedback.

editor@thebookfolks.com

www.thebookfolks.com

Also in this series

A KILLING ON THE COAST PATH
(book 2)

A panic-stricken woman, a man's body on Musselwick Beach, a creepy landlord, a raucous glamping party, plus fireworks going off between Sergeant Vicki Blunt and her boss, amply demonstrate that Pembrokeshire isn't the sedate backwater one might suppose. Can the young officer deal with the mess and prove her worth to the force?

Available on pre-order now for release in March 2025!

More fiction by Nicola Clifford

The Welsh crime mysteries series

Stacey Logan is a reporter based in a small town in the heart of Wales. Her boyfriend Ben James is a detective in the police. They don't always see eye to eye but together they take on some tough cases and somehow always seem to pull through. Follow their exploits in this mostly heart-warming and cozy, but sometimes a little daring and shocking, series full of mystery and suspense.

All FREE with Kindle Unlimited and available in paperback!

Other titles of interest

The DI Winter Meadows mystery series
by Cheryl Rees-Price

Raised on a commune, Detective Inspector Winter Meadows has an open and sympathetic nature. He is driven by a sense of justice, the need to find the truth, and the good in people. If he has a fondness for the close-knit valley communities in South Wales, it is matched by his appreciation of how challenging it is to tackle crime there. Deep, simmering resentments and bitter rivalries can emerge in these remote places, nestled beneath the windswept Brecon Beacons. Residents here are bound by family ties and generations of friendships and the lines of good and evil are often blurred. Penetrating the walls of silence that hide serious crime will take all of DI Meadows' intuition, training and more.

All FREE with Kindle Unlimited and available in paperback!

Pippa McCathie's Welsh mystery series

Since taking early retirement, Superintendent Fabia Havard is struggling with civilian life. Nonetheless, she sets to her new career as an illustrator. However, when a girl is murdered in her town, her old instincts kick in and she is desperate to find the killer. Her ex-colleague Matt Lambert will have to decide whether to stop her or allow his former boss to assist the floundering inquiry. So begins a series of cases in which Havard, with her local knowledge and experience, will play a pivotal if unconventional role. Her bond with Matt grows stronger and they have the potential to become a formidable investigative duo. But only if they both don't overstep the mark…

All FREE with Kindle Unlimited and available in paperback!

MURDER IN THE NEW FOREST
by Carol Cole

When a woman's body is found on the ground next to her horse, it seems an unfortunate accident had occurred. However, DI Callum MacLean, newly arrived in the picturesque New Forest from Glasgow, suspects differently. But hunting a killer in this close-knit community, suspicious of outsiders, will be tough. Especially when not everyone in his team is on side.

FREE with Kindle Unlimited and available in paperback!

THE BOOK FOLKS

As a thank-you to our readers, we regularly run free book promotions and discounted deals for a limited time. To hear about these and about new fiction releases, just sign up to our newsletter.

www.thebookfolks.com

www.ingramcontent.com/pod-product-compliance
Ingram Content Group UK Ltd.
Pitfield, Milton Keynes, MK11 3LW, UK
UKHW011332240625
6557UKWH00023B/229